VOODOO MAN

Antoine's curvy, firmly muscled body was a smooth, light golden brown – flawless, hairless and gleaming. His large lips were glossy and well defined, and he licked them with knowing flirtatiousness as he looked around him at the three fishermen, winding his pelvis to the music on the radio.

The fishermen watched Antoine intently with slightly open mouths as he let his head tilt back, arching a supple, sinewy neck, and spread his strong, smooth brown-sugar thighs wide, bouncing his big melon butt up and down in time to the music as if he was using it to pleasure a seated man's erect, upstanding cock. His large nipples stood out from the domes of his chest like dark-brown bullets filled with a sexual energy that drew men's fingers towards them.

He was starting to work up a sweat.

VOODOO MAN

Johnny T. Malice

First published in Great Britain in 2001 by
Idol
Thames Wharf Studios,
Rainville Road, London W6 9HA

ISBN 0 352 33622 6

Typeset by SetSystems Ltd, Saffron Walden, Essex
Printed and bound in Great Britain by
Mackays of Chatham PLC

SAFER SEX GUIDELINES

We include safer sex guidelines in every Idol book. However, while our policy is always to show safer sex in contemporary stories, we don't insist on safer sex practices in stories with historical settings – as this would be anachronistic. These books are sexual fantasies – in real life, everyone needs to think about safe sex.

While there have been major advances in the drug treatments for people with HIV and AIDS, there is still no cure for AIDS or a vaccine against HIV. Safe sex is still the only way of being sure of avoiding HIV sexually.

HIV can only be transmitted through blood, come and vaginal fluids (but no other body fluids) passing from one person (with HIV) into another person's bloodstream. It cannot get through healthy, undamaged skin. The only real risk of HIV is through anal sex without a condom – this accounts for almost all HIV transmissions between men.

Being safe
Even if you don't come inside someone, there is still a risk to both partners from blood (tiny cuts in the arse) and pre-come. Using strong condoms and water-based lubricant greatly reduces the risk of HIV. However, condoms can break or slip off, so:

* Make sure that condoms are stored away from hot or damp places.
* Check the expiry date – condoms have a limited life.
* Gently squeeze the air out of the tip.
* Check the condom is put on the right way up and unroll it down the erect cock.
* Use plenty of water-based lubricant (lube), up the arse and on the condom.
* While fucking, check occasionally to see the condom is still in one piece (you could also add more lube).

* When you withdraw, hold the condom tight to your cock as you pull out.
* Never re-use a condom or use the same condom with more than one person.
* If you're not used to condoms you might practise putting them on.
* Sex toys like dildos and plugs are safe. But if you're sharing them use a new condom each time or wash the toys well.

For the safest sex, make sure you use the strongest condoms, such as Durex Ultra Strong, Mates Super Strong, HT Specials and Rubberstuffers packs. Condoms are free in many STD (Sexually Transmitted Disease) clinics (sometimes called GUM clinics) and from many gay bars. It's also essential to use lots of water-based lube such as KY, Wet Stuff, Slik or Liquid Silk. Never use come as a lubricant.

Oral sex
Compared with fucking, sucking someone's cock is far safer. Swallowing come does not necessarily mean that HIV gets absorbed into the bloodstream. While a tiny fraction of cases of HIV infection have been linked to sucking, we know the risk is minimal. But certain factors increase the risk:
* Letting someone come in your mouth
* Throat infections such as gonorrhoea
* If you have cuts, sores or infections in your mouth and throat

So what is safe?
There are so many things you can do which are absolutely safe: wanking each other; rubbing your cocks against one another; kissing, sucking and licking all over the body; rimming – to name but a few.

If you're finding safe sex difficult, call a helpline or speak to someone you feel you can trust for support. The Terrence Higgins Trust Helpline, which is open from noon to 10pm every day, can be reached on 020 7242 1010.

Or, if you're in the United States, you can ring the Center for Disease Control toll free on 1 800 458 5231.

One

——————

Under the vast dome of a moonless indigo sky clotted with a billion stars Voodoo drums throbbed, their rhythms compelling, hypnotic. The insistent pulse of the drums floated down over the lush, tangled and steep hillsides that rose into the Caribbean island's mountainous and inaccessible interior, over towering and ancient silk-cotton trees and acres of rustling banana plants, over decayed and overgrown plantations of sugar cane and mouldering colonial mansions, across a patchwork of tilled fields of yams, plantains, cassava, lime and lemon groves, and down to the small fishing village of Croix-Le-Bois, where a darkly emerald sea fringed with white foam pounded the lambent crescent of the shore and lapped the beached boats of the fishermen.

The *oufo*, the Voodoo temple that was the source of the drumming, had been built three generations earlier at the end of a narrow track that began a mile away from the small village and headed into the island's thickly forested interior for a further three miles. Although the red earth of the track was well trodden, compacted into stone-hard smoothness by the passing of many feet, its entrance was purposefully obscured by the villagers with vines and thickets: the government of the island, supported by the Catholic Church and concerned with its image abroad as superstitious and corrupt, was intolerant of Voodoo and persecuted its

1

followers with sporadic violence. But despite this persecution the followers continued to honour the *lwa*, the Voodoo spirits or *Mystères*, taking the icons of the Catholic saints given to them by missionaries and using them as images of the gods and ancestors the Christian priests hoped to displace and overlay with their own: Mama Ezulie, Papa Legba, Damballah Wedo, Baron Samedi taking on the forms of the Virgin, St Peter, St Patrick with his serpents; possessing them as the *lwa* possess the *serviteurs*, the faithful followers.

The *oufo*'s low, windowless, whitewashed walls rose up glowingly against an inky backdrop of darkly verdant foliage and enclosed a number of simple single-storey buildings within. The air was still and solid as glass, breathless, blood-warm, blood-close. The mountains rose sheer and vast and immobile behind the compound, granite pushing up forcefully through forest and crowning bare.

Within the *oufo* compound the relentless, unceasing pounding of the drums pulled at the partly clad bodies of the *serviteurs*, commanding them to dance, dance, dance until sweat oiled their dark skins and their muscles ached, making them pound their thighs and grind their hips until they went beyond fatigue and exploded into ecstasy and entered that state beyond ecstasy that was the aim of all true believers: Possession. To be taken, to be mounted and ridden by the *lwa*. To lose control and become the vehicle of the will and pleasure of *Les Mystères*. Sharply rung handbells counterpointed the complex rhythmic drumming of the *oufo*'s three drummers, and timbrous voices rose and fell as the service proceeded.

It was the night before All Saints' Day, 1 November, the *mange-lwa*, the feast given to feed the *Ghedes*, also known as the Barons, one of the most important families of *lwa*. Tonight a smaller ceremony was being carried out at the *oufo* as a preamble to the larger one the following day, and a rehearsal: the *mange-lwa* was one of the most important ceremonies in the Voodoo calendar, and there were many things to make ready and get right.

Ti-Charles, the handsome young *oungan* or Voodoo priest of Croix-Le-Bois, was busily making his preparations for the special day. The *mange-lwa* ceremony was important for the whole community of believers, but especially so for Ti-Charles, because his temple was dedicated not only to Baron Samedi, Lord of Graveyards, but also and more particularly to the *massissi* Barons Limba and Lundi, lovers it was said, and certainly appreciators of masculine beauty and energy – and Baron Samedi himself, though not *massissi*, was open to the charms of both sexes when he deigned to visit the *oufo* and enter the body of one of the frenziedly moving *serviteurs*. It was before the elaborately piled altar dedicated to Baron Limba and Baron Lundi that Ti-Charles was making his preparations. He took a swig from a bottle of white rum and expelled it from his mouth in a fine, hot mist over the twin skulls that sat raised in the centre of the altar, and muttered imprecations to the *massissi* deities under his breath: 'You understand what I am and what I need. I feed you and I praise you and I ask you help me now . . .'

Then Ti-Charles left the small, whitewashed hut that contained the altar known as the *kay-mystère* and, carrying a lighted candle, crossed the peristyle to another, slightly smaller hut set back from those dedicated to the Barons, the *Ghedes*. This *kay-mystère* was dedicated to the *lwa* or Mystery Ezulie, the goddess of love. He ducked his head and, shielding the candle, stepped through the low doorway and went inside.

Ti-Charles was a good-looking, lean and ebony-dark young black man with a closely shaved scalp at sides and back, but topped by a snakelock-anenome mass of dreads he usually kept wound in a tight white cotton headscarf. He had large, dark eyes, full, sensual lips, broad shoulders, a compact hairless chest from which large, dark nipples projected bullet-like, and a narrow waspy waist. His legs were long and well muscled, his buttocks high and firm and encased in close-fitting white cotton breeches. He had many preparations to make that evening, many small rituals to perform and prayers to offer up before the greater ritual the following day. But he also had a request to make of the *lwa* before tomorrow that had nothing to do with his role as Croix-Le-Bois's *oungan*, a request entirely to do with his increasingly intense attraction to one of the handsome young fishermen of the village, Henri Biassou:

Papa Legba ouvri bayè-a pou mwen
Papa Legba open the gate for me
So I can go through
When I return I will honour the lwa . . .

So Ti-Charles chanted, invoking the Corpse at the Crossroads between the material and the spirit world, Legba Carrefour, through whom all other *lwa* are invoked. But his mind filled with the image of Henri's handsome, large-featured face, his flashing, white, boyish smile, one front tooth framed with gold, the provocative gap between his two front teeth. He saw the sinuously muscular, mocha-brown body, blocky, hard and tanned from each long day he spent out on the limitless blue ocean, a half-moon shiny scar running down his side from just below his bevelled armpit and beside his ridge-muscled belly – the result of an attack by a mako shark when he was seventeen, three years ago – and Ti-Charles longed to reach out and touch it with the very tips of his fingers, imagining Henri shivering in response. He pictured the casual, loping grace of Henri's walk as he strode up the beach late each afternoon with marlins almost too long to carry slung over his shoulders, their indigo-blue tails dragging in the hot white sand, or rows of red snappers strung from a pole, straw hat pushed back on his shaved head, the domes of his hairless chest bare, red shirt open to the waist and knotted over his sharply defined abdominals, showing them off proudly, sun-bleached denim shorts tight around his hips and bulging crotch and across his firm, muscular buttocks.

Ti-Charles lived in a cabin on the edge of the village, screened from the road that ran along the coast towards the nearest town by a row of thick-boled palm trees. A tethered black goat nibbled the lawn around it, keeping it neatly cropped, and purple bougainvillea climbed its walls, releasing sweet perfume from the soft purple-pink petals of its many flowers. Ti-Charles had inherited the cabin from the *oungan* who had initiated him into the Voodoo mysteries, a man who had been like an elder brother to him. Sometimes, when his duties did not require him to be at the *oufo*, Ti-Charles would sit on the raised porch stretched out in a wicker chair and listen to the laughter of the fishermen floating over from the small thatched bar at the top of the beach where they spent their evenings watching the sun sink into the sea, or to their work songs as they gutted the fish and repaired their nets – rich, timbrous calls-and-responses. Sometimes calypso or compas music would drift over from Henri's small portable radio, which he would set up on top of one of the beached boats to entertain the other men while they worked. All the fishermen were beautiful to Ti-Charles, but it was Henri he had fallen in love with.

Henri was a passionate believer, a true *serviteur* of the *lwa*, though not an *ounsi*, a temple initiate. He attended every festival and danced wildly to the pulsing interlocking heartbeats of the drums, ecstatically possessed by the music, the chanting, the sacred rites, the *lwa* themselves – and yet outside the *oufo* he almost completely ignored Ti-Charles, doing no more than show him the respect proper to the *oungan* of Croix-Le-Bois, never meeting the lithe young satin-skinned priest's wide, dark eyes with his own hazel ones. Perhaps Henri was also a little afraid of him, for Ti-Charles was reputed to deal with both hands, the left and the right, that is, to be a *bokor*, a sorcerer, as well as an *oungan* and healer. This reputation was unjust, for while like any *oungan* Ti-Charles made protective charms and spoke with the *lwa*, *Les Mystères*, he did not curse, poison, create zombies or summon up monstrous, dwarfish *baka* to terrorise any villager who crossed him, as a *bokor* would do. Still, he was known to know sorcery. To know evil so as to combat it, as his master would say when Ti-Charles was himself a young *ounsi*.

There was said to be a *bokor* who lived in a ruined plantation house nearby. This shadowy figure was rumoured to take the recently deceased from the grave and resurrect them as zombies, then make them tend and chop the sugar cane in the overgrown fields around the crumbling clapboard edifice. Many of the funerary rituals Ti-Charles performed at the burials and commemorations of loved ones in the village were to prevent this dreadful possibility from occurring: to have one's soul stolen from one's body and trapped in a clay jar in the *bokor*'s peristyle, and one's body enslaved as a consequence, appalled even those who claimed to regard Voodoo as heathen superstition. The Catholic priest, for instance, who made periodic visits to Croix-Le-Bois, was known to wear a protective *wanga* packet of snake vertebrae and thunder-stones around his neck, beneath his surplice.

No one had ever seen the *bokor* – at least knowingly, for who could tell what such a man would look like? – but he was widely believed in, and bad luck was often attributed to his unseen presence in the parish if it continued after the proper obeisances to *Les Mystères* had been sincerely made.

Although he was no sorcerer, the wisdom, knowledge and power of *Les Mystères* was channelled through Ti-Charles, and perhaps that in itself was enough to make the normally bold Henri Biassou shy and tongue-tied in his presence. And Ti-Charles, in his turn, became flustered when he passed Henri in the village or on some country lane, and was unable to push past that wall of shyness.

Still, the young *oungan* did what he could: he made out *veves* for the handsome, muscular fisherman's protection and prosperity, tracing the elaborate symbolic patterns out on the raked black earth of the *oufo*'s peristyle with flour and coffee grounds. And he also made offerings of rum and flowers and small, sweet cakes in the *kay-mystère* that contained the shrine to Agwe, *lwa* of the sea and Ezulie's sometime husband, that Henri's boat should travel safely across the vast and swelling waters.

After several such awkward encounters with Henri, Ti-Charles had gradually resigned himself to the fact that nothing would happen between the young fisherman and himself however much he wanted it to. But then had come the time of the Mardi Gras festival in Lent, earlier that year: the *oufo* had been packed with sweaty, muscular, red-headscarved men of every skin tone from butter-demerara to obsidian, stripped to the waist and throwing themselves around ecstatically to the compelling pounding of the temple's drummers, dancing for hours on end around the *poteau-mitain*, the elaborately carved and painted pole that rose up in the middle of the *oufo*'s peristyle, the sacred pole that joined the earth to the sky and permitted the arrival and channelling down of the spirits from Guinée, from the African homeland of memory, the pole that pierced the ground and crossed the barrier between the material and spirit worlds and became the conduit for the *lwa* from the Watery Place *là-bas* to the worshippers.

Ti-Charles had led the ceremony and danced and chanted for several hours in the sultry early-evening heat, losing himself in the drumming and song until every muscle in his shapely brown body ached and his heart hammered painfully in his chest. Now he sat on a carved, raised chair by the door of the shrine to Legba, the opener of the way, taking a moment to get his breath back. Still he kept the *asson*, the sacred gourd rattle encased in a loose-fitting mesh of beads, moving constantly, hissing out a rapid, shifting rhythm from which the drummers took their cue to set the tempo of the dance. White crosses were painted on Ti-Charles's bare, mocha-dark, hairless chest, representations of Legba, the Corpse at the Crossroads the ceremony had begun by invoking. The crosses were beyond Christian, older and deeper, despite what the Catholic priest sometimes chose to believe when he found them crowning the small altars in the homes of the faithful. They symbolised instead the crossing of the material and spiritual planes and also their mirror symmetry, for in Voodoo the world of the dead mirrors that of the living, and the ancestors and the spirits are as present as a man's reflection in a mirror. Sweat ran down between Ti-Charles's flat pectorals in glittering rivulets, making the white paint blur and run. His large, protruding nipples were stiff and tingling, and his mouth and throat were dry: the air in the peristyle was hotter than blood, and stiflingly humid.

Henri Biassou now led the dancing, tossing his head back wildly, wearing nothing but tight, white, cotton breeches that hugged his full crotch and lean hips provocatively, his rich brown skin gleaming with sweat, his closely shaved scalp and handsome, upturned face a mass of diamonds. A glowing choker of cowries pressed against his rising and falling Adam's apple, constricting the tense cords and inflated veins in his neck. Every sinew in his strong, lean body stood out in flawless symmetry as he moved forward with his curving thighs spread in jerking hops, blocky calves tensing above diving tendons as he hammered the heels of his bare feet into the compacted earth, obliterating the elaborate *veves* that Ti-Charles had laid out there, that obliteration part of the ritual too. Henri flung his strongly muscled arms wide and lifted himself up on the balls of his feet, arching backwards as he did so. Suddenly his whole body began to convulse. His mouth opened, flashing gold and pink and white, and his eyes rolled back in his head: Henri was being mounted, ridden, possessed by one of the *lwa*, his higher soul, his personality, his *gros-bon-ange* displaced by one of *Les Mystères* the Lent festival had tempted forth with its offering of music, food and sacrifice, his body offered to whatever spirit wished to make use of it for the duration of the service.

Ti-Charles impulsively jumped to his feet as two other *serviteurs* moved forward to make sure the sweaty, glistening fisherman did not injure himself in the course of his trance. For some reason the young *oungan* had been particularly excited that night, and full of an inexplicable anticipation: *tonight, something*.

Ti-Charles had, of course, been possessed many times himself. Although it was physically arduous, to be ridden by the *lwa* and come into rapport with the divine principles was the hope and wish of any *serviteur*. To do so was to serve the wishes of the spirits and the needs of the community. There were other benefits also: Like any other *serviteur*, Ti-Charles had been possessed by *lwa* of both sexes, and through this he had come to understand the deeper androgyny, the profounder openness of *Les Mystères*. This in turn had helped him to understand his own nature, that of a man who finds the totality of masculine and feminine experience both in himself and with another man; that he was *massissi*, and that to be *massissi* was not against the spirits. And so, when he had been fully initiated and received his sacred *asson* from his master, he had dedicated his *oufo* to Baron Limba and Baron Lundi, who were, it was said, both male, and lovers. Had he chosen them, or had they chosen him? Perhaps in the end there was no difference: they were his *lwa*, his inheritance, as much so as the cabin in which he now lived or the colour of his eyes.

Ti-Charles had never tried to describe the experience of being possessed, being taken by one of *Les Mystères*. A believer would understand without words while an unbeliever could not understand, and words would convey nothing. The nearest he could have come would be to say that the ecstasy of being fucked anally touched on some corner of the transcendental sensation of being utterly opened at the profoundest level by the mounting spirit, a fearful yielding that gave the 'horse' a pleasure beyond pleasure, a brief moment of insight into the necessary, unbearable essence of life, a moment of passionate connection to everything living and beyond living. And just as the world of the *lwa* was a mirror to the world of the living, so in his private life Ti-Charles looked for a mirror to the ecstasy of possession – a man who would take him as *Les Mystères* took him, deeply, passionately, totally.

The lord of the Barons, Baron Samedi, chief of the Ghede family and Lord of the Dead, was a frequent visitor at Ti-Charles's *oufo*, often possessing one white-cotton-clad, sweaty *serviteur* after another, and entertaining and shocking all those present with his obscene dancing, lewd stories, practical jokes and eccentric behaviour, his crudity and sexual boldness an assertion of the viscerality of life and a gift to the living, however hard their lives, a chance for the villagers to laugh at death, assert life to the full, and finally face successfully death's inevitability.

It was Baron Samedi who possessed Henri that sweaty, breathless night in Lent. The muscular, cocoa-brown young fisherman – naked except for tight white pearl-button-fronted breeches that hugged his crotch and large, muscular buttocks – undulated his way over to the rising pole of the *poteau-mitain*, head still thrown back, neck straining, eyes rolled up in his head, and started to grind his crotch against the painted post with sensual motions of his pelvis. As he did so he reached down with one lanky, well-muscled arm and ran his hand over the offerings that had been laid out for the *lwa* around the base of the pole, picking out a bottle of rum and swigging from it, running long dark fingers through platters of pale rice and yellow-brown chicken stew, finally picking up a battered black top hat and placing it on his head, then fumbling for the dark glasses laid there that would conceal his white, rolled-up eyes. One lens was missing, symbolising Baron Samedi's double vision: into the world of the living and the world of the spirits and the dead.

Slowly, with swivelling hips, Henri made his way towards where Ti-Charles was standing. Ti-Charles looked down at Henri's crotch and saw that the now-possessed fisherman had become sexually aroused, his thrillingly large erection pushing out visibly against the constraining cotton of his close-fitting, knee-length breeches for all those present to see, his small, dark nipples stiff on the curving brown domes of his sinew-striated pectorals. Ti-Charles's cock stiffened to erection inside his own tight breeches in reaction to the intensely arousing sight of Henri's shameless public hardness, and to the proximity of Henri's well-muscled body, its head swelling and its shaft expanding awkwardly across his lean thigh beneath the skin-tight material of his breeches. A red scarf was knotted tightly around Ti-Charles's head, holding his dreads in place, and his loose white cotton shirt was knotted up in front of him across his firm chest and curving ribcage, exposing his supple waist and flat, trembling belly for the Baron's carnal pleasure. Ti-Charles could see every muscle in Henri's sinewy, hairless body tense and flex and swell as Henri moved towards him filled with the chaotic, horny spirit of Baron Samedi, extending a long muscular arm, a strong twine-calloused hand, rotating his hips provocatively as the drums pounded faster and faster.

And Ti-Charles had reached out and taken Henri's – the Baron's – hand and been led into the centre of the peristyle, moving to the relentless, compelling rhythm of the three *Rada* drums as he did so, skin on skin. The other *serviteurs*, sweaty, exhausted, envious, intrigued, had parted and given the two young men space, and Ti-Charles had let Henri grip his narrow, supple waist and turn him around and place his hands on Ti-Charles's hips and grip them and grind his rigidity against Ti-Charles's firmly muscular and upturned buttocks, simulating fucking the young *oungan* up the arse with lusty passion, driving the breathless, painfully erect Ti-Charles to such an unbearable level of excitement that he found himself willing Henri to pull his trousers down and fuck him for real in front of the whole community, give him the gratification he so urgently needed. Why should he be ashamed? Was he not dedicated to the *massissi* Barons Limba and Lundi?

But Henri hadn't done that: he had pulled back from Ti-Charles and turned away from him and danced with others, grinding equally lustfully with both men and women from the village, leaving the lean young *oungan* desperately aroused and so frustrated he had become nearly delirious as he was obliged to turn back to performing the rituals that ensured the orderly passage of the horny Baron and several other *lwa* in and out of the bodies of the faithful.

Afterwards, many hours later, when the moon was sinking in the lightening sky and all the *serviteurs* had left, Ti-Charles had felt compelled to take a thick, pale, wax candle from the shrine to Baron Samedi and pleasure himself by slowly sitting on it in the close stillness of the *kay-mystère*, letting the warm, unyielding wax pole penetrate him deeply, open him up, sink into the core of him. Then with a soft moan he began to move his relaxed, stretched arsehole up and down on it, his thighs aching as he pumped his arse on the candle's thick length, squatting down on it with legs spread wide apart to take its entirety up into himself as far as he possibly could, moving his fist on his rigid erection and moaning Henri's name as he bounced his arsehole up and down on the warm, smooth pole with increasing rapidity, tears squeezing from the corners of his closed, glossy-lidded eyes as the candle filled his anal cavity with each down thrust, repeatedly forcing himself to sit down harder on it and push it even further up inside him, satisfying his arse and his gut but not his heart, his headscarf loose, his dreadlocks tumbling down over his face. Eventually, he took his hand off his dripping dick to concentrate on working his arsehole on the thick wax pole, his large, rigid cock bobbing above heavy, free-swinging balls, bouncing with each push down so vigorously that it slapped his trembling belly. With a sharp gasp he came, the candle slipping even further up his arsehole as his muscles tensed, gripped and slackened, and his come spattered the base of Baron Samedi's altar, a libation to the *lwa* of Ti-Charles's seed. Exhausted and drained, the handsome young *oungan* slowly pulled himself upright, the candle sliding smoothly out of his arsehole as he stood. Although it had not fully satisfied him, Ti-Charles immediately missed its presence inside his rectum. His anal ring had remained open, receptive, as if in anticipation, and Ti-Charles had found himself hoping against reason that Henri might either return to the *oufo* after the service, or visit Ti-Charles's cabin after the moon set. He did neither, but still, that night Ti-Charles felt that Henri Biassou had moved closer to him.

But once again, when he had greeted the muscular young fisherman on his way down to the village the next morning to administer a healing ritual bath of herbs and goat's milk to an elderly woman stricken by a fever, Ti-Charles had been all but ignored by Henri. Of course he knew that those possessed remember nothing of their actions when their *gros-bon-ange* is returned to them and the *lwa* has departed, but it still burned Ti-Charles's heart to be so coolly treated by Henri, a pain that was made all the worse for him when he saw Henri again later that day, at a distance, laughing and throwing his arm casually around the shoulders of one of his fellow fishermen as they made their way home after a day spent painting their boats, the other man feeling little or nothing in response to a touch that would have sent breakers of ecstasy pounding like the surf through Ti-Charles's lean, taut body, rammed him into violent erection and possibly even made him come without so much as touching himself.

And so tonight, the night before All Saints', and after months and months of longing, the young *oungan* had decided that he could no longer bear the intensity of his feelings, his loneliness, his unprofessed, unacknowledged love. Tonight he would invoke Ezulie, the goddess of love, and seek her guidance to help him win Henri Biassou's heart. His own heart began to hammer in his chest at the thought, and he found himself wishing the rest of the preparations for the next day away, then feeling guilty at his selfishness and want of dedication to his role as *oungan* and so attending to them with special care.

In any case, before he could attend to his own business with the spirits, Ti-Charles was to receive a visit from Sudra, the local gendarme, who was seeking the dark-eyed young *oungan*'s advice on his own torments of the heart.

Sudra was the police chief of the southern rural parish that included Croix-Le-Bois and a string of other small fishing villages, extending as far along the coastline eastwards as Arbrerouge, the nearest decent-sized town, twenty miles away, from which daily buses ran to the island's capital, Solaville, which was named after the revolutionary leader who was the first man to challenge the French colonial rulers of the island in the mid-nineteenth century. Jean Sola's rebellion was ultimately and violently crushed by the French authorities, and his bloody, mutilated body was hung by the governor from a spreading mapu tree in the market square of LaFontainelle for all the peasants and slaves to see. After the French were finally driven from the island three decades later LaFontainelle was renamed Arbrerouge ('Red Tree') in commemoration of Sola's heroism and sacrifice. The offices of the Police Commissioner who had appointed Sudra overlooked that square, their windows shaded by the leaves of the same ancient tree from which the rebel leader had been hanged.

Sudra covered his beat on a battered but gleaming and impeccably maintained Harley Davidson that had been left behind nine years earlier when the American troops had withdrawn from the island in 1951, after a 'peace-keeping' exercise. Nothing gave the lean, hard-bodied forty-year-old black man greater pleasure than speeding along the red-dust roads that ran through the sprawling cane and tobacco fields that produced the island's principal exports like arteries, in search of wrongdoers: brawling drunkards, petty thieves and the like. The 'big man' of the neighbourhood, he enjoyed buying drinks for the men of the villages he patrolled and entertaining them with stories of scandalous and decadent big-city doings.

Despite having been appointed by the Police Commissioner in Arbrerouge – an ambitious and self-serving man in the pocket of the Catholic Church and a repressive central government propped up by the American military – Sudra was himself a committed Voodoo *serviteur* who honoured the *lwa*. He saw it as his duty to warn Ti-Charles in advance if he heard of any plans to raid the *oufo* or break up a festival. The economy was once again being mishandled and so persecution of believers was on the rise: any failures could be blamed on the activities of *bokors*, and the authorities had little interest in distinguishing between sorcerers and *oungans*. So Ti-Charles was particularly beholden to the parish's police chief, who, in addition to warning him about raids in the offing, also regularly filed reports of 'No Voodooist Activity' in the area around Croix-Le-Bois to his superiors in Arbrerouge.

The moon was riding high in the cloudless sky when Ti-Charles heard the sound of Sudra's Harley Davidson sputtering up the path to the *oufo*. Finishing his obeisances at Legba's shrine quickly, Ti-Charles picked up an oil lamp and left the *kay-mystère*. He crossed the peristyle, where the drummers were busy anointing and dedicating their drums, and the *ounsis*, the temple adepts, were completing their ritual preparations for the next day's festival, the good-looking young men talking softly among themselves as they worked. Nodding acknowledgement to the other *serviteurs*, Ti-Charles passed by them and out through the open main gate of the compound just as Sudra pulled up outside. The air was a little cooler and fresher now, and Ti-Charles could feel the heat of the motorbike's engine as Sudra kicked out the stand with one army-booted foot, and smell its petrol and the dry pink dust its passing had stirred up.

'Ti-Charles, my friend,' Sudra called out with a broad smile as he dismounted with a fluid movement, holding out a hand to the lithe young *oungan*. Ti-Charles was stripped to the waist, bare-footed and wearing only tight white breeches, a red bandana around his neck, the dreadlocks on the top of his head exploding outwards like palm leaves from the top of the trunk. Sudra had always found the velvet-smooth and curvaceous younger man attractive, and in the past Ti-Charles had certainly seemed receptive to his flirtatious talk, but somehow it had never gone beyond that: they had become brothers rather than lovers, fellow *serviteurs*.

'Sudra,' Ti-Charles replied, smiling too and extending his hand for the shaven-headed police chief to shake. Sudra's hand was large and dark and he wore gold rings on his fingers and chains around his wrists. Sinews corded his forearm as he gripped Ti-Charles's hand firmly. His features were battered but oddly handsome, his eyes sad but sparkling, his teeth large and irregularly gold-capped, his lips large, and he grew a moustache above his wide, mobile mouth. He wore a light-blue short-sleeved police-man's shirt with brass epaulettes, tight across his broad shoulders, soft, worn, black leather trousers that hugged his lean, well-shaped legs, full crotch and large, muscular butt like a second skin, and heavy black boots that rose up shinily smooth to the tops of his calves except for a haze of brick-red dust. His torso was compact, sinewy and densely muscled. Before he had become a policeman he had been a cane cutter, and his physique had retained that ingrained supple solidity. He wore his revolver stuck into the waistband of his leather trousers at the back, its barrel pointing down between the impressive globes of his buttocks provocatively.

'Let us walk a little,' Sudra said, indicating a track that wound up towards a small hill behind the *oufo* with an inclination of his glassily smooth shaven head.

Ti-Charles nodded. Large, pale, velvet moths had begun to gather around his lantern in profusion. One landed on his face, bright creamy-yellow in the lamplight, its wings fluttering. He could feel the prickle of its small feet on his cheek. He brushed the moth away and turned and placed the lantern on a small shelf by the *oufo*'s entrance, for the full moon was still high in the sky, and bright enough to light their way along a path that both men knew well: Sudra, like Ti-Charles, had been born in Croix-Le-Bois.

From the hill they could look out across the dark forest to the pinprick yellow lights of the fishing village far below. A faint luminescence lit the sea beyond, rafts of phosphorescent micro-organisms throwing out a pale blue-green light beyond the shallows, and the breakers on the beach were just barely audible above the ciccadas thick in the trees around them. Sudra and Ti-Charles sat side by side on the inclined lawn that capped the rise.

'It is Antoine,' Sudra said eventually.

Ti-Charles nodded: he had known this visit would be about Antoine, the melon-butted, demerara-brown black youth whom Sudra adored but who was well known to wander. Dark-eyed, big-dicked, easy-access Antoine, who adored Sudra but not exclusively, or so the talk around the village went.

Antoine had lived practically all his life in Croix-Le-Bois, but dreamed of leaving for the island's decadent and exciting capital, Solaville. So far he had got only as far as Arbrerouge, which was where he had first met Sudra, singing in a coffee house one humid afternoon. He played the guitar and sang to entertain folk in the local villages mostly, occasionally in Arbrerouge, and dreamed of one day being on the radio. Antoine would have liked to have moved to Arbrerouge, if not Solaville, but Sudra preferred their home to be in Crois-La-Boix: he and Sudra shared a cabin covered in wisteria and honeysuckle on the outskirts of the village, along a small track lined by banana trees. But Sudra was often away, either patrolling the countryside or on assignment in Arbrerouge, and Antoine was left to his own devices for many days and nights in a row. And the love-struck policeman was being driven mad by tales of Antoine's flirtatious – and more than flirtatious – behaviour during his frequent absences.

'Well, man?' Ti-Charles asked. 'What is he supposed to have done this time?'

'Man, it is the fishermen,' Sudra replied. 'They say he drinks with them and – and more. Much more. With many of them, they say. Night after night, and sometimes in our home.'

'Who say?' Sudra shrugged. 'This jealousy will drive you mad, man,' Ti-Charles warned him, shaking his head. 'The man who takes too often from the pot of gossip will choke on sharp bones.'

'I think it is more than that,' Sudra said, staring out over the indigo forest. 'I think a spell has been placed on him to make him wander.'

'Why do you think that, man?'

'It is as if he acts against his will, man,' Sudra said. 'Like he is being made to stray.'

Ti-Charles grunted. 'Are you so sure that is not his nature?'

'Man, I have *been* with him,' Sudra answered, sounding pained. 'When you have been inside a man, when he has been inside you, when you have tasted his seed hot in your mouth, you *know* that man.'

Ti-Charles's cock stirred in his trousers and he gripped Sudra's shoulder and shook it. 'But still, man,' he said gently.

'Go to the bar where the fishermen drink after hauling their catches,' Sudra said harshly. 'Go and see for yourself what this *bokor* has done. It is witchcraft, undoubtedly, I'm telling you.'

'You have seen?'

'I have heard.'

Ti-Charles sighed. 'Very well, man. Because I respect you, I will do this. And, when I have seen, I will make you a *wanga* packet,' he continued. 'Nail it to the door of your cabin. It will protect both of you from harm. Offer a black cockerel to Baron Samedi. Place three black feathers from its tail beneath Antoine's pillow. Take this stone.' He handed the police chief a smooth pearl-grey stone. 'Put it under your bed wherever you sleep. And speak a charm for Ezulie I shall tell you.'

Sudra nodded, rubbing his thumb over the stone's smooth, warm surface as Ti-Charles spoke the invocation he should make, then repeated it back to him.

'I want his heart to be for me alone,' Sudra said quietly when he had finished. 'His heart and his cock.'

'Come,' Ti-Charles said, getting to his feet, extending a hand to Sudra and pulling him upright too. 'I have some things I must attend to at the *oufo*, and then I will do as you ask.'

'Tonight?'

'Tonight, man. I swear. But the *lwa* may listen or they may not.'

'I understand, man.'

Hand in hand they made their way back to the whitewashed enclosure below. Sudra kissed Ti-Charles on the cheek, leaving a lingering lemony tang, threw a curving thigh over his Harley

17

Davidson, straddled it, turned the key in the ignition and sped away with a roar that briefly ruptured the night.

Ti-Charles turned, took the still-burning lantern from its alcove, and went back into the *oufo* as the sound of the motorbike faded into the distance, swallowed by the constant *zz-zz* of the cicadas in the surrounding forest. By now the *ounsis* had departed, and only Sauveur, the chief drummer, remained in the peristyle, squatting on a low stool before a tall drum with *veves* carved into its sides. The carved wood was decorated in the colours of the *Ghedes*, the Barons. All was still.

'Maît' Ti-Charles,' Sauveur said, not looking up from the drum whose skin he was carefully tautening by twisting turquoise wooden pegs in the twine knotted around its lip, bouncing his fingers lightly off its stretched surface and inclining his head to listen to the drum's timbre. It was the *manman tambour*, the principle drum of the three normally used in a ceremony, and it was his duty to attend to it both ritually and practically.

'I need you, Sauveur, man,' Ti-Charles said, his young face lit from below by the light from the lantern, his eyes dark. 'There is something I must do, now.'

Sauveur nodded. He was handsome in a large-featured way, clean-shaven, with café-au-lait skin that freckled in the sun and sleepy hazel-gold eyes flecked with green, large, arrogant lips and a small chin. A gold stud glinted in one ear. His hair was plaited into cane rows that gathered at the back into a seam running down into a pigtail that hung nearly to his narrow waist. He was thirty-eight or so, smooth-skinned and heavily muscled, both from his drumming and from his work as a blacksmith and a carpenter in Croix-Le-Bois. The village girls loved to flirt with him, teasingly stroke his impressively thick arms, run their fingers down the grooves between his biceps and triceps, feel the pulse of the veins standing proud when he flexed them, or touch the swelling domes of his pectorals, or even reach for his large, muscular buttocks, but Sauveur had no interest in them: like most of the men at Ti-Charles's *oufo*, the well-built drummer was totally *massissi*, totally dedicated to the beauty and power and spirit of men. He wore a loose red vest that gave easy access to his chest and muscularly ridged stomach, and tight, red-dyed denim shorts that left little to the imagination of any onlooker whose eye was drawn to his full crotch or the gravity-defying globes of a magnificently big arse above strong thighs. Red was the colour dedicated to Ogoun Feraille, patron *lwa* of blacksmiths. Ogoun Feraille was also Sauveur's *maît'-tête*, the spirit who most often possessed the drummer at ceremonies, and with whom Sauveur had had a particular bond since he was fifteen and had first been 'ridden'. And so Sauveur always wore red, except for a few very particular rituals, to honour that *Mystère*. Around his neck he wore two leather bags on braided leather thongs, containing sacred and secret objects. His other dedication was to Ezulie, to whom he had become a spirit groom, just as his father had. Ezulie was a jealous *lwa*, so it was fortunate that Sauveur was by nature *massissi*, since she would not have permitted him romantic attachments to, or sexual relations with, another woman.

Sauveur had been the head drummer at the *oufo* since before Ti-Charles had undergone his initiations and become an *oungan*, and shared with the younger man a profound and passionate dedication to the temple and the *lwa*. His belief and devotion amounted to more than just words and participating in ceremonies: he had once memorably held a machete to the throat of a French Catholic priest who had threatened to report the location of the *oufo* to the authorities after spying on a *mange-lwa* festival several years before. Ti-Charles had administered the spiritual equivalent of a blade to the throat afterwards by making offerings to Damballah Wedo and Baron Samedi; and it was said that, when the priest – who had unsurprisingly fled immediately after being threatened by Sauveur to Arbrerouge – had tried to speak to the Police Commissioner there, his denunciation had stuck in his throat and he had been struck dumb. Some said the priest died three days later in great agony, choking on his own tongue, others that he had returned to France a fearful, chastened man with a permanent stammer. In any event he was not seen again, and the authorities did not come to Croix-Le-Bois.

Sauveur got to his feet and lifted the *manman tambour* and followed Ti-Charles across the peristyle, where the *oungan* was setting out lighted candles to mark the four cardinals of the crossroads, the place of transition, carrying his stool in his free hand, and setting both down near to the *poteau-mitain* post in the centre of the area. The drummer made himself comfortable while the younger black man marked out *veves* with flour to Baron Lundi and Baron Limba, that they might mediate with Ezulie, whose passions were powerful and unpredictable. Once this had been done, he disappeared into a small hut in which various ritual and practical things for the maintenance of the *oufo* were stored. He returned bearing a polished wooden dish on which were set his *asson* rattle, a plate of goat curry he had brought with him earlier in the day, a bowl of rice and a glass of rum. These he took to another whitewashed hut, the *kay-mystère* of Ezulie, goddess of love. They were both offerings to please her and sustenance to give her power: if the spirits are not fed they grow faint and weak and irritable, just as the living do.

Sauveur played small rhythms softly on the brightly painted drum between his thighs as soft sounds of chanting drifted out from within the *kay-mystère*, accompanied by the rasping pulsing of Ti-Charles's *asson*: both the drum and the sacred rattle existed to bring the heartbeats of the human and the deity into harmony and facilitate communion on many levels. Sauveur interwove his rhythms with Ti-Charles's and they began to build in intensity.

After several minutes the young *oungan*, still stripped to the waist, emerged from the hut, his dreadlocks now fastened up in a red headscarf to show the freshly-shaved sides and back of his head. Sauveur had wielded a cutthroat razor with a lover's lightness of touch, Ti-Charles semi-, then fully, erect from the total trust it had required of him to let Sauveur do him this simple, intensely intimate service. At first he had been afraid, but now he looked forward to sitting between Sauveur's smooth, bare, curving thighs once a fortnight and looking out at the world blank-mindedly while the strong, caramel-skinned man sitting behind and above him on a low stool tilted the younger man's head this way and that with deft assurance, lathered the back and sides of his scalp with cool foam and slid the blade over his skin with careful, confident movements, leaving it afterwards liberatingly slick and clean, and making Ti-Charles's cock so hard that he had to go and masturbate immediately just to relieve the pressure of sexual excitement created by such complete yielding to another man in this way. Ti-Charles had felt Sauveur's thick rigidity, too, pressing into his back between his bare shoulder-blades each time Sauveur shaved him, so he knew the drummer was as excited by taking control as he was at giving it up. Still, they had never acted on their excitement together.

Sauveur began to pound the drum harder, and Ti-Charles started to move his body in response to the commands of the beat, shaking the *asson* faster, the muscles and sinews in his lean, smooth, outstretched arm standing proud as he intensified the rhythm, sending the beads and snake vertebrae hissing around the lacquered, curving skin of the dried gourd rattle on their webbing, pumping his crotch and clenching his stomach muscles as the *manman tambour* pounded through the whole length of his body. He struck the ground with his bare, slender feet, the pink soles hammering the impacted reddy-brown earth, the contact facilitating possession just as the *poteau-mitain* post's being embedded in the ground connected the physical world with the world of the *Mystères la-bas*, down below. A bangle around Ti-Charles's narrow brown ankle twined black, red, blue and orange thread together, and it flashed as he danced. Becoming increasingly caught up in the ritual, Ti-Charles tore the headscarf from his head and threw it aside, and his dreadlocks exploded in a snakey mass.

Sauveur's drumming became more rapid as Ti-Charles moved up to the brightly painted *poteau-mitain* post, and the air grew heavier. The orange candle flames at the cardinal points flickered and elongated as though deprived of oxygen as the young man began to grind his lean hips hard against the decorated wood of the column that rose up in the centre of the peristyle, crushing his balls against the warm silk-wood *poteau-mitain* patterned with *veves* and symbols, pushing his painfully stiff cock up and down inside his tight, white, cotton pants, undulating his trembling belly and flatly muscled, hairless chest against its warm, smooth surface, a surface worn and polished by many such movements, his large, bullet-like nipples prickling in excitement at the contact. Ti-

Charles could feel a tense, magnetic energy building in his body as Sauveur's drumming increased in intensity, a sense of being pulled upwards through his own chest, drawn towards Guinée, mythic Africa, the home of the *lwa*. He kissed the pole, licked it with a long, pink tongue, caressed it with his hands, all the time flexing the globes of his arse and pumping his crotch urgently against it, trying to bring himself off for Ezulie, to feed the spirit with that energy, draw her with that need. The silk-wood tasted of salt and perfume. Ti-Charles's heart was hammering in his chest, his excitement building feverishly.

'Give him to me, Ezulie Frieda, bride of many grooms,' he implored. 'Give me this man and I will serve and honour you.'

Sauveur watched the young *oungan* caress and grind against the post, stretching his smoothly muscled arms high above his head and moving his hips from side to side as Sauveur pounded the stretched hide of the drum with large, work-calloused palms, skin on skin, sweat pouring down his face, from his armpits and down between his pectorals, his café-au-lait skin shiny, his cane rows glittering. He tossed his head, flicking his pigtail as he increased the tempo of his drumming, working up a good sweat now, his large, thick cock stiffening within his tight denim shorts and pressing against the warm carved curves of the *manman tambour* gripped firmly between his bare bulging butter-brown thighs.

He had offered to perform this ritual with Ti-Charles tonight because Ti-Charles had made him many *wanga* in the past, magical packets that protected him from sickness, misfortune and occult harm. Into each of these Ti-Charles had put certain magic dusts, small bones, twists of hair and other ingredients. But most important of all, in search of the final, most potent ingredient, Ti-Charles had fallen to his knees in front of Sauveur and buried his face in the muscular drummer's crotch, nuzzling it with his nose and full lips until the standing Sauveur had found himself becoming fully, achingly erect.

'I need your seed,' Ti-Charles had said to the beefy older man below a riding crescent moon as the hour neared midnight, as he knelt before Sauveur, fumbling at the brass buttons of his fly. 'To complete the charm. Your come and my spittle.'

And Sauveur had allowed the kneeling *oungan* to unbutton his fly and pull his red-dyed denim shorts down and suck his stiff and throbbing cock, Ti-Charles explaining breathlessly that the *wanga* would be most effective if the young priest's saliva and Sauveur's ejaculation were mingled hot in his eagerly moving mouth. The pleasure the *oungan* gained from sucking the drummer's large and rigid cock was the unspoken payment Sauveur gave Ti-Charles for his trouble as with a throaty grunt he came in Ti-Charles's mouth. Still, Sauveur felt indebted to Ti-Charles for going to such lengths to make his charms effective, that he cared so much for his *serviteur*, and so he was glad to be able to perform this service for the *oungan* in return, to help the large-eyed, full-lipped young man to find love with Henri Biassou, even though it meant he would be tired before the All Saints' Day ceremony had even begun. He pounded the *manman tambour* with renewed vigour.

Suddenly Ti-Charles started lifting himself up on to tiptoe, still grinding his crotch against the *poteau-mitain*, every muscle straining in his lean body, thighs rigid, calves blocky, Achilles tendons standing proud, his flat chest rising as if he was being drawn upwards by some invisible force, both arms extended upwards at full stretch. Then, as if a string had been cut, the sweaty young man fell back on to the dirt floor of the peristyle, convulsing and arching there for a long moment, thrusting his crotch upwards, his large, stiff cock straining against his tight cotton trousers, a dark stain visible where its head pushed against the fabric. He kicked and bucked several times, eyes rolling up into the back of his head, and then became rigidly still.

Sauveur twisted round and lifted up a smaller black-and-red-painted drum standing just behind him and moved the *manman tambour* to one side. He began to play a slow rhythm on this new drum. This was a *Petro* drum, an instrument of magic, of bewitchment rather than worship, and it would signify to the *lwa* now riding Ti-Charles that a specific request for assistance was being made: the *lwa*, too, serve. Ti-Charles's full lips began to move and he spoke rapidly, too rapidly for Sauveur to catch the words. This speech continued for several minutes, during which time Sauveur slowed the rhythm further and further. Then Ti-Charles's large eyelids slowly fluttered down and covered his still upturned eyes and he fell silent. He exhaled and his chest sank and the tension left his body.

'She come for you, *maître*?' Sauveur asked Ti-Charles later, when he had come out of the trance, propping the pretty young man's head up on his large, smooth, brown thigh and tipping a little rum down his throat. Ti-Charles swallowed, coughed, and nodded.

'Yes,' the young priest replied breathlessly. 'She will speak to the *Ghedes* for me. To Samedi, to Lundi and Limba. She will help.' He looked up into the face of the handsome, lighter-skinned man with wide, dark eyes. 'She says I must carry your seed inside me. Up inside my arse, to the crossroads west of here where the lane from the village meets the road to Arbrerouge, and bury it there with other things at midnight. Your seed because you are the groom of Ezulie, as your father was.'

Sauveur smiled gently and bent forward and kissed Ti-Charles on the mouth, reaching down the length of his prone body and cupping the young *oungan's* crotch in his large hand.

'I will fuck you here, man,' he said softly. 'Under the flags and before the consecrated drums.'

'Fuck me now,' Ti-Charles said hoarsely, half-turning towards Sauveur where he lay, making his arse available to the heavily muscled older man. 'Fuck me so that I may please Ezulie, Limba and Lundi and win Henri Biassou.'

Sauveur reached round and slid a hand down the back of Ti-Charles's knee-length trousers, squeezing the young man's beefy buttocks and pushing two fingers firmly up between them against Ti-Charles's trembling sphincter. It was ready for them, and yielded instantly to Sauveur's fingertips. The two men groaned softly. Up above them the moon was full and vast and yellow. Sauveur withdrew his hand, gripped the waist of Ti-Charles's breeches and pushed them down to his knees, baring his arse. Ti-Charles could feel Sauveur's large rigidity pressing into one bare shoulder blade. His own jutted heavily at an angle where he lay, above his balls, which hung loose and tingling over his thighs.

Without another word Ti-Charles rolled on to his front, face-down, his hard-on now pressed against the impacted earth of the peristyle. Sauveur slipped behind him on to his knees and pushed Ti-Charles's smoothly muscled thighs apart.

'Raise your arse up, man,' Sauveur instructed Ti-Charles hoarsely. 'Show me where you want me.'

Ti-Charles obeyed, raising himself up on to all fours, pushing his large buttocks up and back. Sauveur reached into the back pocket of his frayed denim shorts and pulled out a small olive-green bottle of oil that he used to keep the drumskins supple. He pulled the cork from the bottle's mouth with his large, firm lips and poured a warm golden stream down between Ti-Charles's smooth, muscular globes. Ti-Charles exhaled as Sauveur pushed two fingers up past his now lubricated anal opening to the knuckles.

With his other hand Sauveur fumbled his copper fly buttons open and shucked his shorts down over smooth, muscular thighs to his ankles, freeing his large, heavily veined erection to bob above his large, hanging balls. Then he anointed his swollen, mushroom-shaped, pinky-brown cock head with oil, keeping two thick fingers moving in and out of Ti-Charles's arsehole as he did so, dilating and relaxing the *oungan*'s anal ring as, with his other hand, he lubricated his own pulsing crown and shaft with firm, caressing motions. Ti-Charles squirmed and groaned with excitement and anticipation as Sauveur's fingers moved back and forth inside his anal passage.

Eager for his own pleasure, Sauveur pulled his fingers out of Ti-Charles's slick and hungry chocolate star and moved around so he could guide his cock head towards it. He bent his thick, rigid shaft downwards slightly with a grunt and placed the smooth brown dome of its crown against Ti-Charles's glossy sphincter, inclining his hips forward slightly to press and hold it in place. Ti-Charles exhaled in anticipation and braced himself, curving his back like a bow downwards and pushing his buttocks up as high as he could, to ease Sauveur's entry into his body cavity. Sauveur placed one large hand in the small of the back of the younger man before him and moved his hips and thighs forward, slowly but relentlessly easing the large, curving head of his thick, stiff, oily dick into Ti-Charles's hot, smooth rectum, forcing his anal ring to stretch and yield to the invading tool. Ti-Charles moaned and tossed his head as Sauveur's cock began to slide inside him, sending his dreads flying; but he kept his hips and buttocks in place, taking deep breaths as inch after inch of Sauveur's throbbing rigidity slipped inside his anal passage, filling him thrillingly and making his own large, stiff cock buck and drip pre-come between taut spread legs.

For Henri, Ti-Charles thought, wishing it was the handsome young fisherman who was mounting him from behind, who was pushing his nine-inch wood-hard erection up Ti-Charles's arse-hole to the root, who was bracing himself up with a strongly muscled arm and splayed hand and starting to move his lean, sinewy hips backwards and forwards against the mocha globes of the *ougan's* upturned buttocks with the regular slapping sounds of skin against skin, muscle against muscle while gripping Ti-Charles's waspy waist firmly with both hands, who was sending waves of pleasure coursing through Ti-Charles's body, making him sigh and gasp and then groan loudly and uncontrollably.

Sauveur began to fuck Ti-Charles in earnest, pumping his hips against Ti-Charles's upturned arse, pumping his cock back and forth in Ti-Charles's rectum, his own firm buttery-brown buttocks flexing concave-convex-concave-convex as he thrust fast and deep into the tight but accommodating arsehole of the young man facing away from him on all fours on the still-warm red earth, naked except for his trousers tangled around his ankles, determined to satisfy himself quickly and roughly in Ti-Charles's hot and juicy anal cavity.

'Oh yes,' Ti-Charles gasped, his cock now running pre-come like a tap, clear crystal strands coursing down from his piss slit and libating the dry red earth between his legs. He longed to grip his own dick where it bobbed and bounced above his heavy, hanging ballsac, and give himself some relief from the turbulent excite-ment the rapid motions of Sauveur's large, thick, stiff dick in his now well-lubricated arse were giving him, or at least toy with his dark, bullet-shaped nipples. But he refused to allow himself this gratification, this sweet relief: only with Henri would he allow himself to come.

Ezulie teases and tests me, he thought as Sauveur's cock slithered backwards and forwards inside his now stretched and thrillingly aching rectum, making his heart hammer inside his heaving chest and his lungs burn. She teases me and tempts me to give my relief to Sauveur, handsome Sauveur whose body I have enjoyed so many times, who knows how to give a man pleasure, who is giving me great pleasure now as he grips my waist firmly and fucks me deeply, his heavy, swinging balls bumping against mine with every deep thrust of his cock into my arsehole to the base. And I will give this man pleasure, and I will take pleasure from him, but I will save my own release for Henri, Ezulie. You will not misguide me.

Sauveur now straddled Ti-Charles, pushing him forward and down so his large, beefy arse was raised up even higher, and fucked him with a passion, his own large and tautly-muscled chest beginning to heave as he hammered the younger man's arse with his dick, ramming it in and out of Ti-Charles's now fully relaxed sphincter, leaving it glistening and gaping open for moments at a time before shoving his throbbing rigidity up Ti-Charles again right the way to the mesh of glittering black coils at its thick root, thrilling to the feel of the silky-smooth tightness of the lining of the *oungan*'s rectum against his cock head, the grip of Ti-Charles's anal ring around his stiff, veiny, aching shaft.

Ti-Charles was now gasping high and fast with every rough, rapid thrust of Sauveur's cock into his arsehole, and Sauveur could feel a tightness in his chest and a growing weight in his pulsing erection as he fucked Ti-Charles as rapidly as he could. His throat was dry, the domes of his chest were heaving and sinew striated across them and across his aching thighs and hips. He could feel his throbbing dick growing heavier and heavier, until it was his rigid erection that was forcing his hips to pump, drawn in by Ti-Charles's greedy, hungrily sucking arsehole.

'Oh yes, oh yes, oh yes,' Sauveur yelled throatily as he soared past the point of no return and thrust his hips forward with all his strength, pushing Ti-Charles face first into the dry red earth as he forced himself as deeply as humanly possible into the younger man's anal passage and exploded inside him, his aching cock bucking inside Ti-Charles's rectum and pumping hot jism into the face-down, gasping *oungan* he held pinned beneath him. 'I honour the *lwa*, I give you my seed.'

And Ti-Charles gasped, 'Oh, thank you, man, thank you,' as Sauveur's boiling semen flooded his slick, bruised anal cavity, a healing libation of seed, the male principle, his richly dark skin shiny and glistening with sweat, every muscle and sinew aching, exhausted and sexually charged up, filled and firmly fucked yet unsatisfied. Ti-Charles longed to rest, to lie there for a while with Sauveur sprawled on top of him, strong, protective, his cock still up Ti-Charles's now slack arse. But Ti-Charles had two journeys to make tonight, two obligations to discharge.

Still, he couldn't help but sigh regretfully as Sauveur pulled his still-stiff and gratifyingly long and thick manhood out of Ti-Charles's well-stretched rectum as Ti-Charles lay face down on the ground, leaving it empty except for the jism he had shot into the young priest's back passage. Ti-Charles clenched his sphincter reflexively to ensure that none of Sauveur's seed could escape.

With an effort he pushed himself up on to all fours, then sat back on his heels. His whole body ached and his throat was dry. He wanted to rest a while but the candles were burning low, and the moon was beginning to set in the sky. He had no time to waste: *Les Mystères* were waiting.

Two

A straw *macoute* bag filled with ritual objects slung over one dark, lean shoulder, Ti-Charles cut along a narrow, overgrown track that led through a succession of groves of orange and lemon trees, hurrying to reach the lane that led up from the village to the crossroads where he was to carry out Ezulie's instructions. The large moon was riding high, its light making his white breeches and white headscarf glow almost phosphorescently against the darkness of his skin and the lush indigo-veridian verdure around him. Grass had covered over the little-used track, and it felt cool and pleasant beneath the soles of his bare feet. The air was very still and he felt a heightened sense of everything that was around him. Despite the lateness of the hour, he was wide awake, and full of anticipation for what he had to do. Overhanging the track, the dry, smooth leaves of the orange and lemon branches brushed his chest and arms and face as he hurried along, but their touch was more like a caress than an obstruction, an encouragement for his errand. The perfume of their blossoms filled his nose, and that too seemed fitting.

In a little time he reached the lane leading out from Croix-Le-Bois to the road to Arbrerouge. The red clay glowed opalescently in the moonlight, imbued with a magical energy that he felt as he stepped from the soft grass on to its hard, smooth surface, reaffirming his connection to *là-bas*, the place below where the spirits dwelled on their island in the waters. Here the air moved a little, and he could taste a trace of salt on his tongue carried in from the sea.

The lane was empty, deserted. Ti-Charles was pleased: he didn't want all his paths to be known.

Ti-Charles set off uphill, turning away from the village and leaving it behind him. The crossroads was a little over a mile away. The lane wound slowly upwards into the lower foothills and away from the coast, any view obscured by rising walls of palm trees and banana plants. Ti-Charles's skin began to gleam with sweat as he walked fast and with his buttocks clenched – already he could feel that Sauveur's seed was beginning to slip out of his rectum however tightly he was keeping his oily anal ring closed.

Forgive me, Ezulie, he thought. But he fucked me hard and made me slack. I serve as best I can.

The lane levelled off and ran straight for a while, skirting a rise. Suddenly Ti-Charles began to get the feeling that he was being followed, and with malicious intent. Several times he stopped and looked back, but there was no one to be seen – although a pursuer could have stepped aside and into the inky shadows of the palms without much difficulty. He persuaded himself it was most likely his imagination as he hurried forward.

At this point the lane ran along a ridge and the vegetation fell away on the coastal side, giving a view of the valley next to the one at the base of which Croix-Le-Bois sat. This valley had once been cultivated by slaves, and from the ridge the patchwork pattern of fields of tobacco, sugar cane and cotton, now long overgrown, was still visible in the moonlight. In its centre a vast, whitewashed clapboard, colonial mansion still stood, its interior long since gutted, its fabric gradually being reclaimed by the forest, by the soil. Almost against his will Ti-Charles paused, looked down on it, and shivered: his presence here, in this land, his severance from the ancestors and Guinée – all that was bad about his life and the life of his people was represented here. He both wished it obliterated by the creepers and beetles and the weight of time and wanted it to exist for ever, so that nothing could be forgotten, overwritten, whitewashed as the building had been whitewashed by the slaves year after year. Now it gleamed white as bones, jutting up from soil blackened with blood. He couldn't look away.

The tiny hairs on the back of Ti-Charles's smooth neck began to prickle as he stared down at the spectrally moonlit mansion: were those human figures moving slowly and erratically among the overgrown cane fields closest to it? He screwed up his dark, feline eyes, trying to sharpen his vision. Perhaps it was only the breeze off the ocean stirring the leaves down there: at this distance it was hard to be sure. Ti-Charles had never quite believed the tales that a *bokor*, a sorceror, lived there and worked the fields with zombies, but still he knew there were such men. It was indisputably true that some years ago the grave of Sauveur's cousin had been opened, and the body had been removed and never recovered.

The cousin had not been a believer, and nor had his wife – they had both been fervent Catholics and disavowed *Les Mystères* (unlike many who simply combined their faiths; and indeed Ti-Charles himself honoured the Christian trinity before invoking Legba in his ceremonies at the *oufo*) – and so she had failed to take the proper precautions, not even watching over the grave for the requisite period or taking the precaution of burying her husband near to a busy byway in a solidly constructed concrete vault. And so his body had been taken. Did it toil even now in the cane fields as its ancestors had toiled? Was it enslaved as its ancestors had been enslaved, its spirit trapped in a bottle on a *bokor*'s altar?

A light flickered briefly in an upper-storey window of the mansion and Ti-Charles inhaled sharply. Perhaps it was no more than one of the few remaining panes of glass in an old window pane swinging in the sea breeze and catching the moonlight, although it had seemed yellower than that: more like the light of an oil lamp. Now the house was dark again.

Ti-Charles looked round sharply, scanning the lane in both directions: still nobody was there. With a shiver he hurried on, feeling as if the old house, or some will within it, was trying to waylay him, make him miss his appointment with the *lwa*. The crossroads lay only a little way ahead. The moon was now almost directly overhead: it was time.

There was a slight breeze stirring the leaves of the palm and cinnamon trees and the air was cooler at the place where the lane that went from Croix-Le-Bois to the steeply mountainous interior crossed the main road to Arbrerouge, which wove its way all along the island's southern coastline a mile or two inland. Two years earlier it had been widened and surfaced with tarmac to facilitate the movement of government and foreign 'peace-keeping' troops in trucks and jeeps, but already the land was reclaiming it, roots and suckers splitting its surface, torrents of red mud washing chunks of it away and rendering it impassable except on foot or by mule or cart. Even Sudra's Harley Davidson struggled over the ruts and the rubble.

Except for the soft hiss of the shivering leaves, all was quiet. The feeling of being followed had left Ti-Charles, and he could now attend to the task at hand. He set down his straw bag, produced a small trowel and dug a hole at the exact centre of the crossroads. A strange energy surged through him as he did so: the power of the crossroads, *carrefour*, the place that mirrored the intersection of the world of the living and the world of the spirits, the dead and the *lwa*. For in Voodoo there is both a mirroring and a constant interpenetration of these worlds: the spirits and the dead are not elsewhere but always present, always informing and acting in the world of the living, and in turn being nourished by it.

'Papa Legba, *ouvri bayè-a pou mwen*, Papa Legba open the gate for me,' Ti-Charles muttered as he placed white candles at the four cardinal points. Under his breath he spoke quick imprecations to the Voodoo trinity – *Les Mortes, Les Mystères, Les Marassa* – the spirits of the dead, the *lwa*, and the twins who symbolise divine androgyny and creation giving birth to itself. He took a mouthful of white rum and sprayed it in a fine mist over the hole and the candles. The flames caught the alcohol and flared up in response.

Ti-Charles quickly stripped off his breeches and put them aside, standing there naked, his cock thrust forward, semi-erect, his mouth slightly open. From his straw bag he took a small bottle of perfume given to him as payment for a healing bath by Sudra from Arbrerouge, and poured half its contents into the small hole. Then he thought again and poured the entirety into the darkness, placing the cut-glass bottle carefully in the hole after it. This was followed by a twined circlet of laurel leaves and a small mirror with a mother-of-pearl back that had belonged to Ti-Charles's grandmother, given to her, it was said, by a lady in the Big House where she had once been a maid. And now it was a gift to Ezulie. On top of it he placed a small offering of saffron rice wrapped in a silk handkerchief and a *wanga* packet he had prepared some days beforehand containing the bones of a song thrush and certain magical dusts.

Invoking Ezulie so rapidly and quietly as to be inaudible, Ti-Charles squatted above the hole, spreading his smooth thighs wide and lowering himself so the globes of his arse were a little way above it. Then he reached back and pulled his buttocks apart, exposing his glossy sphincter to the cool night air, and pushed, his lean ebony belly tensing. Sticky white strands of Sauveur's jism, intermingled with oil and kept hot for Ezulie inside his body, slid from Ti-Charles's relaxed arsehole. Ti-Charles glanced back round as the dollops of come dropped from his relaxed anal opening into the hole, excited to see its satiny, cock-stretched shininess reflected up at him in the mirror, see the thick, white, pearly come drip out of it.

Sauveur gave me a good load, Ti-Charles thought. Ezulie should be pleased: he has honoured her too. He pushed until all Sauveur's come had slipped out of his rectum, then slowly stood up. His cock was fully erect now, wagging in the breeze and pulsing.

'Ezulie Dantour, accept this offering and answer my prayers,' Ti-Charles said softly. Then he extinguished the candles, pinching out the wicks between spit-wetted thumb and forefinger, and put them back in his *macoute*. Afterwards, he pulled on his breeches and quickly filled in the hole, careful to leave the earth as undisturbed-looking as possible so that no one would know a ritual had been performed there.

Ti-Charles felt strangely elated as he started back down the lane towards Croix-Le-Bois, but also tired. He wished he had not given his word to Sudra that he would go to the bar where the fishermen spent their evenings that same night to see if there was evidence of his lover Antoine's infidelity, and whether sorcery was indeed in any way involved. Earlier that evening he had been sure that this was not the case, although he had been happy to give Sudra what spiritual aid and protection he could offer, but now he wondered. Hadn't he been followed by someone – or something – earlier? Hadn't that been a lamp at the window of the old Sonnelier mansion? He set his jaw, resolving to keep his eyes and ears open.

Because tomorrow was the *mange-lwa* ceremony and both a celebration and a feast day, and they did not have to sail that day, Ti-Charles knew the fishermen would be up drinking, talking, singing or listening to the radio until well past midnight. But still he found himself hurrying forward.

See what there is to be seen, he thought. Perhaps nothing, perhaps something.

The lane forked a little way above the village. Ti-Charles took the narrower left fork that led down through a grove of satin-wood trees to the beach, petering out among the dunes above the stretch of sand where the brightly coloured fishing boats were beached.

Ti-Charles made his way down to the boats, feeling uneasy. The tide was turning, darkly emerald waves mantled in white starting to rush in over the smooth, expanses of white sand pitted by the feet of night birds and the tracks of ghost crabs, reaching up towards the sterns of the tethered boats. He recognised Henri's boat, painted with images of Agwe and Ezulie. Ti-Charles had watched Henri paint them, admiring his skill as an artist as he admired Henri's broad, tapering and smoothly muscled back, longing all the while to kiss the elegant indentation between Henri's shoulder blades.

He ran his fingers over the painted wood. It was cool to the touch, and slightly rough. His cock stirred in his breeches.

Rara music came floating on the breeze from the fishermen's radio a little further down the beach, the thatched bar screened from Ti-Charles's sight by a thrusting clump of palm trees. He made his way forward silently.

The beach-hut's front opened towards the sea, and the sides and back windows set into its straw-woven walls were louvred, so Ti-Charles could see nothing except slats of yellow light as he came up to it, hear only the radio, and talk and laughter. Nor could he be seen. He disliked the idea of spying on the fishermen, particulary as Henri would be there. But he had given Sudra his word. And, if he was honest with himself, he was curious about what he would see as well. He slipped forward almost on all fours and silent as a shadow, and peered in.

There were five men inside the hut, their wide range of skin tones – from demerara to cinnamon to mocha brown to obsidian – lit warmly by a row of tin oil lamps hooked from a beam in the low ceiling, yellow-orange flames flickering as they swung slightly in the breeze off the sea – four fishermen, and Antoine.

One of the fishermen was Henri Biassou. He leaned back against the narrow, chrome-fronted bar – bought from an American hotel in Solaville – on his elbows, straw hat pushed back on his shaven head, clearly etched stomach muscles stretched out long in flat, supple blocks beneath a white mesh vest, lean hips slanting in crotch-huggingly tight, sun-and-salt-bleached denim shorts, a bottle of beer hanging loosely in one large hand. Ti-Charles's eyes roved over Henri's compact chest, his smooth, richly brown thighs, his leanly muscled arms, and the young *oungan*'s cock expanded rapidly to full hardness inside his breeches.

Henri laughed then, at something one of the other fishermen had said, his full, well-shaped lips splitting into a boyish white and gold smile, and Ti-Charles felt his balls clench and his chest tighten so sharply in response to the young man's smile that he almost gasped aloud.

'Man, I'm going to go out and get some air,' Henri said with a stifled yawn. 'Look at the stars.' He wiped the back of his hand across his mouth, his hazy golden eyes looking suddenly sleepy. Then he pushed himself up from the bar and loped across the room, his gait sexily bow-legged, and stepped out onto the low verandah at the front of the hut that looked out on the endless Atlantic, and down into the coolly velvet night.

Towards Guinée, Ti-Charles thought. Towards home. Would I have thrown myself from the slaver's ship as I saw all that I knew disappear over the horizon for ever? Can I regret all that my life is because it was born of that passage? He felt a longing to go and join Henri down by the sea and take his hand and watch the eternal stars and the endless breakers with him, melancholy and love and desire mingled in his chest, his loins.

With a soft sigh he resigned himself to staying where he was – for Sudra – and turned back to see what the remaining four men in the hut were doing. Antoine was centre-stage now, dancing provocatively to the music on the radio. He was a short, curvy, butter-brown-skinned youth of twenty-two, with a round, pretty, hairless, freckled face, full lips, and an easy smile showing gappy teeth, the front two gold-framed, and large greeny-brown eyes. The sides of his head were shaved glassy-smooth and his hair on top was conked and slicked back glossily. He wore pearl studs in his ears and a choker of pearls given to him by Sudra high around his neck. His full name was Antoine Dieudonne, which meant 'given of God', and he had been blessed – or cursed, perhaps, Ti-Charles thought now – with a God-given gift for pleasing and teasing men.

All Antoine was wearing was a pair of skimpy, skin-tight, white lace briefs – another present from Sudra – that could barely contain his full and bulging crotch at the front, and at the back dived down between his large, high, smooth and beefy buttocks invitingly, a narrow gold chain around his hips, the pearl choker around his neck, and a pair of battered army boots stolen from Sudra's wardrobe. His well-packed crotch pushed forward provocatively, as if inviting any man who wanted it to reach out and take hold of it for his pleasure.

The rest of Antoine's curvy, firmly muscled body was a smooth, light golden brown, flawless, hairless and gleaming with sweat.

His large lips were glossy and well defined, and he licked them with knowing flirtatiousness as he looked around him at the three remaining fishermen, winding his pelvis to the music on the radio.

They watched him intently with slightly open mouths as he let his head tilt back, arching a supple, sinewy neck, and spread his strong, smooth brown-sugar thighs wide, bouncing his big, water-melon butt up and down in time to the music as if he was using it to pleasure a seated man's erect, upstanding cock. His large nipples stood out from the domes of his chest like dark-brown bullets filled with a sexual energy that drew men's fingers towards them. He was starting to work up a deep sweat now.

Ti-Charles could see why Sudra was besotted with Antoine, and also that Antoine was a natural wanderer who might love the lean, handsome policeman very much, but would never be able to say no to whatever life might bring his way – above all, if it involved the attention of men. Who would not want to say no, even if he could.

But perhaps it is only flirtation, Ti-Charles thought, excited himself by Antoine's near-nudity and smooth, muscularly swivel-ling body, and the expression of wanton abandon on the youth's face. Although he generally preferred to be passive with another man, to be fucked, Ti-Charles felt a sudden hot desire to bend the brown-skinned youth over the bar, pull those tight lace panties down to his ankles and shove his achingly stiff cock up Antoine's no doubt already greased and receptive anal star to the root, to make Antoine gasp or squeal in pleasure as Ti-Charles fucked him hard. Ti-Charles found himself rubbing his hand over his rigid, trapped erection through the soft, tight cotton of his breeches and breathing a little harder.

As he glanced round at the faces of the three fishermen watching Antoine, Ti-Charles realised that Antoine was having much the same effect on them as he was on him. Their names were Petro, Ti-Coyo and Bossuet, and they watched the scantily-clad boy with hungry eyes. Not that they didn't have sex with each other, Petro, Ti-Coyo, Bossuet and Henri Biassou: there wasn't one of them who hadn't sucked his friend and fellow mariner's cock to the root, swallowed his friend's hot come as he climaxed or taken his stiff dick up his arse – or sometimes even both at the same time – and loved doing it, either here in the beach hut at the end of a long day at sea, or out on the vastly swelling blue ocean while waiting for the swordfish, the marlins, the red snappers or small sharks to bite; or cradled his friend in his arms against the vastness of the sky, warm, smooth muscular bodies pressing close in trust and affection. They were bonded by the sea, by their craft with net and line, rigging and sail, and by their kisses, their laughter, their sudden, quickening desire for each other's lips and cocks and arses. But Antoine Dieudonne was different: he was brazen, and wilfully provocative. They were fishermen, first and foremost; the rest came after. With Antoine his lips, his eyes, his nipples, his buttocks – all these came first.

'I never say no to anything,' Ti-Charles had once heard Antoine say while buying cocoa yams and plantain at the market in Croix-Le-Bois, smiling a wide white smile and adjusting the bulge in the ball-crushingly tight denim shorts he wore to tease and please Sudra – and any other man he happened to pass by. Sudra had had his lanky ebony arm around Antoine's muscular café-au-lait shoulders, and the shaven-headed, darker-skinned man had smiled too, pulling Antoine to him, eyes hidden behind mirrored shades, his cock visibly expanding within his tight leather biker's trousers in anticipation of getting Antoine back to his house for some lovemaking.

'Anything?' Ti-Charles had said.

'Anything to do with love,' Antoine had replied.

And now Antoine looked like he was spreading his love far and wide, further and wider than Sudra had believed he was going to back then anyway, as he arched his body back in front of Bossuet, Ti-Coyo and Petro, pushing his bulging, lace-covered crotch out for any one of them to grip or fondle, then pumped his now shiny body hard to the beat of the music on the radio.

The fishermen applauded and laughed as he began to caress himself with his own hands, putting on a show for them, adjusting their own now lumpy crotches, toying with their own nipples, exchanging half-shy glances at each other, wondering who would be first to throw his inhibitions aside and do something, put on a

show himself, put on a show with Antoine, or indeed with one
of his fellows.

Ti-Coyo was the shortest of the three fishermen, perhaps a
little under five foot six, mid-brown, lean and hard-bodied, every
well-defined muscle etched with sinew and striated with veins.
His handsome face was framed by an Afro-like mass of dreadlocks
that exploded bushily from his head; his wide mouth was filled
with large white teeth and his lips were full and arrogantly
defined. His nostrils flared. A little hair coiled in the centre of his
compact chest, and he had a golden ring in one darkly protruding
nipple – a souvenir of a drunken night in Arbrerouge with some
Brazilian sailors three years before.

Ti-Coyo was a little over thirty and had a sinuous, angular
body defined by the toughness of a countryman born and bred.
Cheap imitation-gold rings adorned his twine-hardened, squared-
off hands. He wore a flimsy white singlet that didn't cover his
nipples or chest, and a pair of tight, soft, white, cotton shorts that
did nothing to conceal the largeness of his balls or the size and
thickness of his huge, missile-like cock. It wasn't just because Ti-
Coyo was so short that his manhood seemed so immense: his dick
really was unusually and impressively large and long. It measured
– as he was more than keen to prove to any man who provoked
him by doubting his assertions as to its magnificent proportions –
eleven inches in length, and was almost six inches around when
fully erect – a beer-can-thick prick that any man would be proud
to get on his knees and get his lips around.

And Ti-Coyo's dick was fully erect now, provoked into rigidity
by Antoine's large, glossy lips, accommodating smile, bulging
crotch, bouncing butt and swivelling hips, pushing itself sideways
across his lean ebony-hard thigh beneath the close-fitting fabric of
his shorts at an awkward angle, its rounded head thrusting
outwards and casting a revealing blue shadow on the white cotton
in the lamplight.

Painfully aroused now himself, Ti-Charles was suddenly eager
to see Ti-Coyo's cock in all its renowned splendour, and found
himself wondering whether Antoine could accommodate the
whole of its length up his arse, or whether even he would find

taking eleven thick inches an effort. Ti-Charles suspected not, however, remembering Sudra telling him about a private show the beefy young light-skinned man had put on for him one afternoon with an exceptionally large cucumber bought from the market.

'I swear, man,' Sudra had said, his eyes widening as he told the tale. 'More than a foot of it went up him, easy. Straight up his arsehole with just a dab of grease to slick himself. He gasped but he took it up there and his dick got even stiffer, man.' He never lost it, he was so turned on. Then, I'm telling you it turned me on so much I thought I would lose my mind, he *bounced* on that cucumber, man. Got it right the way up him until it was satisfying him deep-deep. It was this thick.' Sudra had made a ring with both fingers that was eight inches around. 'And I stood there in front of him with my trousers round my ankles,' he had carried on. 'And he squatted on that cucumber and bounced while he sucked me off. Bounced hard, you know, man? Pushed down and *ground* on that cucumber. It made me wish that there were two of me so I could please him at both ends at the same time. Man, that was one memorable afternoon!'

Ti-Charles wondered what Ti-Coyo enjoyed doing when he was with a man. He seemed to remember having heard rumours of Ti-Coyo having unusual tastes, liking things beyond just cocksucking and being sucked, and fucking and being fucked, but what they were exactly escaped the young *oungan's* mind as he stared at Ti-Coyo's massive dick straining against the fabric of his white cotton shorts through the slatted shutters of the fishermen's hut, and licked his dry lips.

Hard-bodied and hard-living, a great better on cock fights, Ti-Charles suspected Ti-Coyo liked his sex rough, but he wasn't sure. And, even then, how rough? He imagined being gagged by Ti-Coyo's enormous cock, Ti-Coyo fucking his face, his throat, pleasuring himself in the pretty young Voodoo priest's mouth with lustful callousness, and the idea excited Ti-Charles. He imagined gagging and gasping for breath as Ti-Coyo forced eleven rigid inches down into his oesophagus, the taste of Ti-Coyo's sweet, salty pre-come on his tongue and lips. He was glad Henri

Biassou had left the hut, and hoped he wouldn't return or, if he did, that he wouldn't participate in whatever looked like it was inevitably going to happen: it would break Ti-Charles's heart to see his sweetheart giving himself to these other men, even as their handsomeness and horniness aroused him strongly.

Bossuet was the darkest of the three, and the tallest, heavily muscled, with broad shoulders and a shaved head, and a little over six foot in height. All his teeth were gold and he wore gold studs in both ears. He was handsome in a battered, thick-necked way, clean-shaven, with black, heavily lidded eyes and a large, beefy, blocky umber body whose bulgingly muscular symmetry was thrown off by his missing most of his right arm – the legacy of an attack by a mako shark that had become entangled in the nets one time they had been out night-fishing.

It was Henri who had pulled Bossuet back into the boat out of the boiling, inky sea and made a tourniquet from his shirt to staunch the bleeding and held it in place as the five of them rowed back to shore and the rising sun turned the sky crimson, and so there was a particular bond between the two men. Bossuet now had a stainless-steel framework arm ending in a pair of hooks and attached to his thick upper arm with a leather brace, which he had had to go to Solaville to find. As if by way of compensation, his left arm was exceptionally heavily muscled and strong, and there was no one in Croix-Le-Bois who could beat Bossuet in an arm-wrestling competition. This evening Bossuet held a lighted cigar between his chrome hooks, and dragged on it as he watched Antoine dance, letting the smoke slide sensually out of his mouth and up over his full lips.

Bossuet sat back on a zebra-print bar stool, arms folded, legs extended, heavily muscled thighs spread wide. He wore nothing but a pair of leopard-skin briefs bought from an American mail-order catalogue that arched revealingly over his narrow hips at the sides, and a necklace of cowries: Bossuet was always ready for action. His cock was large and thick and pushed straight out against the stretchy black and yellow fabric above the bulge of his ballsac. His erect, half-inch-long nipples pushed out from the great, dark domes of his chest above the ridged curve of his belly, and his butt was big and high and solidly muscular. His missing an arm was, perhaps unexpectedly, not offputting: he had an aura of strength and self-possession even without it, and a directness of manner that made any man he spoke to forget it, or even find it oddly exciting.

'More than a few men have asked me to caress them with my hook, man,' Bossuet had said to Ti-Charles one time. 'I always say, "Sure, providing my cock is down your throat or up your arse at the time." You would be surprised how eagerly they take down their pants or drop to their knees. Very good-looking men.' And he had laughed.

'But you know what turns me on most of all, man?' he had carried on. Ti-Charles had shaken his head, blushing slightly at being taken into Bossuet's confidence so fully. 'When I say that and the other fellow says, "You're so masculine, such a big man, but what I really want to do is fuck you, man. Fuck your big beefy arse." I had a hand up my arse one time, man. Right up there. I did not think I could be so accommodating. This light-skinned fellow with the greenest eyes, fine features and a hard, lean, smooth body. He said he was an artist. We had been drinking and smoking in the cafés and bars and eventually he suggested we took a hotel room. He knew a place. We went up to the room and undressed, and he rolled me on to my front and began to finger-fuck me. When he saw that I liked it, he greased his fingers and began to work them in me, one, two, three, four. Backwards and forwards. It felt good. Hot, you know? He moved his hand on my cock and I relaxed in the excitement and my arsehole opened up and before I really knew what was happening I realised his hand had slid up my arse. I felt my anal ring slip shut around his wrist. And that felt even better.

'He moved his fist backwards and forwards inside me and I came almost immediately from the fullness of it. It was in Arbrerouge, in a hotel room with yellow silk curtains around the bed and black-lacquered furniture from China. Man, I enjoyed it. Of course,' he had added, 'I had to let him fuck me afterwards, satisfy himself in my hot, slack hole.' Bossuet had sighed nostalgically. 'Men are more conservative in Croix-Le-Bois,' he had said.

'Less experimental.' Then he'd smiled to himself. 'But they love to suck and fuck, and so I love them. They are filled with love. In Arbrerouge they are often colder, less giving.'

Ti-Charles wondered if Ti-Coyo had ever fucked Bossuet. The idea of the taller, bulkier, darker man lying back on the pearly top of the bar with his smooth, solid, well-muscled thighs spread wide, his legs up in the air and his smooth mocha arse with its flawless chocolate star exposed, Ti-Coyo gripping Bossuet's ankles and thrusting his thick, rigid eleven inches all the way into the shaven-headed older man's rectum hard and fast to the root, forced Ti-Charles to grip his own throbbingly erect dick through the fabric of his breeches and move his hand slowly back and forth on it to give himself a little relief.

How would it begin?

Maybe Bossuet would beckon with his hook, or with his large, veiny left hand, to Antoine to get on his knees, pull down the well-muscled, shaven-headed, darker-skinned man's leopard-skin briefs and suck his thick, dark and – judging by the stain on the front of the fabric – dripping cock, swallow it to the root and make him groan. Sweat was running down Bossuet's totally shaved scalp, and his features were bloated with excitement as his black eyes ran over Antoine's shapely, near-naked body.

'Face, head and arse, man,' Bossuet had told Ti-Charles. 'I shave them all, every other day. It is one of the pleasures of the safety razor. Now I always feel clean. And I feel that to shave my arse is an invitation to any man that I am happy to be eaten out or fucked. Sometimes I shave my crotch, too.'

Looking at Bossuet's bulging crotch, his rigid cock thrusting out, stretching the leopard-skin material taut, Ti-Charles found himself envying Antoine's chance to suck Bossuet off, or to push Bossuet back on the stool and lift his thighs up and tongue and lick and eat his shaved chocolate star out.

If I had Henri Biassou by my side I would not be thinking these things, Ti-Charles thought to himself, looking last at the youngest of the fishermen, twenty-two-year-old Petro Labwa. Petro was named after the drum he drummed alongside Sauveur at rituals at the *oufo*, and answered to no other. An orphan, abandoned by his unknown mother outside the Voodoo temple, he had been brought up by Ti-Charles's teacher and the adepts there without ever knowing his birth name or why he had been left in their care. Petro often said that he considered Ti-Charles's teacher to be both his father and his mother, and that he had no curiosity about the woman who bore him, or the man who impregnated her. Ti-Charles became a sort of uncle to Petro, despite their similarity in age. Regardless, it was a fisherman rather than an *ounsi*, an adept, that Petro became when he grew up – although he also always drummed at the ceremonies where the *Petro* drum was required. At other ceremonies he sometimes drummed the *seconde* drum.

The *Petro* rituals were the ones that tapped into the darker side of the *lwa*, the bitter side, the side that dealt in sorcery and manipulation, rather than healing and knowledge. They were derived from the beliefs not of the African slaves, but of the native people who lived on the island before it was colonised by the French and the slaves had been brought there from Africa. The natives, called 'Indians' by the French, had been at first oppressed and then eventually enslaved themselves, or murdered by the colonial authorities. Those who could had fled to the island's steeply mountainous and inaccessible interior, where they banded together and became a force of resistance to *les blancs*, which courageous slaves could escape to and join forces with.

Voodoo is a belief system that incorporates other beliefs rather than trampling over them, and so the beliefs of the native people came to be seen as representing aspects of the *lwa* of Guinée not normally seen in the more stable West African countries from which they had been brought, and became part of Voodoo too. They represented the magical, chaotic, violent and revolutionary aspects of the *lwa*, *Petro*. Perhaps it was for this reason that they had appealed to the orphaned, abandoned boy who chose his drum on his seventh birthday and called himself Petro Labwa.

Had it not been that his need had been so personal, it would have been Petro that Ti-Charles would have asked to drum for him when he was performing his ritual for Ezulie earlier that evening – how many hours away that all seemed now! But Petro was too much like family for Ti-Charles to have asked him to do what he had asked Sauveur to do without hesitation – fuck him for La Sirene. Also, what Ti-Charles was doing was asking Ezulie to intervene with Barons Lundi and Limba in his favour in his pursuit of Henri Biassou, not simply make a charm to bewitch the handsome fisherman: *Rada*, as much as *Petro*.

Petro was a very dark, smooth-skinned, slightly feminine young man of twenty-two, a little under six foot in height. He was broad-shouldered and narrow-hipped and willowy, with long, defined muscles and high, firm buttocks. He had wide eyes and a wide mouth and, like Henri, wore a straw hat pushed back on his slickly shaven head. Unlike Henri, Petro liked to accentuate his large eyelids and lips and high cheekbones with a little make-up and lip gloss he ordered by post from Solaville. He often wore a blue-and-white-striped top that slipped off his shoulders and tight white breeches to just below his knees, and sovereign rings on his long fingers. The other fishermen gently mocked his appearance at times. 'What colour lipstick you wearing today?' they would ask when he sashayed up to the boats in the morning. 'Cock-suck purple,' Petro would reply, or 'Dick-suck scarlet.' And they would laugh, and excitement would thrill through their loins.

Despite his languid appearance, Petro was as tough and hard-working as the other men, his smooth skin turning sinewy with muscle as he wrestled nets heavy with writhing blue and red fish on to the boats or dragged their painted hulls up the beach at the end of a long day on the open ocean, or pounded the ceremonial drums all night at the *oufo*. Ti-Charles had also seen Petro box bare-knuckled and lay the other fellow out cold with a single punch. Playing with femininity was his release, and the other men were pleased to indulge him.

Petro tipped his head back, stretching his long throat, and drained his bottle of beer, his Adam's apple rising and falling as he swallowed the last of the cool liquid. Today he was wearing black cotton shorts hung low on his hips and a black mesh cut-off vest that intentionally revealed his flat, muscular stomach. From the bulge in the front of his shorts, Ti-Charles could see that Petro too was heavily turned on by Antoine's supple, provocative movements to the music on the radio, and also by the obviously aroused state of his fellow fishermen.

Ti-Charles watched dry-mouthed as Bossuet suddenly reached inside his straining leopard-skin briefs, pulled out his stiff, thick, blunt-headed cock and began to move his fist on it, lidding his eyes as he did so. As if this was a signal, Ti-Coyo and Petro Labwa stepped forward, Ti-Coyo behind Antoine, Petro in front of him. They sank to their knees simultaneously, pulling Antoine's lacy briefs down over smooth café-au-lait thighs to his ankles as they did so. He didn't resist them. His large, circumcised dick sprang up and slapped against the firm curve of his belly, and he laughed hoarsely and gasped and tossed his head theatrically, flicking the slick, glossy tousled hair on the top of his scalp back out of his now closed eyes.

Petro kissed the demerara-brown dome of Antoine's cock head with large, dark, purple-stained lips, then teased its piss slit with the tip of his soft, pink tongue, making Antoine's shaft kick and his slit bead stickily. Petro twisted his head sideways and began to nibble his way along its underside towards Antoine's heavily hanging ballsac, pushing his face between Antoine's strong, hairless thighs and sucking the lighter-skinned man's balls into his mouth, closing his lips around them and working over their smooth surfaces rapidly with his rough tongue. Antoine's stiff, heavy dick wagged above Petro's smooth, dark head as Petro knelt before him, its tip brushing the brim of the hat Petro had pushed right back on his head and making Antoine moan.

'Suck it,' Antoine ordered Petro excitedly. Petro pulled his head back immediately and did as he was told, beginning to suck Antoine's throbbing cock deeply, his cheeks glossy velvet concavities as he pumped his mouth eagerly on the standing, lighter-skinned young man's stiff, hot erection.

Behind Antoine, Ti-Coyo was kissing his firm, beefy, hairless brown buttocks and nipping them with his teeth, all the while stroking the outsides of his golden-brown thighs with strong, dark, twine-calloused hands. Antoine moved his feet in their army boots wider apart, constrained in an exciting way by the stretch of the elasticated lacy briefs around his ankles. While Petro sucked him off, Antoine reached back with both hands and pulled his well-shaped buttocks open.

'Eat me out,' he ordered Ti-Coyo.

Ti-Coyo pushed his face forward without hesitation, kissing Antoine's bittersweet anal star with his full, well-defined lips, his close-clipped goatee brushing against Antoine's spit-slick, now freely swinging ballsac, tasting Antoine's arsehole, then teasing its puckering, shiny entrance with the tip of his long, firm tongue. Ti-Charles watched excitedly as Ti-Coyo opened his mouth wide and pushed his tongue determinedly against Antoine's sphincter until it yielded, and the sinewy, kneeling man behind him began to work his tongue up into Antoine's rectum and eat the policeman's boyfriend's arsehole out greedily.

While being simultaneously blown by Petro and rimmed by Ti-Coyo, a sweaty, bloated-faced but still pretty Antoine turned his head and eyed Bossuet's thick, darkly erect and heavily veined cock, its foreskin sliding backwards and forwards over its rigid shaft and smoothly domed head as Bossuet moved his fist on it slowly, lolling back on the zebra-print barstool and pushing his dark-brown pole forward like a soldier bracing a rifle. Pre-come beaded in its pinky-brown slit and slid to the palm-matted board floor between his spread thighs in a glistening thread.

The shapely, curvy and lighter-skinned young man turned his body around in small shuffles to face the shaven-headed, muscular older one, making sure to keep his own stiff and throbbing cock in the kneeling Petro's mouth as he did so, and reaching back behind him and burying his fingers in Ti-Coyo's exploding locks at the same time, holding the shorter, darker, kneeling man's face in place against his juicy, demerara-brown arsehole as he, Antoine, bent forward over the kneeling, cocksucking Petro and began to work his open mouth on Bossuet's pulsing and rigid erection with greedy enthusiasm.

Ti-Charles watched excitedly, fighting an urge to push down his breeches and work his fist on his own now aching erection in the cool night air. He fought the urge, although with difficulty, feeling it would be disloyal to both Henri and Sudra to give himself pleasure and relief in that way. He thought briefly about leaving: after all, he had seen what he had come to see, had he not? And yet he remained where he was, held by two contrary thoughts. One was that something might still happen to suggest that it was something other than an appreciative eye for men and an accommodating nature that saw Antoine sucking dick, being sucked and rimmed in the fishermen's hut; that sorcery was involved. The other, more compelling, thought was that he needed to see it all through to the end to make sure that Henri did not return and take part. And behind both those reasonings Ti-Charles had to admit to himself that the sight of four handsome men taking pleasure in each other's bodies in the most intimate ways was both beautiful and arousing. So he watched on, doing no more than rubbing his painfully stiff cock through his breeches, refusing to grip it and bring himself off in that way.

Bossuet pushed Antoine's head back so his rigid, shiny dick slipped out of the younger man's greedy mouth and sprang up with a slap against the ridged curve of his stomach above his heavily hanging balls. Antoine gasped breathlessly, his full, ruddy features bloated with lust, his well-shaped lips glistening with saliva and pre-come, his greeny-brown eyes wide, pupils dilated to pools of black in his excitement under the flickering lamplight.

Bossuet swivelled round on the bar stool, turning himself belly down and, hyper-extending his broad back, thrust the globes of his large, muscular and shaved mocha arse back into Antoine's face. Antoine immediately reached forward and pulled Bossuet's big, smooth, high buttocks apart, then plunged his tongue into the muscular, shaven-headed man's waiting, hairless anal star. Bossuet wiggled his large arse excitedly in response to Antoine's attentions, pushing himself back on to Antoine's face harder, pressing his pleasurably dilating anal opening against Antoine's wide-open mouth, firm lips and probing tongue. The head of his stiff, twitching dick rubbed slickly on the underside of the bar stool he was sprawled over face down as he swivelled his arse to get Antoine's tongue further up him adding to Bossuet's pleasure at being anally penetrated in that way. He arched his glittering shaved head back, showing off the broad V-shaped spread of his shoulders, braced up on one well-muscled arm, the steel one holding the still-smouldering cigar off to one side.

Ti-Coyo now pulled his head with its wild Afro of shortish dreadlocks back from between Antoine's firm café-au-lait buttocks. His lips too were shiny from rimming. He wiped his broad mouth and stood up behind Antoine, placing a hand possessively on Antoine's narrow, supple waist. Ti-Coyo quickly shucked off his white singlet and shorts, kicked them to one side, and stood there naked. His eleven-inch, beer-can-thick, circumcised dick wagged heavily in front of his hanging ballsac, his lean, dark stomach and sinewy thighs, disproportionately large but beautifully shaped. It was so heavy and rigid with blood that the sinews that supported it stood out in clear, etched relief as elegant lines rising up either side of his pelvis and his flat, chiselled stomach. Its thick shaft was only lightly veined, but strongly ridged below, and its lighter, well-shaped head gave Ti-Coyo's erection a missile-like, streamlined appearance: perfectly designed for penetration. For fucking. Without a word he gripped Antoine's narrow hips in both hands and began to push his outsize dick up and down between Antoine's smooth yellow-brown buttocks as if preparing him psychologically for a good, hard fucking.

'Oh, yeah, man,' Antoine moaned, pulling back momentarily from tonguing Bossuet's arsehole and feeling the throbbing shaft of Ti-Coyo's cock sliding up and down over his own pulsing sphincter.

Petro was still in front of Antoine on his knees, pumping his mouth on Antoine's slick, stiff dick, eager to give Antoine pleasure with his lips and throat and tongue, greedy for a hot mouthful of the tensely muscled and sweat-shiny standing man's creamy white jism. Petro had found a moment to push his own shorts down to his ankles, revealing a solid, heavily veined cock with a satisfyingly mushroom-shaped head that looked like it would please a man's arsehole. He moved his fist on his cock slowly, carefully, needing to give himself some relief but clearly determined not to bring himself to climax before Antoine had come in his mouth. So far he had been unable to pull off his black mesh top as that would have meant taking his mouth off Antoine's hot, rock-hard cock, something he obviously wasn't willing to do. 'Because I'm a *born* cocksucker,' he would say later.

From his vantage point outside the hut Ti-Charles admired the kneeling Petro's high, firm, almost ebony-dark buttocks and hoped he would see Petro getting fucked up the arse tonight as well as Antoine.

Ti-Coyo reached over to the bar with a lean, lanky arm for a half-finished bottle of beer, still sliding his large, stiff mocha cock up and down between Antoine's beefy demerara buttocks, and tipped the bottle so that the golden, sparkling liquid poured down in a fast-moving stream between Antoine's shoulder blades, descending the groove of his spine and spreading out over his buttocks, libating them shinily. Antoine gasped as the cool beer caressed him and ran in lines down the outsides of his taut, hairless thighs as if he was sweating champagne. Ti-Coyo poured the remainder of the bottle over his own cock head as it slid up and down between Antoine's golden-brown globes as if he was a mechanic lubricating a piston with oil for its shaft.

Without a word Ti-Coyo pulled his flat, lean hips back and bent his painfully stiff cock down so its smoothly swollen head was aimed at Antoine's now shiny sphincter, pressing his free hand into the small of Antoine's arched back, then gripping the slender golden chain around his waist to hold him in place. Ti-Coyo took a small step forward so his lean, dark thighs were outside Antoine's beefier, lighter ones and pressed his throbbing crown against Antoine's spit-and-beer-shiny sphincter.

Antoine broke off eating out Bossuet's arsehole to glance around at the short, lean, well-endowed and heavily aroused man behind him, his lips shiny with his own saliva and Bossuet's pre-come from sucking his cock earlier. Seeing that he was about to be fucked with Ti-Coyo's massive tool, Antoine inhaled deeply, then exhaled and pushed his arse slowly back on to Ti-Coyo's cock head, bracing himself up on the kneeling Petro's broad, flat shoulders as he began to spear himself on Ti-Coyo's enormous tool.

Ti-Charles watched in amazement through the slatted window as, sweating profusely, Antoine slowly pushed himself back on to

Ti-Coyo's erection, inch after inch of its thick rigidity slowly slipping up through his achingly stretched anal opening and into his rectum. At five inches Antoine paused for a moment, grunting and letting his head tip forward so his flushed face was hidden from view. Then he took another breath, and began to squirm his arse back again. Gradually his arsehole swallowed Ti-Coyo's cock to the root. A shudder ran up Antoine's body as he forced himself to take the entire eleven inches up himself, and he lifted up his head then and looked straight ahead of him with unseeing eyes glazed and dulled with the ecstasy of having his anal cavity so completely filled. Ti-Charles felt sure Ti-Coyo's stiff enormity must have pushed past the second sphincter at the top of Antoine's rectum and up into his anal canal, taking him to a greater level of pleasure than a smaller dick would have done: he remembered Sudra's story of the cucumber.

Petro had let Antoine's stiff, dripping dick slip out of his mouth for a moment so that he could bend forward and peer round and up between Antoine's spread legs and watch Ti-Coyo's massive erection disappear up Antoine's forcibly dilated arsehole. Satisfied that Antoine was going to be thoroughly fucked as he saw the two men's swinging ballsacs knock gently together, as Ti-Coyo achieved full penetration of Antoine, Petro went back to his place, kneeling in front of Antoine and sucking his painfully rigid, light-brown cock with long, firm movements of his full lips up and down on Antoine's veiny shaft.

Looking round, Bossuet saw that Antoine's attention was going to be absorbed in being sucked and fucked simultaneously, and that he would be too distracted to return to rimming him. Wanting some of whatever satisfaction was on offer, Bossuet pushed himself to his feet, pulled down his leopard-skin briefs, stepped out of them, and went and knelt behind Petro, between his legs, his thick, stiff prick standing proud from his muscular thighs and belly. Bossuet's knees pressed against the insides of Petro's calves. Petro immediately and wordlessly moved his knees wider, opening his legs and pushing his high, smooth mocha buttocks back, making his arsehole available to be fucked, while keeping his mouth moving regularly on Antoine's cock as he did so.

Bossuet reached up to the bar with his hook arm and pulled a jar of Vaseline that had been standing there all evening towards him. He lifted it up and placed it in the small of Petro's flawless, tapering back, rucking up his black mesh top, then gripped the plastic jar with his hooks and unscrewed the lid with his large, real, flesh-and-blood hand. He slid his fingers into the greasy petroleum jelly within, then boldly pushed two of them straight up the cocksucking Petro's arsehole. They slid into the ebony-skinned youth's back passage to the knuckle without the slightest resistance. Bossuet pulled them out and pushed in three fingers. This made Petro gasp around Antoine's dick, gurgling when Antoine carried on plugging his throat roughly regardless. Petro arched his body upwards, lifting himself up off Bossuet's pushing hand, but then slowly lowered himself again, relaxing his sphincter, accepting the fingers in his anal cavity. He broke off working his mouth on Antoine's hot, rigid tool momentarily and glanced round behind him, sticky, shiny pre-come dripping in strands from his lower lip.

'Give me your cock, Bossuet, man,' Petro gasped. 'It's dick I need up there. Don't just finger my man-hole. Fuck me like a man!'

Then Petro was back sucking Antoine's rigid hard-on again.

Bossuet withdrew his fingers, inclined his heavily muscled body forward, resting his hand and his hook on Petro's broad, braced-up shoulders, and in one forceful thrust pushed his stiff, thick dick all the way up Petro's butthole until the tight coils of his neatly clipped pubic hair were being ground against the darker-skinned youth's sphincter. Petro grunted and waggled his firm, well-shaped ebony arse slightly from side to side in a struggle to accommodate Bossuet's throbbing cock in his anal cavity, but didn't resist Bossuet's invading manhood sliding up him to the root. Every muscle standing out on his beefily built body, Bossuet began to fuck Petro hard, pumping his buttocks as Petro greedily and repeatedly sucked Antoine's spunk-heavy dick to the back of his throat.

At the same time Ti-Coyo was starting to work Antoine's arsehole, swivelling his cock around inside Antoine's elastic, accommodating rectum, making Antoine gasp hotly with each sideways or up-and-down motion of outsize hot, hard cock inside his anal canal. Then Ti-Coyo began to slide his massive rigidity in and out of Antoine's slick, slack anal star, slowly at first, making sure Antoine was sufficiently dilated to accommodate him, then slightly faster, then faster still. Antoine began to toss his head, but not theatrically this time: now his responses were being dictated by the big thick dick filling his arsehole. The pearl choker gleamed around his glistening neck, and shining rivulets of sweat ran down his shiny, muscular body, adding to the glinting highlights of the narrow gold chain around his waist.

'Oh, you're stretching me, man,' Antoine gasped as Ti-Coyo ground his hips against Antoine's freely offered buttocks. 'Your thick cock is stretching me like I'm having a baby!'

Ti-Coyo laughed, and cracked the palm of his hand on one of Antoine's large, upturned buttocks, and began to fuck him harder.

Ti-Coyo knew how to use his cock, Ti-Charles could see, gripping Antoine's waspy waist with both hands and leaning forward so he could ram it in and out of Antoine's surely slack arsehole faster and faster and harder and harder, pumping it in so hard that Antoine was forced to lift himself on to his toes with every deep and unrelenting thrust into his rectum to give himself some relief from the hot, throbbing pole forcing its way up into his guts. Every sinew, every segment of every muscle stood out clearly on Ti-Coyo's lean, dark body as he fucked Antoine. He slapped Antoine's arse again, hard, and Antoine gasped.

'Oh, man!'

Ti-Coyo's palm cracked down on Antoine's buttocks a third time.

'Oh, yes!' Antoine's voice was higher now, with a hoarse crack in it. He was playing with his own nipples to add to his pleasure, teasing their bullet-like stiffness, biting into them with his nails as he was sucked greedily and fucked hard, transported to ecstasy by Petro, now on all fours, and the standing Ti-Coyo.

Petro was also being gratified at both ends, in a different way. 'I'm a two-cock man,' he had once said to Ti-Charles, smiling cryptically. Ti-Charles understood now, watching Bossuet hammer

Petro's upturned dark-brown butt as Petro opened his mouth wide and swallowed Antoine's hard-on down his throat in greedy gulps, his cock bucking between his spread legs as he was pleasured by two well-endowed and horny men at the same time.

Sweat was pouring down between the striated domes of Bossuet's chest, dripping from his nose and lips as he slammed his cock in and out of Petro's well-lubricated, wide-open battyhole. Ti-Coyo was equally shiny with exertion as he rammed his huge weapon deep into Antoine's anal canal, then out, then in again, making Antoine squeal with each penetration, both Ti-Coyo and Bossuet building their fucking rhythms, their breaths coming shorter and harder as they pounded the muscular, upturned arses of the two men in front of them, hips hammering, heads inclined forward, neck muscles straining, concentrating on what they were doing, concentrating on the building heavinesses in their dicks as they slammed their throbbing erections in and out of the lube-slick rectums of the accommodating Petro and Antoine.

Both top men moved rapidly towards their climaxes, pounding their eager bottoms as hard as they could, yelling aloud with hoarse shouts as they exploded inside the anal passages of the sweaty, ecstatic and now totally dilated Petro and Antoine, shooting gouting loads of hot jism deep into their bodies in shuddering waves as they came violently.

Antoine arched back and yelled aloud too, the combination of Ti-Coyo's eleven inches repeatedly battering his prostate and the exciting, demanding suction supplied by Petro's greedy mouth bringing Antoine to his climax as Ti-Coyo exploded volcanically inside the lighter-skinned man's bruised anal cavity. Antoine's come flooded Petro's mouth as Bossuet shot his load up Petro's arse with one final, gut-deep thrust of his throbbing rigidity.

Petro slumped face down on to the floor, filled with man juice at both ends. Bossuet lowered himself protectively on top of him, moving his still-stiff cock inside the youth's rectum with slow, teasing provocativeness, making him moan. Bossuet arched his neck forward and kissed Petro's small, neat ear. Petro smiled with his eyes closed.

Meanwhile Ti-Coyo pulled his eleven-inch cock out of

Antoine's slack, well-fucked hole. Antoine's well-satisfied anal star didn't close immediately, perhaps in the hope that it would receive more attention soon. His thighs aching and his lace briefs still around his ankles, Antoine stumbled forward, and a pearly white drop of jism slid from his open arsehole. It landed by chance on Petro's lips. Impulsively, Petro licked them, then opened his eyes and twisted his head around to look up at Antoine standing almost astride him.

'Sit on my face, man,' Petro said suddenly. He lifted himself up, pushing Bossuet off him gently, letting Bossuet's large but now softening cock slip out of his greasy and come-filled arsehole. Bossuet pushed himself up into a squatting position as Petro rolled on to his back. Everyone else's erection had softened by now, but Petro's veiny, mushroom-shaped tumescence thrust up proudly. Bossuet reached forward and gripped it firmly, making Petro gasp, and began to move his fist on it slowly.

Antoine slowly sat down on Petro's eagerly waiting face. Ti-Charles saw a thick rope of come sliding out of his areshole and into Petro's open mouth as Antoine squatted all the way down until his well-fucked sphincter was pushed firmly against Petro's full, sharply defined lips.

'Open your mouth wide, man,' he ordered.

From the expression on Antoine's face and the sudden bucking of his softening dick, Ti-Charles guessed Petro had done as he was told, and was tongue-fucking the lighter-skinned man while Bossuet began to wank him off vigorously.

Bossuet was a skilled handler of men's cocks, and the strength in his thick and very muscular remaining arm was enough to make him much sought-after for manual relief. Familiar with Petro's dick and its particularities from many such sessions out on the open ocean, Bossuet bent it straight upwards and moved his fist on it while rubbing his thumb slickly over its head and piss slit. In less than thirty seconds Petro was gasping muffledly into Antoine's butt, kicking, arching, and pumping a large hot load of creamy jism out over Bossuet's fist.

Antoine stayed sitting where he was, smothering Petro with his butt, while Bossuet slowly, methodically milked all the come out of Petro's cock as shudders passed up and down the darker-skinned young man's body. Once he had done that, he lifted his fist to his lips, opened his mouth and began to lick it clean.

And then it was over.

Antoine pulled himself up off Petro's face and stepped, semi-erect, bow-leggedly to the bar for another drink, choosing this time a Coca-Cola from the small, glass-fronted Frigidaire that sat at one end of it. Ti-Charles could see the small tremors running up and down Antoine's aching thighs as he stood there holding the bottle, looking around blankly for the opener. Bossuet struggled to his feet and took the bottle from Antoine and twisted the metal cap off with his hooks. He took a swallow himself, then handed the Coke back to Antoine, who drained it.

Ti-Coyo bent over and pulled Petro upright. 'I think it is your hole I am going to fuck next time,' he said, with a gold and white smile.

'Maybe next time *I* will fuck *you*,' Petro replied.

'Maybe,' Ti-Coyo said, still smiling. 'It has been a long time since I have had a cock up me.'

'A long time?' Bossuet echoed. 'How long is that?'

'I mean more than a *week*, man,' Ti-Coyo replied, his smile becoming a boyish grin. 'But men, they love my good big cock more than my nice tight hole.'

'Maybe next time we will *all* fuck you, man,' Antoine said, laughing. 'Then you won't be so tight.'

'Maybe.' Petro laughed too.

There was clearly nothing more to see. Ti-Charles moved away from the window and sat leaning back against the wall of the hut to think: the young *oungan* had noticed nothing about Antoine's manner that suggested he was in any way acting against his true nature, had been bewitched, influenced or blackmailed. Sudra would be heartbroken to hear this, Ti-Charles knew, though Antoine's inclination to wander had been well known to the policeman before they became involved. But what else could he do as a friend but tell Sudra the truth?

Ti-Charles slowly pushed himself upright, relieved at least to be able to stretch out his aching thighs, although his aching erection would be less easy to deal with. With a soft exhalation he arched back, pushing the kinks out of his spine, and looked up at the endless stars high above the island. The moon had set now.

Henri Biassou hadn't come back.

Ti-Charles was about to head back discreetly to the path leading to the village when the feeling that another person was nearby came to him sharply. He crouched down quickly and looked around. What if Henri saw me watching? was Ti-Charles's first thought. What would he think of me? But he could see no one. Steeling himself and holding his breath, he stood upright again, then crept along the side of the hut and, with his heart hammering in his chest, peered around the corner along the back wall of it.

He was just in time to see the shadowy figure of a man stealing away across the sand towards a nearby grove of coconut palms that jutted out green-black against the softly glowing white of the starlit beach.

Someone else had been watching.

But who? And why?

Perhaps sorcery *was* involved, Ti-Charles thought as the figure disappeared into the solid black shadows beneath the trees. Should he follow, or let the mystery remain a mystery? he asked himself, although he already knew the answer: he would have to follow.

With a sinking in the pit of his stomach as he wavered momentarily, Ti-Charles realised that beyond the palm grove was another path, a path that had been disused for many years, or so everyone in Croix-Le-Bois believed. A path that had once been broad and trodden by the feet of many slaves; the path that led up from the heaving Atlantic through the old sugar-cane plantation to the ruined Sonnelier mansion. There was little doubt in Ti-Charles's mind that it was that path the figure was making for.

Ti-Charles took a deep breath, and hurried after it.

Three

The quickly moving figure had left light footprints that cast clearly visible blue shadows in sharp relief on the white sand of the beach, so Ti-Charles had no problem making his way to the exact spot where it had slipped into the coconut grove. Beyond that he could make nothing out in the darkness beneath the trees. He listened for a moment, but all he could hear was the soft sound of the surf behind him, and the wind stirring the dry palm fronds high above his head. A clattering, scuttling sound close by his head made him look round sharply. It was just a robber crab climbing a curving tree trunk in search of coconuts, but in the darkness its size – well over a foot across – and quick, erratic movements seemed strange and disquieting, and made Ti-Charles think of stories he had heard about *bakas*, small, savage dwarflike monsters summoned up by *bokors* for malign purposes. He had never seen one, but knew such things could be.

There had once been a well-to-do woman in Croix-Le-Bois called Madame Celine. She was said to have gone to a *bokor* in Arbrerouge and asked him to invoke a *baka* to punish her employee, a wealthy man who had mistreated Madame Celine and made advances towards her. Nothing went right for the man after she had done this, and some little time later he died in a car crash, swerving, it was said, to try to avoid something small that had darted out from the roadside and under his wheels. A week later Madame Celine's newborn son also died, drowned in the enamel basin she was bathing him in. She seemed distraught with grief, and cursed God, but it was widely held in the village that the child was the price the *baka* had demanded for its assistance, and that Madame Celine had drowned the boy herself, a belief confirmed for many by Madame Celine and her husband's sudden disappearance a few days after the funeral, along with their few goods and clothing, although nothing could be proved for certain.

Ti-Charles knew more than most, however, for the day before she left Madame Celine had come to him to ask him to make her a *wanga* packet, the most powerful he could devise, as she was afraid that the *baka* would not be satisfied with her child, but would take her husband as well. Ti-Charles had stared deep into her sad, dark eyes, trying to decide whether she was trying to deceive him or whether her apparent fear was genuine. She had broken his gaze and fallen to her knees, weeping and begging him to help her.

In the end he had made her the charm even though he had not been certain he believed her. What else could he do? He was her *oungan*.

Ti-Charles decided to strike as directly towards the old Sonnelier path as he could, trusting his memory to steer him straight even at night. A lantern would have helped him, although, of course, even if he had thought to bring one, he would not have dared to light it. Whoever he was following knew the way without light.

The palm trees gave out, and Ti-Charles found himself passing through a glade of sweet-smelling bougainvillea and rhododendron bushes, his forward progress impeded by tangled undergrowth. He had to jump a small, steep-sided rivulet and, shortly after that, he found himself on the path, as he had hoped he would.

The path was overgrown but was still erratically outlined with white stone markers that caught the starlight and ran away in both directions – towards the sea and inland. Once there had been a landing jetty at the seaward end, and a quadrangle of two- and three-storey clapboard buildings used for storage and administration, and the processing of slaves from Africa, but all these had burned many years ago, and the charred timber had long been reclaimed by the wind, the rain and the sea. Only the odd stump or rusty echo of an iron link or fetter remained as reminders of what had been.

Ti-Charles turned away from the sea and followed the path inland, reasoning that the man he was trailing would surely have reached it before him, and would hardly be returning almost exactly the way he had come. The path curved away into the darkness, screened on both sides by a solid wall of sugar cane that rose taller than a man and rustled ceaselessly in the fading sea breeze. The cane seemed to extend out endlessly in every direction.

'Baron Limba, Baron Lundi, I have dedicated my life to serving you,' Ti-Charles whispered, rubbing his thumb over the *wanga* packet that hung around his neck, a protection he was never without. 'Protect your *serviteur* from harm.'

The path, overgrown by grasses and rutted and uneven as it was, ran on in a long curve without forking or crossing any other tracks, so Ti-Charles was able to move forward quickly without any fear that he was missing his way.

In front of him the bone-white façade of the decaying Sonnelier mansion began to rise up gradually above the sugar cane, still distant, but near enough to make him feel uneasy. Dark cypresses flanked it like great twisted sentinels. Seen from above, it had seemed almost like a doll's house, macabre in its reminder of the past, disturbing even, but unthreatening. Now he was aware of how massive it was – heavy and somehow powerful, even in its decay. It loomed blackly, a vast block of night cut out of the backdrop of stars.

There were at least no lights in any of its windows.

Ti-Charles was almost beginning to wonder whether he really had seen a figure back at the beach hut, despite the plain evidence of the footprints. Certainly there seemed to be no one on this path, ahead of or behind him, or any suggestion that anyone had passed this way recently. Perhaps whoever it was who had been watching the fishermen had some other motive that had nothing to do with Antoine at all, and nothing to do with sorcery. Not wanting to find himself at the old Sonnelier place on his own, in the middle of the night, Ti-Charles slowed and stopped, wondering what to do next.

At that exact moment a man stepped out from the wall of sugar cane just in front of Ti-Charles, blocking his way, an opaque silhouette. He was dark-skinned, hard-bodied, stripped to the waist, and wore a red bandana embroidered with *veves* around his dark, shaved skull. Several *wanga* packets hung around his neck and a machete was hanging loosely from his right hand. Its well-polished blade glinted in the starlight as he tightened his grip on it.

'Why are you following me, man?' the man said, pushing his face towards Ti-Charles's aggressively, his muscular chest rising as he did so. There was gold in his mouth. 'Who are you? Why are you in my business?'

'Faustin?' Ti-Charles said, surprised, suddenly recognising the man's voice. 'Faustin Marcelin?'

The man suddenly looked confused and immediately backed down.

'Ti-Charles?' he replied, his dark eyes clouding. '*Maître Oungan?*' There was a trace of fear in his voice.

Ti-Charles nodded. 'Yes, Faustin. It is I.'

'I, I did not mean you harm, *maître*,' Faustin stammered, gesturing sheepishly with the machete. 'I could not sleep. I was just out walking to clear my thoughts when I became aware I was being followed. We are near the Big House and I became uneasy. Who would be following me at such a late hour, and in such a place? So I concealed myself among the canes and waited.'

Ti-Charles met Faustin's eyes intently. Faustin Marcelin was the postman for Croix-Le-Bois and three other fishing villages along that stretch of coastline. He was a dark, stocky, well-muscled man, around five foot ten, in his mid-thirties with a wide nose, high cheekbones, and full, soft lips framed by a close-clipped goatee. His feline eyes were set far apart in his wide, sculpted face.

He couldn't match Ti-Charles's gaze, and quickly looked away from the *oungan* with a lopsided half-smile.

'It is lucky I challenged you and did not just set about you straightaway, man,' he said, shrugging.

'Yes, it is lucky,' Ti-Charles said, trying to catch his eyes again. They stood in silence for a while, Faustin studiedly looking at the ground.

'Why were you watching the fishermen in the hut, man?' Ti-Charles asked him eventually, when it had become clear that the postman wasn't going to volunteer any other information or opinions.

'Why were you, *maître*?' Faustin replied.

'You were going towards the Big House,' Ti-Charles said, ignoring Faustin's question.

'Like I said, I was just walking, *maître*,' Faustin said. His grip tightened slightly on the machete again.

With a rapidity that took Faustin by surprise, Ti-Charles reached out and snatched one of the *wanga* packets from around his neck, snapping the plaited straw rope that held it in place.

'I did not make you this charm, man,' Ti-Charles said quickly, before Faustin had a chance to react. Ti-Charles ripped the fabric packet open with strong, dark fingers. Blue-grey dust spilled out, graveyard dust. Inverted crosses were sewn into the charm's lining, and the small bag also contained the bones from two fingers and several opals. Ti-Charles scrutinised them carefully, then bundled the now split *wanga* back into Faustin's hands, although Faustin seemed unwilling to take it from him, as if that simple act would confirm his guilt beyond all doubt, or at the least bring other troubles down upon him. But it was too late for evasion.

'You have been dealing with a *bokor*,' Ti-Charles said.

'Yes, *maître*,' Faustin answered.

'Tell me,' Ti-Charles ordered him.

Faustin didn't speak at once. Instead he looked round at the ruined Big House looming up behind him. He knew that if Ti-Charles told the other villagers he was dealing in sorcery he would find himself totally without friends, and that if Ti-Charles told Sudra that he had had a spell put on Antoine he would be in real

62

trouble, and possibly even danger: Sudra was a hard man, tough and unforgiving. And Ti-Charles was an *oungan*, and, without the Voodoo priest's interventions on his behalf, Faustin knew he would be unprotected from the caprices of *les mortes* and *Les Mystères*. But at this moment he feared the Big House more than Sudra, or Ti-Charles, or the loss of his own reputation.

'I will tell you, *maître*,' he said, not looking at Ti-Charles. 'But not here. Come with me to my cabin and I will tell you there.'

Ti-Charles followed Faustin's gaze to the shadowy mass of the ruined plantation mansion. 'Then it is true, a *bokor* does live there?' he asked.

'Come, let us go,' Faustin said, not answering the question but looking afraid as he glanced back at Ti-Charles. 'It is not good to speak of such men, such things in such a place. Come now, *maître*.'

Ti-Charles nodded and let Faustin lead him. At first, to Ti-Charles's surprise, they headed further towards the old mansion. But, a little way on, the path branched, and the fork he and Faustin took, the left-hand one, led away from the house in a long loop back towards Croix-Le-Bois through the cane fields. The cane rose high above the two men on both sides, and soon cut the Big House off from their view. Ti-Charles was relieved not to be overlooked by gutted windows that were only seemingly tenantless. At this distance from the sea there wasn't the slightest breath of wind, and all was still and silent as a graveyard.

Then, somewhere off to his right and obscured by the cane stems, Ti-Charles thought he heard the soft sound of hoeing: metal turning earth with clumsy regularity. Somewhere nearby, and without light, more than one person was digging in the dry plantation soil. It was an unexpected and disturbing sound. Ti-Charles slowed, peering into the shadows between the sugar-cane stalks. He would perhaps have crept towards it, but Faustin caught at his arm and gestured sharply that they should go on, his eyes wide with fear. Ti-Charles was about to ask him what he was so afraid of, but Faustin cut him off wordlessly with a movement of his thumb across his throat, turned, and hurried away down the track. Ti-Charles had to break into a half-run to keep up with him, as Faustin was clearly near to panicking.

The sound of digging faded away and Faustin slowed his pace a little, although he refused to speak until they had left the plantation far behind, and were passing through a long grove of lemon trees half a mile beyond its boundaries.

'Those digging. They were – zombies?' Ti-Charles's voice caught in his throat as he spoke the word.

'Yes, *maître*.'

'You have seen them?'

'Only in the distance and by night,' Faustin said. 'I did not want to go closer.' He shuddered.

Ti-Charles understood Faustin's dread and fear all too well. The fear of a zombie is a different fear from that of a ghost or a *loup-garou*, a werewolf. A zombie frightens not because it may do you harm, although such a thing is not impossible, but because of what it represents: a body from which the *gros-bon-ange*, the soul, has been stolen. Who would not be horrified to find themselves reduced on death to a brainless, soulless, perpetual slave? For those who are themselves descended from slaves, the horror is intensified in magnitude. It is perhaps the ultimate degradation. Every believer knew that many precautions had to be taken on death, many rituals observed, to prevent some *bokor* from gaining access to the bodies of their loved ones, and also to make sure that their *gros-bon-anges* could not be captured by the *bokor*. It was the idea that, if he saw the zombies closer to, he might recognise a friend or, worse, a family member, that had made Faustin give them a wide berth. Because what then?

'Here, *maître*,' Faustin said. 'My home is nearby.'

Faustin lived in a small shack at the top of a lane running alongside the orange grove that he and Ti-Charles were now cutting through. Its plaster walls were whitewashed outside, and La Sirene, the *lwa* Ezulie, had been painted in bright blues and pinks by the front door, in the form of a mermaid. Faustin went in ahead of Ti-Charles, bent over a small oil lamp that sat on a bamboo table by the door and lit it with a match. Then he stood back and turned and gestured to Ti-Charles to come in.

Ti-Charles found himself standing in a modest parlour with a brightly coloured rug in the middle of the floor, a camp bed divided off from the rest of the room by a red-and-orange curtain, and two wicker chairs with sagging embroidered cushions flanking a table under the small window opening on to the lane. A doorway led off to a small kitchen. In the corner stood Faustin's personal altar, loaded with the familiar devotional articles: a calabash, candles, mirrors, two crosses, a bottle of rum, a coconut cake, a heart-shaped box of chocolates bought in Arbrerouge, and a lithograph of the Virgin Mary, representing the *lwa* Ezulie, La Sirene, who was Faustin's *met-tête-lwa*, the *lwa* to whom he had been dedicated as an *ounsi*. Several *wanga* packets were hung on twine around the crosses, and Ti-Charles scrutinised these carefully. They all seemed to be of his own making.

'Sit, *maître*,' Faustin said, indicating one of the chairs by the window. Ti-Charles sat. Faustin disappeared into the other room, returning in a moment with a pitcher of lemonade and two glasses, which he filled in front of Ti-Charles. Then he took the other chair.

'Well, then, man,' Ti-Charles said, waiting for Faustin to drink before sipping from the glass that had been placed before him. Not that he believed that Faustin would try to poison him, but the sound of zombies and the talk of a *bokor* made him wary: *bokors* were not above speeding people to the grave in order to add to their unpaid, uncomplaining workforce.

'It is true I was watching the fishermen in the hut, *maître*,' Faustin said slowly. 'And Antoine Dieudonne.' He spoke with contempt as he named Sudra's young lover.

'Why were you watching them?'

'To see if the bewitchment had been effective, as I had been promised,' Faustin said, looking down at his glass.

'So Antoine Dieudonne has been bewitched?'

'Yes,' Faustin said. 'But who is to say if it worked? The truth is – you know this, *maître* – that he is – he has always offered his favours freely. Everyone in Croix-Le-Bois knows this.'

He looked up at Ti-Charles then. Ti-Charles said nothing,

inclining his head in the ghost of a nod, his eyes intent on Faustin's.

'Everyone except Sudra,' Faustin went on. 'Man, he is a fool. He –' Faustin cut himself off, shaking his head, and fell silent.

'Why did you put a spell on Antoine Dieudonne?' Ti-Charles asked.

Faustin looked down, embarrassed. 'Well, it was this way, *maître*,' he began awkwardly. 'You know I like the cockfighting.'

Ti-Charles nodded: Faustin Marcelin had three good birds, and fought them every weekend in one or other of the villages around Croix-Le-Bois, and had even once taken his best cockerel to a fight in Arbrerouge and come back with a winner's purse.

'It was six months ago,' Faustin said. 'To tell it plainly, *maître*, I was accused of fixing a cockfight. It was said that I had replaced a weaker bird with a stronger, having taken bets on the weaker. That I had painted a white spot upon the stronger bird's breast to deceive others that it was the bird I had fought first. Naturally I protested, *maître*, but I was not believed.'

Ti-Charles nodded. He had heard about the fixed fight at the time, of course – there are few secrets in a village.

'I found myself having to repay all the bets, and on top of that what I would have had to pay had my bird lost,' Faustin continued. 'I could not afford to do this, and so I found myself in the jail in Sous-L'Eau.'

Sous-L'Eau was a nearby village slightly larger than Croix-Le-Bois, named for the magnificent waterfall above it, to which the Voodoo faithful made pilgrimages on Christmas Day to take *bains de chance*, anointing herbal baths that brought good fortune. Unlike Croix-Le-Bois, it was large enough to have a jail, even though it had only three cells.

'I was sentenced to two weeks there by the visiting magistrate, and was very fearful of losing my job, although I had a friend who collected my mail for me and made sure that it was all delivered. He and I had been lovers some years before, and we had remained friends, so he was happy enough to do me this favour without taking credit or asking for a reward. But my jailor was Sudra. He would wake me in the morning in my cell with food, and visit me each afternoon or evening to ensure that I had at least water to drink and had not come to any harm.'

'Sudra is a fair man,' Ti-Charles said. 'So why did you do this thing, after he had treated you fairly?'

'*Maître*, I have always found Sudra attractive,' Faustin said awkwardly. 'Very attractive. And to be in his power, it almost excited me, although of course I did not wish to be in jail. And he was kind, and I would make a little conversation with him, and smile, and perhaps flirt a little to encourage him to stay longer before driving off on his motorbike. After a few days he brought in a chequerboard and sat it on a barrel and we would play and talk. And I would gaze at him and wish I could kiss his firm lips and grip his strong, lean arms, open his shirt and kiss his chest . . .' Faustin's dark eyes went hazy with longing as he remembered.

'One night he took my hand through the bars and gripped it, and then he opened the cell door and came inside. He was looking fine and handsome in his short-sleeved blue policeman's shirt and his tight leather trousers, his legs so long, his arms so strong, his chest so large, his head shaved, his moustache so neatly trimmed. We kissed, and then I found myself kneeling in front of him. It was so natural, *maître*, you understand me? It was irresistible.'

Ti-Charles nodded.

'I unbuttoned his fly and pulled his leather trousers down to his knees and sucked his cock. Man, he has the most beautiful cock I have ever sucked! It is –' Faustin cut himself off again, shrugged. 'It inspired my mouth and I pumped my lips on it, determined to give him as much pleasure as I was able, even swallowing his crown to the back of my throat, *maître*. It is surprising how much length of a dick you can swallow if you like the man who it belongs to enough.'

Faustin's voice was a little hoarse, and he broke off to take a sip of lemonade. Ti-Charles discreetly adjusted his hardening, lengthening cock inside his breeches, hoping Faustin wouldn't notice.

'I was stroking his smooth, dark thighs, running my hands over his big, muscular arse, massaging his balls,' Faustin went on. 'All the while sucking his dick as hard as I could. I could taste his bittersweet excitement filling my mouth.' He took another sip of lemonade. 'I sucked and sucked, my knees getting bruised on the cell floor, my neck aching, my throat getting bruised from swallowing that big, hot cock head down there – although that bruising was very pleasurable, man, you know? And I can feel that he is getting sweaty, and his breathing is getting heavier and heavier. And all at once he grips my head in both hands tight-tight and comes in my mouth! *Maître*, it was ecstasy to me to receive his pleasure in that way – although, truth to tell, I didn't taste his come as much as I would have liked, as his explosion happened in my throat, not over my tongue or lips. Still, I squeezed the last few drops out of his shaft and on to my tongue and brought myself off with his cock still in my mouth, and he let me do that. And then he let me go.'

'I don't understand, man,' Ti-Charles said.

'He released me, man. After only five days in the jail,' Faustin said.

'I mean I don't understand why you are now doing him ill by having a bewitchment placed on his lover Antoine Dieudonne.'

'Sudra believes I only sucked his cock to get out of jail early,' Faustin said. 'But the truth is, I have fallen deeply in love with him. I would like to make my life with him. But of course I was shy to approach him, and I was fearful that he would think I was someone who would exchange sex for favours, someone heartless. And then the next thing I heard was that he had fallen for Antoine Dieudonne, who I knew would only break his heart. So I had a spell placed on Antoine Dieudonne to make him reveal his true nature. It made him do nothing he would not do anyway, in time, *maître*.'

'No?'

'Antoine Dieudonne is faithless, *maître*. I wanted Sudra to see the truth of that and reject him so that I would have a chance to win his heart. And that is my tale.'

Faustin drained his glass. Ti-Charles sat in silence, thinking. He himself felt that what Faustin had said was true: Antoine was faithless. And Ti-Charles was naturally sympathetic towards any man who pined from afar. But still . . .

'Who did you go to to have this spell placed?' Ti-Charles asked eventually. 'You did not come to me for either guidance or help, although you know I deal with both hands.'

Faustin shook his head in agreement, avoiding Ti-Charles's piercing gaze and saying nothing.

'Tell me the truth, Faustin Marcelin,' Ti-Charles ordered him. 'If you do I will know what to do. I will consult the *lwa* and make my decision. But this is a serious matter, man. It is not a light thing to bewitch another man's lover. If you do not tell me the truth –'

Faustin nodded.

'I consulted a *bokor, maître*,' he admitted finally. He met Ti-Charles's dark, feline eyes now, his own filled with defiance and fear.

'He lives in the Big House?'

'Yes, although he does not live there all the time; but a few rooms in the east wing are still habitable and have been furnished.'

'What is his name?'

'He calls himself Zoboyo,' Faustin said.

Both men knew that the name the *bokor* had given was not a true name. All it did was indicate that he was, or claimed to be, a member of a secret society that operated in that part of the island, and was said to be responsible for many criminal acts, large and small, of the sort that could not be attributed to sorcery.

'Zoboyo Lamartine,' Faustin continued.

'Tell me what happened when you saw this *bokor*.'

'I was given a charm that I was to place under a floorboard in Sudra's bedroom. I stole in there one evening when Sudra and Antoine were out dancing in the square in Croix-Le-Bois to a *compas* band.'

'What payment was demanded?'

'Money, *maître*. Much money. And that I should not tell anyone that I had dealt with a *bokor*. But why would I, if the charm was effective? I was to remove it a month later and bury it in the graveyard by the road to Arbrerouge. And that is all my tale,' Faustin said again.

'Not all,' Ti-Charles said. 'How did you meet this *bokor*, this Zoboyo Lamartine?'

'The friend who delivered my letters and packages for me while I was in the jail,' Faustin said.

'Who is your friend?'

'Bertrand.'

No other name was needed: Ti-Charles knew Bertrand well. Or used to know him well. The aggressive and rangy, big-featured, handsome, light-skinned young man had for a time been an adept, an *ounsi*, at Ti-Charles's *oufo*. Although sometimes charming, he had not been popular owing to his argumentative and sometimes abusive temperament. He had eventually renounced his vocation, left Croix-Le-Bois and not been heard of for over a year. When he returned he had had money in his pockets and a taste for jewellery and fancy clothes – silk shirts, embroidered waistcoats, boots of the softest leather, wide-brimmed hats – and his talk was filled with vague but menacing hints of things he had learned in Arbrerouge, and people he had met there. A year after that he had disappeared again, and had not been seen since. That had been five years ago, and naturally all sorts of rumours had circulated, including one that he had been murdered by a *baka*, and another that he had travelled to Europe with a wealthy white man. Now Ti-Charles felt sure Bertrand had fallen in with the Zoboyo, and through them had met the *bokor* who dwelled in the Sonnelier mansion.

A chill ran through Ti-Charles: these were dangerous people. Although he was confident in his faith, in his *lwa*, the good *lwa-Ginen*, and in his role as *oungan* of Croix-Le-Bois, and not without personal courage, he didn't relish the idea of having to fight on both the spiritual and physical levels at the same time.

'So. It was Bertrand who took you to the Big House?' he asked eventually.

'Yes,' Faustin said. 'And he assisted the *bokor* in making the charm.'

Ti-Charles nodded. 'So he was not just a bystander?'

'No, *maître*. He knew what to do without being told at any time.'

70

They sat in silence for a time. Ti-Charles felt suddenly extremely weary. He pushed himself to his feet.

'I will prepare you a *wanga* packet,' he said, as he made to leave. 'It will protect you from retribution from the *bokor* if he learns you spoke to me tonight. I will speak with Baron Limba and Baron Lundi, my *met-tête-lwa*, and ask for their guidance. Pray to La Sirene in the morning and come to me early, and we will resolve things.'

'Thank you, *maître*,' Faustin said, obviously genuinely grateful Ti-Charles was consenting to help him rather than abandoning him to his difficulties or going straight to Sudra.

'Do not deal with this *bokor* again,' Ti-Charles ordered Faustin as he departed.

'No, *maître*.'

Ti-Charles made his way quickly down the lane, passing shacks with plaster walls painted white, pink, blue and orange, their colours dulled to a near-uniform blue-grey by the tail end of the night. All was quiet: no insect-noises sounded, no birdsong was to be heard. No villager or tethered animal stirred. And yet there was something in the air, some strange expectancy.

In ten minutes he had reached his own home. Exhausted, he threw himself down on to his bed. Tomorrow was the *mange-lwa*, and there would be much to do. Despite the myriad thoughts whirling around inside his head, sleep swept quickly over the young *oungan* of Croix-Le-Bois.

The early morning found Ti-Charles kneeling in the immaculately whitewashed *kay-mystère*, the hut containing the shrine devoted to Baron Lundi and Baron Limba, his *met-tête-lwa*, in deep meditation, moving his *asson* in a fast, light, reflexive rhythm, muttering prayers and invocations under his breath.

Aidez-moi . . . Guide me . . .

Slowly the answer to Faustin, Sudra and Antoine's problems was beginning to form itself in Ti-Charles's mind. He took a mouthful of rum and expelled it in a fine mist over the candle he had lit to the Barons, making its flame flare up brightly for a moment, bringing himself more fully into rapport with the *lwa*, and with the *esprit* of his departed teacher, which was stored in a *govi*, a clay pot, in the shrine at the back of the *oufo* – a state of being in the right and proper place that was completely the opposite of having one's spirit imprisoned by a *bokor*.

On rising just before dawn, and after a night of significant and revealing dreams, Ti-Charles had washed himself carefully from head to foot, anointing his skin thoroughly with certain magical oils and herbs, as well as familiarly aromatic ones such as orgeat and jasmine flowers. Then he had made obeisances at the private altar to Lundi and Limba in his home. Afterwards, symbolically purified and prepared for the festival ahead, he had put on a fresh, white, sleeveless, cotton shirt and white breeches, and tied a new, clean, white, cotton headscarf around his head.

The dawn of the first of November had broken flaming red and orange, with gold searing the underbellies of clouds that piled high and puffy in the pale sky above the steep-sided mountains of the island's interior. Birdsong loud in every tree and bush around him, Ti-Charles had left his home just after sunrise to go to Sudra and Antoine's cabin. There he had spoken briefly with the hard-eyed policeman on the verandah steps, not telling him about the events of the night before, but instructing him only that he was to meet Ti-Charles at the *oufo* in two hours' time, and was to make sure to bring Antoine with him.

Having come home extremely late, Antoine had still been asleep in bed when Ti-Charles came calling, and hadn't been awoken by his knocking at the mint-green front door. Sudra, worn out by lack of sleep and worry, had pressed Ti-Charles for information about what he had seen his sleeping lover do the previous night in the fishermen's hut, but Ti-Charles had only repeated his instructions, adding that the *lwa* had spoken to him in his dreams, and that everything would be resolved later that morning. Then Ti-Charles had returned to the temple and made various preparations for the evening's *mange-lwa* before retreating to the *kay-mystère*, confident he could leave the drummer Sauveur in charge of things in the compound for an hour or two.

The whole village of Croix-Le-Bois was swept up in the

excitement of the *mange-lwa*; it was, of course, first and foremost a day of devotion to the *lwa*, but it was also a holiday and a feast day all rolled into one. Within the brightly whitewashed plaster walls of the *oufo* preparations were intense. The peristyles, where the ceremonies were to be performed, were swept. The sacred Voodoo flags, painstakingly and colourfully embroidered and sewn with sequins in representation of the various *lwa* and their symbols, were taken from their storage chests and unfurled in the morning sun. Ritual movements were practised by the *ounsis* who, like Ti-Charles, wore clean white headscarfs and tight white cotton breeches, and had been anointed and purified that morning with herbs and oils that made their brown skins gleam. A small fire had been lit on which food for the *lwa* was to be cooked and it burned brightly as a large cast-iron pot of water, herbs and spices was set to boil.

One of the *ounsis* was set to watch that fire and make sure that it did not smother and make smoke, as that would be clearly visible from some distance off, and might alert unfriendly eyes to the whereabouts of the temple compound. An attempt by the police or the army to disrupt the service was not expected, however, as Sudra would have received notification from his superiors in Arbrerouge by the day before at the latest if they were planning a raid. Even so, a sudden police or military appearance in the village – sparked by some event or change of government policy in Solaville – was certainly not impossible. In any case, the believers were used to being careful not to draw any more attention than necessary to the whereabouts of the *oufo*. So the fire was always watched.

Sauveur and Petro, both men in high spirits, were practising rhythms and fine-tuning their drums, the *manman tambour* and its smaller neighbour, the *seconde*, on the shaded side of the peristyle. Both drums had been hollowed out from the trunk of a fallen mapou, or silk-cotton tree, which is sacred in Voodoo. Petro was filling in for the usual drummer, who was feeling too unwell to perform. He was less familiar with the *Rada* rhythms of the *mange-lwa* service than he was with the *Petro* rhythms he was so steeped in, and his brow was furrowed with concentration as he followed Sauveur's lead.

The clouds that had filled the sky at the start of the day melted away, leaving clear azure as far as the eye could see, and the air was fresh as Ti-Charles emerged from the *kay-mystère*. He thought of Henri Biassou, and wondered if his own prayers to Ezulie, Limba and Lundi had been successful. He felt hopeful, but knew there were no guarantees where the caprices of the *lwa* were concerned.

Ti-Charles went over to the peristyle, the roofed, open-sided area of the *oufo* where the bulk of the ceremony would take place that night, picking up a machete as he went. The roof was made up of tightly plaited palm leaves and arched up above the brightly-painted *poteau-mitain* post in its centre through which the *lwa* would be channelled. Ti-Charles marked off the cardinal points with the machete, gouging the hard, red-brown earth, a ritual gesture marking the perpetual intersection between the worlds of the living and the dead that is Voodoo – the cross, the crossroads, *carrefour*. Then he took up a shallow wooden dish piled with white flour mixed with white sugar, and began to painstakingly trace out the first of several large *veves* on the smooth, well-brushed earth floor of the peristyle. He began with the *veve* to Baron Samedi, the chief of the *Ghedes*, the *lwa* that tonight's service was to honour above all others.

Faustin, Sudra and Antoine Dieudonne all arrived together as Ti-Charles was completing that first *veve*, Faustin having accidentally caught up with the other two as they walked up the dusty red clay track that led from the edge of the village to the *oufo*. All were freshly shaved, washed, and dressed in white, or white and red. All of them were awkward, as Sudra had guessed that it was not coincidence that brought Faustin to the temple at the same time as Antoine and himself that morning. Antoine, too, sensed trouble was in the air, and was unusually quiet and unboisterous.

Ti-Charles stood and gestured for the three men to follow him over to a small hut at the side of the *oufo* where he received visitors and gave consultations on various matters: health, rituals to pacify and curry favour with the dead or with the *lwa*, advice on many practical matters, and also on matters of the heart. Sudra, Antoine and Faustin sat on low bentwood chairs, all now looking tense and watching Ti-Charles expectantly as he took his seat, a hand-carved cedarwood armchair that had belonged to his teacher, and that he himself had decorated with images of the *lwa* when he was a boy, using turquoise, scarlet, yellow and black paint.

'Well, then,' Ti-Charles said, once he had made himself comfortable, the few moments he took doing so emphasising that this was a serious situation.

'*Maître* Ti-Charles –' Antoine began, interrupting him. Ti-Charles raised a hand palm outwards as though to stop him carrying on and blurting out something he might regret. Antoine fell silent.

'I have consulted the *lwa*,' Ti-Charles continued. 'And the *lwa* have answered me.'

The air in the small room was still, and charged as though with static. Ti-Charles's smooth, handsome face with its black feline eyes and large, sculpted lips was suddenly masklike, removed from the everyday, oracular. The belief of the other men in him as a conduit of the *lwa* was absolute. The sound of Petro and Sauveur drumming outside pervaded the room like an accompanying heartbeat, the ever-present heartbeat of *Les Mystères*.

'Antoine Dieudonne –'

'Yes, *maître*.'

'The altar in your home is to the *Mystère* Ezulie, is it not, man?'

'Yes, *maître*.'

'When you were initiated, Ezulie became your *met-tête-lwa*?'

'Yes, *maître*,' Antoine said. 'I am dedicated to her. And to love, because she is the goddess of love. I am her *serviteur*, and love's *serviteur*.'

Sudra looked at Antoine with dark, suspicious eyes as he spoke, then turned his gaze sharply on Faustin. What was the postman he had once arrested for cheating in a cockfight doing here? Was he in love with Antoine? Had he placed the spell on Antoine to steal him away from Sudra? If the answer to either of these questions was yes, why would Ti-Charles not only permit Faustin to be here, but actually invite him? Surely not. But, if Faustin had nothing to do with what had happened to Antoine, why was he here at all?

Sudra remembered the good feeling of Faustin's mouth on his cock, the sense that here was a man dedicated to giving another man oral pleasure, who enjoyed giving a blow job for its own sake, as well as in the hope of shortening his time in jail. As if he could read Sudra's mind, Faustin flushed darkly, avoiding the policeman's eyes, toying with a charm of plaited grass he wore around one sinewy coffee-coloured wrist.

I could have been interested in you, Sudra thought. If I hadn't met Antoine only a week or two afterwards. He wondered if Faustin enjoyed being fucked as much as he did sucking dick, imagining taking him up the arse in the jail cell in Sous-L'Eau, imagining Faustin's moans of pleasure as Sudra pushed his stiff cock up him to the root.

'Antoine Dieudonne, Ezulie has chosen you,' Ti-Charles said. 'She has chosen you to be her husband.'

This unexpected statement brought Sudra's attention back to where he was with a crack.

'Husband? *Maître*, I do not understand,' Antoine said, looking from Ti-Charles to Sudra and back again, his golden-hazel eyes intense in the darkness of the unlit room, his pretty face slightly flushed. 'I serve, but –'

'You wander, man. You give your love and your cock and your mouth and your arse freely to many men lightly and cannot stick to any one single man –'

'Ah!' Sudra said sharply. 'So everything I heard was true!' It was his turn to flush now. He got to his feet, and for a moment he almost wanted to explode into anger and physically attack Antoine, but Ti-Charles gestured to him to retake his seat with an open hand. Sudra mastered himself with difficulty, nodded, and sat back down again, hunching up on his chair, glowering at Antoine and shooting hurt, fiery and embarrassed glances at Faustin and Ti-Charles. Faustin watched Sudra intently. It was as if he felt that his own heart was breaking to see the policeman's pain.

'This is because Ezulie will not permit you to give your heart fully to any one man,' Ti-Charles continued, as if there had been no interruption. 'Ezulie demands your heart, Antoine. She demands a mystical marriage. She demands that you honour her fully, and in return she will give you freedom to wander as you will.'

Ti-Charles stopped speaking. Antoine said nothing. Ti-Charles seemed to see the myriad thoughts that were no doubt passing through the young man's mind as he tried to take this strange news on board. Several times he seemed about to speak, but each time he cut himself off, touching a finger to his full lips doubtfully.

It was Sudra who eventually broke the silence. 'Man, this explains so much,' he said, almost excitedly. To Antoine: 'I thought you had been bewitched, or that you had betrayed me for another man. But now I see it is something else. You could never give me all your love, never, because Ezulie always had first call on you. And she will not suffer you to give what love you have left over all to one man. Perhaps I always knew this, but refused to accept it –'

Sudra stopped abruptly, as if he had been choked off. His eyes were suddenly brimming, and tears began to run down his cheeks. 'Perhaps I always knew,' he repeated. Faustin reached out and gripped Sudra's bare knee, and shook it gently. Sudra placed his hand on Faustin's, and squeezed it distractedly, reassured by the human contact and unable to say any more.

'What must I do, *maître*?' Antoine asked Ti-Charles, his voice anxious. 'What will Ezulie demand of me?' He knew men whose whole lives had been consumed in service to their demanding spirit brides or grooms, and his carefree nature rebelled against such strictures. But, as an initiate or *serviteur*, he also knew that the will of the *lwa* cannot be flouted without bad consequences following. Besides, Ezulie had brought him health and romance and good fortune in his life, and he was grateful for her blessing and protection.

'You must prepare a bridal chamber for Ezulie, here in the

oufo,' Ti-Charles said. 'You must decorate it to please your spirit bride. Place flowers on the altar and strew it with laurel leaves. Hang ribbons of all colours from the roof, and mirrors on the walls. Drape the tables in lace and the bed in embroidered silk. In this room the marriage service will be conducted, in the presence of witnesses and one versed in the rites of the Church. To this room you will come one night each week, and on that night you will not be intimate with another man. Otherwise you may do as you please, never forgetting that La Sirene has first call on your heart. Do you understand?'

'I understand, *maître*,' Antoine replied. 'But – she does not mind that I love to suck cock, or take it up the arse?'

'She is your *met-tête-lwa*, man,' Ti-Charles said. 'If she objected, you would have known a long time ago. Perhaps she even prefers that you are not intimate with any women of flesh and blood, that you prefer cock.'

Antoine nodded. But he still seemed doubtful.

'I do not question your knowledge, *maître*,' he said after a moment. 'But how do I learn for myself what will be required of me?'

'At the *mange-lwa* tonight she will ride you, and you will know,' Ti-Charles replied. 'And you will know when the marriage service should be performed.'

Antoine nodded again. 'It will be costly, *maître*,' he said worriedly. 'All the finery she will demand, and I have little money of my own.' He looked sideways at Sudra, who grunted and looked away without speaking.

There was another silence.

'I will help, man,' Faustin said suddenly. It was the first time he had spoken since they entered the room. His eyes were bright in the gloom. 'I have a little put aside that I can spare.'

'Good, man,' Ti-Charles said, pleased that Faustin was both facilitating things and finding a way to pay off the undisclosed debt he owed Antoine and Sudra for attempting to bewitch the younger man. Ti-Charles looked at Sudra.

'I will help, too,' Sudra said grudgingly, with a shrug of his broad shoulders and after a long moment of hesitation. He turned to Antoine. 'I will help you in this, Antoine. But for now it seems better if you do not remain beneath my roof, man. Now we know Ezulie's wishes, we would offend her by being together.' His manner was matter-of-fact, but there was a slight tremor in his voice. He cleared his throat. 'I know you have many friends you can stay with, man. You won't be homeless.'

'No, man,' Antoine said. 'I'll be all right.'

'I understand things now,' Sudra continued. 'But still, I don't think we can be friends, Antoine. Not for a little time, at least. Afterwards, perhaps, it will be as the *lwa* will.'

Antoine nodded, rose from his chair, bent forward and kissed Sudra on the forehead. The older, darker-skinned man closed his eyes as if the kiss hurt him.

'Forgive me, Sudra,' Antoine said gently.

'Perhaps one day I will believe there is nothing to forgive, man,' Sudra replied, his eyes still closed. 'Just pain to endure, and leave behind.'

'With your permission I will go and make my preparations for tonight, *maître*,' Antoine said, speaking to Ti-Charles now. There was an edge of rising excitement in his voice. He reached out to Faustin with a well-muscled café-au-lait arm and shook his hand. 'Thank you for saying you will help me out, man.' Antoine stepped over to the doorway and turned, silhouetted momentarily against the bright, whitewashed walls outside.

'Thank you for your guidance, *maître*.'

And he was gone. Ti-Charles slowly got to his feet. Faustin's hand was still on Sudra's knee, and Sudra's hand was still on top of it. Ti-Charles gripped Sudra's shoulder and shook it gently. 'I'll leave you to compose yourself, man,' he said, glancing at Faustin, who nodded that he would stay with the still-upset policeman. 'Take as long as you need.'

'Thank you, Ti-Charles, man,' Sudra said hoarsely as the young *oungan* left, his shaved head bent forward, his face obscured by shadow. Wordlessly Faustin slid closer to him and put a bare, smooth arm around his shoulders, and Sudra found its warm strength comforting. Almost without knowing what he was doing, Sudra half turned in his chair and pushed his face into Faustin's chest. Faustin's sleeveless white vest smelled of soap powder, and his body was clean, with the slight bitter scent of aftershave and cocoa butter. Faustin wrapped both lean arms around Sudra and hugged him tightly.

'It'll all be all right, man,' Faustin whispered, his goatee brushing the slick dome of Sudra's shaved head.

'Will it, man?' Sudra asked in a papery voice, his eyes screwed tight shut.

'I'll make it all right,' Faustin said, kissing him on one temple, trying to sound light.

'I remember your lips, man,' Sudra said, keeping his eyes closed. 'The good feeling of your lips on me.'

'I spent so many nights wishing I was in your arms since that day, man,' Faustin replied quietly, feeling his dick stirring in his white cotton breeches at the memory, and at having Sudra so unexpectedly close to him now.

'Did you?' Sudra asked, feeling the movement in Faustin's crotch, which was pushed against his hip, and glancing up at him enquiringly.

'When I knelt before you it was because I wanted to, Sudra. Not because I thought you would let me out from the jail sooner.'

'Is that true, man?'

'Oh, yes, man. It is true.'

Sudra raised his head and gazed into Faustin's eyes. He sniffed. Slowly, hesitantly, the two men moved their faces towards each other, closer, then closer still. Tentatively they kissed, delicately at first, then more hungrily, excitement rising in them rapidly as their lips fused and melted into each other, love discovered against the odds on the morning of the *mange-lwa*.

As *Les Mystères* will.

Outside, in the temple compound, and sheltered from the sun, which was now riding high in the sky, by the palm-tree roof of the peristyle, Ti-Charles returned to marking out the beautiful and intricately patterned *veves* for the evening's ceremony. Now that he had resolved the situation between Sudra, Antoine and

Faustin, with the help of the *lwa*, his mind was free to turn to thoughts of Henri Biassou.

Funny that I can sort out the problems of three men all at once but I cannot sort out my own, Ti-Charles thought as he allowed the mixture of flour and sugar to pour smoothly between his fingers and thumb, marking out an ornate swirl on the darker earth beneath, beginning the *veve* for Baron Lundi.

Although the *lwa* had come to him in dreams the night before, both Baron Lundi and Baron Limba, revealing Ezulie's wishes to him, Ti-Charles still found himself wondering whether Faustin's spell would have worked on Antoine, and if a similar but differently intended spell would work on Henri. He pushed the notion from his mind: what would be the point of bewitching Henri to desire him? His victory would be an illusion, a defeat.

In an adjacent part of the *oufo*, Sauveur's and Petro's drumming built up to a sudden explosive pitch, then stopped abruptly, and both men burst out laughing. Ti-Charles's heart beat harder in his chest and a slight breeze set the dried palm fronds rustling above his head.

This evening, he thought.

Antoine Dieudonne made his way along the hard-baked, red-clay path leading from the *oufo* back to the village, his mind running away with itself: On the one hand he was thinking of all the obligations he would have to fulfil to appease Ezulie, his *met-tête-lwa*, and feeling burdened. On the other, he was thinking of all the men he could enjoy with a clear conscience, and feeling free. Images of orgies filled his head, and his dick stiffened in his breeches as he imagined his every fantasy being acted out, untainted by guilt or inhibition.

Perhaps Ezulie will aid me in my musical career, he thought to himself. Once I am married to her. And I will sing songs of love and desire in the bars and cafés of Arbrerouge and the people will take me to their hearts, and I will cut records that will be played on the jukeboxes of all the towns and cities. And one day the fishermen of Croix-Le-Bois will hear my music on their little radio in their thatched beach hut and remember the nights they took it in turns to fuck me and suck my cock, and have me suck and fuck them, and they will laugh at the way the world turns, and how things fall out, and say, 'It was our come that oiled his throat. It was our cocks that stretched it, and our love that sweetened it.'

Not wanting to return straight to his home – or no longer *his* home, but Sudra's home, as he reminded himself – Antoine took a small, little-used cross-track that skirted Croix-Le-Bois and wound its way up to a rocky bluff topped with cedar and lime trees that overlooked the village and the beach, and offered a wide view of the countryside all around. This was the place where Antoine had first been with another man, a childhood sweetheart, shy, but with a dominant manner as he put Antoine's ankles to his broad, muscle-capped shoulders and pushed his well-greased cock into Antoine's virgin arsehole for the first time. And Antoine had cried out at the sudden ecstatic pain and the other youth had stopped, afraid he had hurt Antoine, and Antoine had had to beg him to carry on, needing to be fucked then as much as he needed food or drink, transported by the throbbing rigidity sliding in and out of his rectum with increasing rapidity, feeling his whole body dissolving . . .

But now Antoine's mind was full of thoughts of travel, not sex, and as he reached the top of the bluff he wanted to see as far as he possibly could in all directions, and dream of change and the wide world.

The air was clear, and the countryside was laid out before him like a map. On his right the sea sparkled like sapphires being stirred up by the hand of God. The cascading houses of the village, their plaster walls painted pink, blue, yellow and white, looked like candy, and this seemed right, because Croix-Le-Bois was where Antoine had spent his childhood and tasted the sweetness of male love.

He turned and looked along the coast, following the dusty red winding of the road to Arbrerouge as it snaked through a patchwork of dully lambent green fields of cane, corn, tobacco and coffee. Beyond Arbrerouge, and far further than his eyes could see even on the clearest day, the road ran on to Solaville, to which Antoine had never been, except in dreams.

Gazing at the curving road, he felt a sudden pang of remorse, remembering the times he had hurtled along it sitting behind Sudra astride his Harley Davidson, the throb of the engine between his thighs and against his balls turning him on, his hands gripping Sudra's leather-clad crotch as they sped through the tobacco fields kicking up salmon-pink dust, sometimes turning aside and making love with violent passion in the shade of rows of carefully tended and sweet-smelling tobacco plants.

If only Sudra had been less possessive, Antoine thought, shaking his head. But then it was Sudra's jealousy that had led to the truth coming out: that Ezulie was demanding a mystical marriage with him. So regret made little sense. But still he felt it.

In the far distance he saw a vehicle speeding along the dusty road, first its trail, then the vehicle itself. As it grew nearer, he saw that it was a truck.

An army truck.

Antoine watched it as it bounced along the rutted road, waiting to see what it would do at the crossroads, whether it would take the smaller fork to Croix-Le-Bois, or head straight on towards Sous-L'Eau. It did neither, but instead pulled to a stop at the place where the roads met. Disturbed, Antoine squinted and screwed up his eyes in an effort to make out what was happening.

Three soldiers in khaki green, with rifles slung over their shoulders, jumped down from the back of the truck. They seemed to be scanning the ground there for signs of disturbance. Antoine knew at once that they must be part of some anti-Voodoo drive by the military, because why else would they be searching at a crossroads? *Carrefour* to the believers, and highly symbolic, representing as it did the intersection of the material and spirit worlds, to a nonbeliever it was nothing more than the meeting of ways.

The soldiers found nothing, and began to look around more generally, scanning the horizon, shielding their eyes from the brightness of the day with their hands. Antoine caught the glint of something being lifted up by one of them. Realising abruptly that it was the lenses of a pair of binoculars catching the sun, he immediately threw himself to the ground. Hoping that he hadn't been seen, he wormed his way forward on his belly through the brush so he could continue to watch without being visible. Very faintly, he heard the crackle of a radio.

Peering through a tangle of aromatic sage and jasmine, Antoine saw the three soldiers disappear under the coconut palms that clumped around the crossroads and start off in the direction of the village. The truck started up a moment later, and headed off fast in the direction of Sous-L'Eau.

Realising there was no time to waste, Antoine slipped back from the edge of the bluff and, once he was out of view, got quickly to his feet and hurried back down the hill towards Croix-Le-Bois as fast as he could go.

Four

As Antoine was racing down the hill towards the village to warn his fellow believers about the arrival of the military, another young man was making his way through the sugar-cane plantations towards the old Sonnelier mansion. He wore an expensively cut white linen suit, an open-necked black silk shirt and alligator shoes. In his jacket pocket was a black silk handkerchief embroidered with *veves*, and he wore a white panama hat with a black feather in it at a jaunty angle on his head. A diamond-encrusted watch glittered on his wrist, and gold hung around his neck and shone on the fingers of both hands.

He was light-skinned and handsome, almost pretty, honey-coloured with amber eyes, full, arrogant lips and a pencil-thin moustache. His close-cropped, immaculately barbered hair was rust-coloured under his hat. Despite his apparent confidence, he was extremely nervous, and his fear grew as he drew nearer to the delapidated mansion. His name was Bertrand Laverre, and he had at one time been a Voodoo *serviteur*, studying under Ti-Charles at the *oufo* at Croix-Le-Bois. Then he had fallen out with Ti-Charles and abandoned his training for a different sort of quest for knowledge, knowledge he had thought that he would not get if he remained in the small fishing village, knowledge that he knew Ti-Charles would refuse to give him.

Knowledge! Bertrand almost laughed aloud, bitterly, at the thought: how simple life had seemed then, how likely to turn out well! If he had known then what he knew now . . .

Those happier years all seemed like the dreams of a thousand lifetimes ago to Bertrand as he hurried forward under the intensifying heat of the sun towards an appointment he dreaded either keeping or failing to keep. The air was dead still, and already warmer than blood in the bowl of the valley in whose centre the mansion sat.

He had seen and done so many things since he had left the *oufo* – exciting things, strange things, dark things, disgusting things. Things he wished he had never seen or done, or could somehow unsee, undo.

Too late now.

Crows circled the old plantation house, alighting intermittently in the branches of the sprawling cedar trees that hugged it close, and whose roots now forced their way into its foundations, splitting them. Bertrand Laverre's father had been buried in a cedarwood coffin. Bertrand wished that he had never seen the Sonnelier mansion, never met the *bokor* Jean Lamartine, and most of all, that he had never become entangled with the Zoboyo in Solaville.

He had left Croix-Le-Bois five years ago, when he was a lad of nineteen, in search of adventure and the answer to some dark yearning deep within him that he could neither define nor deny. As he packed his few possessions into a borrowed duffel bag he had had no clear plans beyond heading for Arbrerouge, and then, perhaps, if Arbrerouge wasn't big enough for him, going on to Solaville.

Bertrand Laverre had never been further from Croix-Le-Bois than Sous-L'Eau in all his young life. Most men of the village who felt an urge for wider skies became fishermen, and expanded their spirits through dedication to the *lwa*. But Bertrand, filled with a particular restlessness, had needed something else.

The first stage of his journey had been easy: he had been standing by the crossroads for less than two hours when he managed to thumb a lift on a banana truck headed for Arbrerouge.

They had pulled over after driving twenty miles or so and talking pleasantly of this and that, and the driver had put his hand on Bertrand's knee and flashed an enormous, gap-toothed smile framed in gold. He was a tough, rough-looking but sexy man of forty or so, with large hands and a bold manner that had made Bertrand's dick snap to stiffness in the arse- and crotch-hugging shorts he had purposefully worn to hitch-hike in.

'It was those tight white shorts made me stop for you, man,' the driver said, still smiling. 'The way you were showing off your assets, I knew you'd be an open-minded fellow.'

The two of them had got down from the cab and clambered into the back of the truck among the great jumbled tiers of mostly still-green, smooth-skinned bananas, and there in the cool darkness Bertrand had fucked the lean-bodied, aubergine-dark truck-driver, pushing his face down into the bananas and instructing him to lift his high, muscular arse up into the air so Bertrand could drive the whole length of his rigid caramel cock into the driver's anal cavity to the root. The driver worked his gold-ringed fist on his own large, veiny, uncut dick while Bertrand pumped his aching rigidity in and out of the driver's tight, spit-slicked ebony star as fast as he could. In his youth and excitement, Bertrand came quickly, before the horny truck driver felt he had been properly anally satisfied.

'Break off one of them bananas, man,' the driver had ordered Bertrand throatily after Bertrand had pulled out of him, glancing round at the younger man and gesturing, keeping his large, firm arse pushed back and out. 'Pick a nice big one, man. The biggest you can lay your hands on.' Bertrand nodded and did so vaguely, not quite sure what the driver intended. 'Well, fuck me with it, man,' the driver said insistently as Bertrand held up a thick, smooth and bright-yellow banana almost a foot long, starting to move his fist on his hard-on again. 'Your spunk will be my lube.' Turned on by the idea, Bertrand pushed the first six inches of it straight up the driver's arse without resistance. 'Yeah, that's it, man,' he grunted as he opened up to take it. 'Oh, yeah. Pump it.'

Bertrand slid the banana all the way up into the man's arsehole, making sure to keep a tight grip on the stalk, fascinated as the man's anal ring opened smoothly to take it in, the delicate skin around it glossy as a horse's flank.

'Ram me with it, man. Oh, Christ, yeah,' the driver gasped as Bertrand worked the smooth, unpeeled and increasingly warm banana in and out of the hard-bodied, shaven-headed man's upturned butthole, becoming half aroused again himself as he pleasured the driver, and the driver's fist pumped on his cock as he pushed his arse up as high as he could, and he started to grunt with each invasive thrust of the banana into his rectum, the grunts getting sharper and higher as he neared his climax and Bertrand pumped the banana in his arsehole as fast as he could. A moment later, sinews tautening under smooth dark skin, the driver came in excited spurts over the matting beneath him, thighs tensing and butt cheeks flexing with impressive muscularity as he orgasmed, splitting the banana's skin as he clenched and expelling the pulped yellow flesh within.

'Next time I want to be up you when you come, man,' Bertrand said breathlessly, full of admiration for the tightness and suppleness of the truck driver's anal ring, and wishing he hadn't come so early. 'To feel your hole and your buttocks grip me so hard I know I would come myself.'

'I have a room in Arbrerouge, man,' the driver said, pushing himself upright and wiping the sweat from his lean, hairless chest with the red handkerchief he wore tied around his neck. 'If you like you can stay with me for a couple of days until I have to make my next trip along the coast,' he offered matter-of-factly. He pulled up his breeches.

'I have no money, man,' Bertrand said, pulling up his shorts too, and buttoning them over his still half-hard cock.

'You have a good dick, though, man,' the driver had replied. 'And you're young and horny and you like my arse, yes? Give me a good hard fucking every morning when we wake, and every night before we sleep, and I will be satisfied and we will be quits.'

'What if I want to be fucked, man?' Bertrand asked, pretending innocence.

'Then I will fuck you,' the driver had said, smiling widely again.

And Bertrand had laughed, delighted that his adventures had got off to such a promising start.

What had the man's name been? Bertrand could not remember now, although he could remember the tightness of his anal ring as it gripped Bertrand's long, stiff dick, and the hoarse breathlessness of his voice as he begged Bertrand to fuck him harder, deeper, longer, the aubergine darkness of his skin against the whiteness of the sheets, the Spartan, white-walled simplicity of the driver's bedroom, the peeling green shutters, the coolness of glazed terracotta tiles beneath the soles of his feet, a fragrant candle burning on a small altar to Ayida Wedo, the *lwa* bringing good fortune – sensory memories, but the man's name had long since faded from Bertrand's mind.

Arbrerouge, with its shaded and brightly canopied town square, its bustling paved streets, its shops selling fancy imported and manufactured goods, its cafés with French cakes and pastries, its peeling, pilastered, colonial courthouse and mayoral mansion, had almost overwhelmed Bertrand at first, and he had felt very provincial, very much a peasant in his dress and manners. It was not a feeling he liked. He didn't know how or where to start in making a place for himself, but he was young and handsome and open to experience, and he already had the shrewdness to see that that was all he would need to pay his way in Arbrerouge.

The truck driver put a roof over Bertrand's head for a few weeks as he had promised, and introduced Bertrand to his friends, mostly transient working men like himself who travelled all over the island on one piece of business or another. One of these friends gave Bertrand trousers and a jacket he was no longer wearing – not the most fashionable of cuts, it was true, but better than what Bertrand had brought with him from Croix-Le-Bois; another gave him a blue-and-white-striped Breton shirt and cast-off but comfortable shoes with plenty of wear still left in them. A third was a barber in the choicest part of town, the Old Quarter just behind the square, and he gave Bertrand a truly fashionable *coiffure*: shaved at the back and sides, and glossily conked on top, and pomaded with the most expensive unguents from Solaville.

After the truck driver left town, Bertrand moved in with the barber. Leon Debrasser. Leon was a lean, fey, coffee-coloured man in his late thirties with an immaculate process and elegantly arched eyebrows. Despite his feminine manner and habitual pose of sophisticated ennui, in the bedroom Leon was both extremely horny and uninhibited and very much the man. He also had an impressively large and circumcised cock, very straight and smooth when fully erect, and he made what he wanted from Bertrand sexually very clear from the outset.

'I'm going to fuck you, man,' he had said to Bertrand, gripping the young man's high, muscular buttocks with both hands as the two men ground their crotches together to some compas music in a small bar off the old square which was called the Black Cat, but was known to its patrons as the Boy Pussy. Not 'I would like to fuck you' but 'I am going to fuck you'.

Initially hesitant about getting his legs in the air for Leon and letting the older man ram his considerable endowment into his tight and relatively inexperienced anal star, Bertrand soon found that he got great pleasure out of having a long, stiff and well-lubricated dick pushed up his arse to the balls. One memorable night Leon had tied Bertrand face down on the brass four-poster bed in the spacious but delapidated rooms he lived in above the barbershop, spread-eagling Bertrand on his belly and with his arse in the air by knotting silk scarves around the caramel-coloured youth's wrists and ankles, then tying them off to the four wrought-iron posts.

'Now you won't be able to touch your cock when I fuck you,' he had whispered into Bertrand's ear provocatively, pushing a finger into Bertrand's already-greased anal canal as he spoke. 'You will experience it all up your arse. And you will love it, man!' he had added as he mounted Bertrand from behind, pointing his swollen cock head towards Bertrand's trembling sphincter.

Bertrand had found being restrained exciting, and Leon had fucked him harder and deeper than ever before, pounding his butt without mercy as he satisfied himself in Bertrand's rectum, enjoying the fact of the lighter-skinned man's being made totally available for his pleasure, delighting in Bertrand's futile wriggling and gasping with excitement as he vigorously penetrated Bertrand from behind and pleasured him anally.

Afterwards Leon had noted with an exploring hand that the face-down Bertrand had remained fully erect the whole time Leon had been fucking him, and was still fully hard even now that Leon had flooded his anal cavity with come after three-quarters of an hour of intense, relentless butt-fucking. As he gripped Bertrand's hot, aching rigidity and pulled it back and up between Bertrand's buttocks, making Bertrand gasp, Leon had said, 'Maybe I will leave you like this and invite some friends up, man. Six or seven men friends we both know. I have told the men at the Boy Pussy bar many times what a tight, smooth ride you are. Maybe I will let them see if I am speaking the truth. Let them *feel* I am speaking the truth.'

Bertrand had struggled against his bonds as Leon caressed his firm, caramel-smooth, upturned butt, feeling both panicky and aroused by the idea at the same time.

Not yet totally hardened back then: he still had boundaries, even if they were only drawn in sand.

'Being gang-banged by those fuckers in the bar? Fuck that, man,' he had said to Leon defiantly. 'I ain't into that sort of scene at all.' But as he spoke he found himself imagining handsome, well-endowed men of every skin tone standing around the bed he was tied face down on, running their eyes and then their hands over his restrained body as they debated in which order they would take him up the arse.

It was a fantasy that was to become a reality in a hotel room with heavily brocaded gold curtains in Solaville. To Bertrand now, looking back, it seemed like a prefiguration – a prophecy of ecstasy and a warning all in one.

Bertrand had known from the very beginning the thing with Leon wouldn't last: unlike Leon he liked to play every role, not just the one, and so he couldn't imagine being satisfied being with a man who always and only wanted to fuck him up the arse, however much he enjoyed being the passive partner – and he certainly did. But more than that, he hadn't come to Arbrerouge to settle down with a barber, however fashionable, and the job

Leon had given him, washing clients' hair and sweeping the black-and-white-tiled floor of the Art Deco barbershop, wasn't what Bertrand had had in mind for himself when he slung a duffel bag over his shoulder and left Croix-Le-Bois on that spring morning that already seemed ten years ago.

It is so easy to forget your dreams. To get sidetracked by the bones life throws you. And then one day you awaken and look around yourself dazedly, and realise that where you are is no more than a way station, not your final destination, and life is trying to trick you, rob you of those dreams. You have sucked the bone of its marrow. For the time being. So you leave.

One morning, after he had been living with Leon for almost three months, Bertrand rose early while the barber was still asleep, and packed a bag – not only with his own clothes, but also with some of Leon's, as well as money and jewellery Leon had left about the place. Then he slipped out of the apartment and made his way to the railway station, where he bought a ticket and caught the train to the island's capital, Solaville.

Dreams, Bertrand thought, mopping his face and looking up at the Sonnelier mansion, which now loomed before him, still imposing in its massive dereliction. Dreams, man? he challenged himself. Dreams? Perhaps at first, hazy and dark and rich. But they became nightmares soon enough. Nightmares of death and desire. Oh, yes.

In Solaville Bertrand had become lost, both physically, in the city's tree-lined boulevards, winding lanes and myriad labyrinthine back alleys, and spiritually in its bars and fancy houses, in its high-ceilinged hotel rooms, and in the secret attics within the balconied and balustraded mansions of the wealthy. These colonial edifices, mostly built by the French before they were expelled from the island, stood on zigzagging lanes that wound up the face of the cliff that overlooked the rest of Solaville, in a district known to the poor as Sugarcane. Sugarcane, where the living was always sweet, or so those who had never penetrated the wrought-iron gates and pilastered porticoes believed.

It was in one such house that Bertrand became involved with the Zoboyo.

Bertrand had fallen in by then with a gang of tough, handsome young men who sought wealthy male patrons to support them. Most of the patrons were of the island, but there were also some foreigners, too, mostly French, American or English, along with the occasional Arab, African or Indian man of means. In return for this financial support, the young men offered companionship of varying degrees of intimacy and intensity, depending on what their better-off partners wanted from their streetwise paramours. Sometimes it was romance, sometimes it was the slaking of lust, and occasionally it was no more than the desire to be seen with someone aesthetically pleasing.

On one level the relationships between the young men and their patrons were, although convoluted and often melodramatically passionate, straightforward: Bertrand's good looks and sexual expertise, for instance, as well as his willingness to experiment, ensured that he was well rewarded by the various men he consorted with. They themselves were surprisingly often imaginative lovers, and attractive, rather than – as he had feared they might be – grotesque, men who needed some difference of class and status, or sometimes race or nationality, to find a partner sexually arousing. Some were good, some were bad, but, like men everywhere, most were a mixture of the two.

There was, however, another level of interaction which was not one bit straightforward, and it was on this level that Bertrand became involved with the Zoboyo, and sorcery.

Of course, some of the streetwise young men sometimes robbed their patrons – never a wise move, as news got around quickly among both groups, and the young thief would soon find himself without money, support or even friends among his own, as anyone who continued to be seen with him knew they would be damned by association and so lose patronage. More seriously, such young men would often disappear. 'He went back home,' the story would go among those who remained. 'Broke and disgraced.' But behind that story was another, unspoken one: that the thief had been disposed of by the wealthy patron. Not by the patron himself, of course, but by some intermediary. And it was in that context that Bertrand first heard the name Zoboyo mentioned.

Despite all that he came to know later, Bertrand never learned the real extent of the Zoboyo, never learned who was a member of that secret society, and who only pretended to be to impress or intimidate others. Perhaps no one knew how numerous they were, and even for those in the know – and they could have numbered only a handful – the picture was confused by feuds and internal rivalries. There were various other secret societies in Solaville and scattered across the whole island, but the Zoboyo were unquestionably the most powerful and feared.

Rumour is a distorting and usually exaggerating mirror, but Bertrand came to know through his own personal experiences that the Zoboyo were involved at the least in robbery, blackmail, murder and sorcery, and that they held considerable sway with the island's elected officials.

It was the scion of one of the island's wealthiest families who actually introduced Bertrand to members of the society. His name was Valris Saint Jacques, and his family owned estates all over the island, some in use, some neglected. One of the neglected estates was very close to Bertrand's home village of Croix-Le-Bois, and had once belonged to a French slaving family called Sonnelier, but this Bertrand learned only much later on.

Valris Saint Jacques had just turned twenty-two when Bertrand was first introduced to him, but he had already experienced more in the way of bizarre and extreme all-male sex than most men twice or even three times his age. The bodies of beautiful men and their erotic possibilities were his passion and his obsession, and he had the money and influence to get what he wanted out of almost anybody. The entertainments he staged in his lavishly decorated top-floor apartment in the decadent quarter of the city were legendary among those in the know, the connoisseurs of homosexual desire.

Valris Saint Jacques's father was Caribbean, his mother Chinese. He was handsome, almost pretty, with a creamy café-au-lait skin, a rangy physique, a wide mouth, high cheekbones and strongly sculpted features. He pulled his wavy black hair back into a plait into which gold braids were woven, and wore gold in both ears. Always he wore dark glasses, sometimes tinted pink, sometimes blue, but more often opaquely black; and he was also never seen without gloves – lacy ones, soft kid leather pairs in a rainbow of colours, studded black leather gauntlets. He was an intense, intoxicating young man, who could have got most things he wanted in life without being wealthy or connected, although no doubt it was coming from wealth that gave him his total confidence: it never occurred to him that a request he made would be refused.

Perhaps it was inevitable that a man like Valris, who had no respect for limits, who actually enjoyed pushing them until they ruptured, should be a member of the Zoboyo, and dabble in sorcery, and it was in Valris's notorious suite of brocade-hung rooms that Bertrand had met the *bokor* Jean Lamartine, and been reminded for a second time of his quest for knowledge from the darker side of the human heart and mind.

The invitation to Valris's apartment had been in the form of a gold-backed playing card with the ace of hearts on the front, and it had had scribbled across it a date – the fifteenth – and a time – midnight – but no address: if you didn't know already you obviously weren't meant to be on the list. Bertrand had been handed the card by a fellow street-corner boy he knew, Auguste, a petite, pretty and dark-skinned young man with a neat moustache who always wore a bowler hat on his shaved head at a jaunty angle, and had an aptitude for dominance surprising in a man only five foot four in height – or perhaps not surprising at all, for exactly that reason. He was a favourite of Valris's because he could be guaranteed to push the boundaries of any man he was dealing with.

Because of their lack of inhibitions, Auguste and Bertrand were normally rivals in their quest for patrons with more extreme tastes, but the party Valris was planning was going to be so wild that there would be more than enough guests to keep everyone more than busy. In any event, it would be memorable, and, like so many men before him, Bertrand found that he had a taste for luxury and finery as well as excess, so he took the invitation from Auguste's hand and guarded it carefully, knowing he would not be able to get himself admitted to Valris's block without it.

Bertrand had come to Valris's notice at another sex party, where he had asked the host to tie him face down to the bed for the evening, so that any guest who wished to fuck him – either in his arse or in his mouth – would be free to do so. The host had been pleased by the request, and Bertrand had serviced, or been serviced by, perhaps twenty men that night. After the first eight or nine he had started to lose count. His only certainty had been that he was being pushed towards an extremity of ecstasy he had been able to no more than dream about when he first had this fantasy in the barber's rooms in Arbrerouge. He had a feeling Auguste had probably fucked him at some point, but, being face down, he couldn't be sure. Not that he would have cared at the time – and if Auguste's big, stiff dick had given him pleasure, and if his hot, slack, greasy hole had given Auguste pleasure, then so much the better for both of them, and why should he care later, either? Afterwards, bruised, battered and sated, he had wandered the streets for days in a euphoric stupor, bow-legged, and with a pleasantly aching arse and throat. Valris had not fucked Bertrand at the party, but he had been impressed by the young man's enthusiasm and stamina.

The evening of the party arrived, and Bertrand dressed with special care in a white trilby, a leopardskin-print silk shirt slashed open to the waist, tight black silk trousers that hugged his bulky crotch and high, firm buttocks, and Cuban-heel boots. He draped a thin gold chain around his neck and touched musky, lemony scent behind his earlobes and on his wrists. Underneath his trousers he wore a leopardskin posing pouch that he thought would show the bulge of his cock and balls and the curves of his arse off to best advantage, and also go with his shirt if he wanted to remove his trousers but keep his shirt on.

It took him about quarter of an hour to walk from his small, plainly furnished room to the railinged courtyard in front of Valris's apartment block. The wrought-iron gate squeaked as he swung it open and stepped through. The courtyard was neglected, its flowers dead, its palm trees dusty, its fountain long since dried up, and the façade of the building that enclosed it claustrophobically on all three sides was peeling and cracking. Valris didn't seem to care, or perhaps he even enjoyed the atmosphere of decay. Bertrand didn't understand the rich: how *could* they not care? He crossed uneven flagstones to a large green door overhung by ivy.

Before he could knock, the door swung open noiselessly. Standing before him blocking the way was a tall, broad, dark-skinned man in a black double-breasted suit, wearing sunglasses. He held a walkie-talkie in one gold-ringed hand and didn't speak. Trying to project a nonchalance he was far from feeling, Bertrand showed him the invitation. The man took it from him and looked it over carefully, grunted his satisfaction, then handed it back to him.

'Upstairs, man,' he said, turning to gesture towards a great sweeping stairwell behind him. 'Sixth floor.'

Bertrand mounted the stairs two at a time, nervousness rising in his chest and stomach as he climbed. He wondered if Valris's parties were as extreme as he had heard, and if even he might be pushed beyond his limits. But it was too late to go back now: what would the doorman think? Or do? A sheen of sweat had broken out on his face by the time he reached the top floor of the mansion block in the close humidity of that August night.

A corridor lit with candelabras and lined with a scarlet velvet carpet ran on ahead of Bertrand, and he followed it until he came to a doorway draped with a crimson cloth, beyond which he could hear hot jazz music and the sounds of sex. His cock stirred in his tight black trousers. He was afraid, but he didn't want to go back.

Taking a deep, oxygenless breath, Bertrand lifted the drapery and stepped into the room beyond.

The shutters were closed and draped with heavy, dull-gold brocade, and the room was dimly lit with candles, the high ceiling fading away into obscurity. A record – Miles Davis's 'Birth of the Cool' – was playing on a large front-lit teak-veneer music centre almost the size of a jukebox that stood against one wall, a flashy

American import. The floor was strewn with Arabian rugs, and doorways opened suggestively into other, darker and more private rooms. In the centre of the main room was a great round bed like a raised dais with black and red silk sheets on it, around which chaise longues were arranged strategically, emphasising its stagelike quality. Chains with manacles attached to their ends and complicated pulley systems hung down from the ceiling in one corner of the room, and they were not unused.

On that bed, on the chaise longues, and in every corner and alcove in the place, man sex of every conceivable kind was going on. The heat of it and the smell of it had Bertrand fully turned on before he could properly take in what his eyes were seeing in the flickering candlelight: at first all he saw was a mass of writhing, muscular male flesh without beginning, end or boundaries. Then, in a series of flashbulb moments, the mass resolved itself into twosomes, threesomes, foursomes and more.

A dark-skinned black man with large, arrogant features, a totally shaved head and body – no eyebrows, no pubic hair, smooth as an obsidian carving, but supple – a sapphire stud in one ear and gold on his eyelids, was squatting in the middle of the circular bed with his thighs spread wide apart, almost a hundred and eighty degrees, and pushing his large, firm, beefy brown butt down on to Auguste's thickly greased upward-pointing fist. Auguste, his bowler hat on his head at a jaunty angle as always, was bracing his smooth, muscular mid-brown forearm to keep it fully upright, his elbow being pressed hard into the mattress below it as the hairless man bounced and squirmed his big arse down on to the shorter man's greasy hand, pushing himself down on it with his whole body weight, his anal ring finally dilating enough to swallow the hand completely, then cinching itself around Auguste's wrist in a moment of comparative relief, then stretching shinily again as the darker, shaved man slowly carried on sitting down, and inch after inch of Auguste's broadening forearm disappeared up into his capacious and highly-elastic rectum.

As the man squatted down, tossing his shaved head and groaning with closed eyes as he forced Auguste's fist and arm further up into his anal canal, a second man, young, cinnamon-brown, clean-shaven and handsomely long-faced, with an orangey-brown fade, wearing a waiter's white matador-jacket and nothing else, was on all fours before him, sucking the shaved black man's curving, veiny, throbbing and achingly rigid cock hungrily and with theatrical relish, opening his mouth wide and swallowing its crown repeatedly down his throat with greedy gulps.

At the same time as he blew the shaved man being fisted by Auguste, this lighter-skinned young man was having his own smooth, caramel-brown and upturned butt fucked vigorously by a mocha-brown, heavily muscled man with a gold-pierced nipple, moustache and tight cane rows, who was wearing only bike boots and a chain of steel links around his waspy waist, and was kneeling on the large round bed behind him. Every sinew tensed as every vein dilated across the muscleman's bulging upper arms, the domes of his chest, and even over his ridged, totally fat-free stomach as he gripped the waist of the slender man on all fours before him and began to pump his lean, narrow hips against the youth's large and upturned butt as hard as he could, holding the young man's arse in place as he shafted him, lifting one leg with theatrical relish as he pumped his thick, darkly erect cock in and out of the dick-sucking young man's well-greased anal star to give anyone who cared to watch a good view of the penetration.

Bertrand watched, his cock straining at his tight black trousers, envying both of them, eager to join them but still uncertain as to whether he needed to ask permission.

The large, rigid cock of the young man being fucked kicked and bucked excitedly with each thrust of the cane-rowed muscle-man's dark, slick erection into his slack, well-fucked arsehole, and Bertrand saw that the hair in his crotch had been clipped back to stubble, and that he had shaved his arse. Other naked or scantily clad and well-muscled men moved sinuously around this trio, caressing them with their hands, their lips, their tongues, at the same time offering up their own stiff dicks and muscular arses to whoever wanted to explore or take hold of them, toy with them or pleasure them. More than one large, beeswax candle had had its wick pinched out prior to insertion into an already-lubricated anal opening.

This floorshow was informal, with participants moving back and forth between it, the chaise longues, the shadowy alcoves and the other darkened rooms Bertrand hadn't yet seen. The chaise longues themselves were being used more for hard sex action than for languid voyeurism: a very muscular older man with butter-brown skin, a heavily pumped chest, long, rangy legs and a shaved head arched back on one of them face up, while a pretty, plain-chocolate-skinned and boyish young man with a beefy booty bounced on his lap, pleasuring the older man's cock with his slick anal star and obviously thoroughly enjoying the sensation of a hot, stiff dick pushing its way deep into his back passage, judging from his own jutting, wagging erection. This younger man wore glasses and had a parting shaved into his close-clipped hair, and would have looked the quintessence of the respectable university student if he hadn't been working his arsehole so enthusiastically on another man's cock.

The older man's face was obscured by another youth's butt being pushed down on to it. He was even darker than his friend, and wore gold earrings, and had his hair in cups-and-saucers. He was lean, but with a very big butt that Bertrand suspected would be much in demand in the course of the evening, judging by the skill with which he squirmed it down on to the beefy older athlete's face, gasping with pleasure as the lighter-skinned man ate his battyhole out greedily.

The two pretty youths were facing each other, and they tongue-kissed with spit-slicked lips as they worked their chocolate stars on the heavily turned-on muscleman beneath them, gripping each other's small, dark, pert nipples and teasing and nipping them with short, well-manicured nails, enjoying playing the role of horny bitches for the pleasure of the man they were on top of.

One of the distinctive features of Valris Saint Jacques's parties was that once you got inside, once you had been vetted at the door by his security men and were allowed to enter, all social distinctions collapsed. Rich or poor, light or dark, educated or street-smart, none of that mattered: all that counted in the apartments of Valris Saint Jacques was sexual prowess and an appetite for exhibitionist shamelessness. It was liberating for the street boys, who were so often despised in everyday life; a space where what they had to offer not only came into its own and was appreciated, but it was all that mattered, all that impressed. Perhaps less expectedly, Valris's orgies were also liberating for the rich young men of the capital: many of them felt trammelled by the rigid social conventions of their class, and the suffocatingly conservative expectations of their families that they should settle down and marry a respectable girl, with whom they would consolidate a family fortune, and from whom they would produce an heir. Their own wishes were of little concern to their parents.

At Valris Saint Jacques's they could briefly forget all that, and for the course of the night feel free and unconstrained by bourgeois notions of respectability. An outsider would have been unlikely to guess, for instance, that the two horny, dark-skinned bottoms pleasuring the older, pumped-up bodybuilder on the chaise longue were both sons of government ministers playing whore for the evening, rather than true professionals selling their arses with good-hearted enthusiasm. And here they *could* play whore, because who would judge them? After all, it was known to anyone who knew anything that no witness here stood back and was not involved: if any man was to say he had seen another man do so-and-so or such-and-such, his listener would immediately wonder, Ah yes, but what were *you* doing while all this was happening? Perhaps when you tell me the governor's son was begging to drink piss hot from the cock he got the idea from seeing you on your knees . . .

The bodybuilder the two dark-skinned young men were pleasuring with their enthusiastically offered booties ran a private gym, where he and his instructors beefed up its profitability by offering a wide range of extras to its well-off male patrons, from massage to sucking and fucking and more: he demanded complete versatility and extreme open-mindedness as well as fitness and good looks and manners from his employees.

On another chaise longue was a mocha-skinned man in his late thirties with shoulder-length braids and spectacular features accentuated by elaborate make-up. He had a lankily muscular frame whose V shape was emphasised by a black leather basque laced tightly up the back, and was driving his ten-inch erection firmly into the upturned arsehole of a slim, buttery-peach and shaven-headed young naval officer who liked to keep his patent-shiny knee-length black leather boots on while being fucked up the arse, and by some quirk of the psyche could enjoy being screwed only by feminine men – although they still had to have big dicks.

The otherwise naked officer braced his muscular, smooth, yellow body and pushed his arse up high, making it available to the man behind him, his handsome face a mask of resilience as his hole was roughly pounded, the drag queen's lean, flat hips slapping repeatedly against the firm globes of his arse. As Bertrand watched, an ebony-dark and well-muscled young man with studded leather round his wrists and neck went up to the sailor being fucked, gripped his sweaty shaved head, lifted it back, stretching the passive man's throat into a long, straining curve, and pushed his bobbing erection into the young officer's mouth. The officer offered no resistance as the standing man pushed his eight-inch dick straight down his throat and began to fuck it roughly, the impressive plain-chocolate globes of his arse flexing concave, convex, concave as he pumped his hips against the yellow-skinned man's face, brazenly using the sailor's mouth for his own gratification.

Within moments a second man, cinnamon-brown and slim and lanky, with a very large, circumcised cock that was slick from having already been deep in several arseholes that evening, a smallish Afro and a gold front tooth in his boyish, freckled face, positioned himself behind the muscular drag queen who was ploughing the sailor's arse hard. Moving his hips into position, and following the drag queen's rhythm, the lanky young man pushed his dick straight up the drag queen's muscular arse to the root, adding to his rhythmic thrusting as he continued to fuck the face-down sailor in front of him without a pause. The ornately made-up man grunted as he was penetrated but didn't allow it to disrupt his fucking of the butter-skinned man on the chaise longue for a second. If anything, having a cock slammed right the way up his arse while he was fucking added to his own dick's excited rigidity and swollenness, and the weight of having two men pounding their hips against his upturned butt certainly also added to the sailor's submissive pleasure at being taken up the arse face down while his face was being fucked hard and deep.

On the other chaise longues similar scenarios were being played out as the champagne flowed freely and marijuana smoke hazed the air. One youth, smooth, pretty, large-lipped, with wavy brown hair and golden eyes, and a smooth, shapely, long-legged and cinnamon-brown body other men would caress idly as they passed him, sprawled back on the button-backed pink velvet in a black silk posing pouch and nothing else. He held a glass of champagne languidly in one hand, and beckoned to any man who wanted to straddle his face and fuck his throat until he came.

The young man would wank himself vigorously through the fabric of his pouch as he sucked greedily on the cock of the man mounting his face, his flat, smooth chest rising as he gasped for breath, his stomach twitching as the dick-head of the man above him rammed repeatedly over his gag-reflex and down his throat towards climax. After the topman had fucked his way to orgasm in the youth's mouth, and shot his load over the brown-skinned young man's tongue and full lips and down his throat, he would withdraw his glistening, semi-erect dick and stagger back, exhausted, muscles aching, desire sated – at least temporarily – and the youth would lick his large spunk-slicked lips, take a sip of champagne, and look around immediately for the next cock to suck. Despite his apparent predilection for oral action only, he too would be turned face down by the end of the evening, have his pouch pulled down to his ankles and off, and be given a good, hard fucking, finally taking stiff cock and steaming jism up his other end and coming without touching his own erection as the third man in a row slammed his greasy cock head hard against the youth's prostate over and over again.

A well-muscled, light-skinned man with his straightened black hair pulled back in a ponytail stood with his legs spread and his hands manacled above his head, silver clamps on his nipples and a small silver block hanging from a cord tied around his large ballsac, which was being stretched shiny by the weight of it. His cock, which was thick and stiff and veiny, wagged above his constricted testicles, and bucked each time a dark-skinned youth in a black leather eye mask and a leather pouch cracked a studded belt on his blocky, muscular buttocks. A kneeling, older, mocha-brown man with a shinily shaven head, a moustache, and a preternaturally long tongue, teased the manacled man by flicking his tongue tip into the piss slit of his bobbing erection, drawing out shiny threads of pre-come that caught in the candlelight like spidersilk covered with dew. After a little while of this, the kneeling man's urge to suck cock for real overcame him, and he drew the manacled man's veiny rigidity into his mouth and began to pump on it, inspiring the masked youth to wield the belt on the manacled man's muscular, pinkening buttocks all the harder.

In an alcove near to where Bertrand was standing, a dark-skinned and firmly muscled man with a blond fade and dark eyes lay back on red velvet padding. His long, shapely and hairless legs had been tied up and out to a rail at the top of the alcove with white silk ropes so they were kept perpetually spread open, the pink soles of his feet bright in the candlelight, and his large, smooth arse was raised up like an inviting chocolate peach, so that his anal star was on constant display to every man who passed by him. Its greasy, relaxed state showed clearly that it had already seen a good amount of action. The blond black man's erection jutted up shinily against the folds of his lean belly and his balls hung down loosely and invitingly between his smooth thighs.

As Bertrand watched, a naked youth with light skin and a ten-inch dick stepped up to the blond man in the alcove and, without a word, pushed his throbbing erection all the way up the darker-skinned man's slack, well-fucked hole, sensing that his need and his pleasure were to be used by active men without the courtesy of an introduction: with his legs tied up in the air, there was no way he could prevent any man from fucking his arse, and Bertrand could see that was how he liked it. Bertrand noted that the blond man never touched his own aching, bucking cock the whole time he was being fucked, even though it beaded and dripped clear glittering pre-come with each thrust of the man standing between his legs. The most he would do was caress his dark, protruding nipples to add to the sensuality and intensity of his anal experiences.

All this Bertrand took in in less than half a minute, by which time the fluidity of the situation meant that many positions and combinations had changed and shifted: bottoms became dominant, tops were turned face down and fucked, twosomes became threesomes, foursomes ... The smells of sweat and come and candle wax filled Bertrand's nostrils. Before he could think about what he wanted to do first, and with whom, he became aware of his host coming towards him through the writhing throng, and offering him a flute of champagne that sparkled with powdered gold.

Valris Saint Jacques wore nothing but a pair of white lace gloves, a choker of diamonds around his café-au-lait neck, diamond studs in his ears, and white leather bike boots with silver chains on them on his feet. His eyes were hidden behind rose-tinted shades. He smiled and revealed a diamond stud in his front right tooth. He had trimmed his pubic hair back to the stubble and had pushed his big ballsac and sizeable, bobbing erection through a silver cockring. His butter-brown skin was flawless, his elegantly lean and solidly muscled physique free of fat, his pinky-brown nipples stiff and protuberant, his pinky-brown cockhead a full and curving dome.

'You came, Bertrand,' Valris Saint Jacques said, handing Bertrand the glass of champagne. Their fingertips brushed and Bertrand shivered excitedly.

'Yes, m'sieur,' Bertrand said, glancing down awkwardly at Valris's wagging dick with its large, smooth, spade-shaped head and ridged shaft as he took the glass, half wanting to sink to his knees in front of his host at once and take his hot, stiff cock into his mouth and suck Valris off as quickly and greedily as he could, to prove he was worthy of his invitation. Bertrand's mouth started to water at the thought of the salty taste of Valris's pre-come flooding over his grooved tongue and full, pouting lips.

'Here I am just Valris,' Valris said. 'Or man. Or boy. Or bitch. Or hole. Or slut.' He shrugged, still smiling. 'My body, my cock and arse, they are all the rank I need.'

Bertrand sipped his champagne nervously, and said nothing in reply. His painfully stiff and constrained cock was being bent sideways uncomfortably inside his posing pouch. He gazed into Valris's rose-tinted eyes, and felt himself starting to fall forward inside his own head, as if he was becoming hypnotised by his host.

'Don't think, Bertrand,' Valris continued. 'Just *do*. Whatever you want to do is permitted here. No,' Valris continued, his voice compelling, 'more than that: it is *demanded*. Fuck, be fucked. Suck, be sucked. Eat arse, drink piss, be whipped. Whip others. Take a hand or a candle, or give these things. Fill your rectum to bursting point. Suck cock till you gag.'

Bertrand nodded wordlessly, and sank to his knees in front of his host. Valris looked down on him with a smile as Bertrand kissed his bobbing cock head, teasing its piss slit with the tip of his tongue, then slowly pushed his mouth down over it, inching his lips along Valris's shaft, savouring the excitement of sucking a hot new cock for the first time, gradually swallowing Valris's cock head down his throat until he was pressing his full lips firmly against the silver ring that Valris wore around his dick and balls, Bertrand's nose brushing the stubble of the standing man's crotch, Valris's ballsac stretching smoothly over his chin.

'Now pump,' Valris ordered, and Bertrand obeyed, eagerly.

Of course Valris hadn't let Bertrand suck him to the point of climax, not so soon in the evening, but having his host's dick down his throat had freed Bertrand of any shyness or inhibition he had been feeling, and he had flung himself into the rest of the party with wild abandon, quickly stripping down to his leopard-effect posing pouch while keeping his leopard-print shirt on – though totally open, needless to say, to ensure total free access to his chest and the large and protuberant nipples Bertrand was justifiably proud of, having teased them into their current state of fullness with the regular, discreet use of tit clamps under his shirt. A good few men took turns in pinching, twisting and tweaking them, egged on by his high, shuddering gasps of pleasure at having his nipples so firmly used.

106

Feeling an unexpected desire to have the palm of a hand on his beefy, demerara-brown buttocks, Bertrand had thrown himself on to the circular bed face down and stuck his arse up in the air, announcing, 'Man, I need to be spanked!'

Several men responded immediately, taking turns slapping his butt with stinging blows until it felt good and hot. After several increasingly exciting minutes of this attention, during which time Bertrand began to suspect he could actually come from being spanked, judging from the thrill that lanced through his crotch with each sharp crack on his upturned buttocks, he called out over one shoulder, 'Oh, man, that was good. But now I need to be stuffed! I need hot cock up me now!'

His briefs were immediately pulled down and off and he felt a pair of hands grip his waist firmly and a moment later a thick, stiff and greasy cock head was pushed hard against his sphincter, slowly forcing it open, then sliding solidly all the way into his rectum, opening him up inside. Bertrand grunted, then relaxed into it as the man behind him started to pump his cock in and out of Bertrand's smooth and elastic anal canal: now he was open he knew he would be able to take as many cocks up there and as much hard fucking as the evening required of him. Like the blond-haired man in the alcove, he was determined never to say no.

That man fucked Bertrand with deep, firm strokes until, with a throaty yell, he came. Then another man took his place behind Bertrand, using the first man's spunk as lube for his fucking. Then a third. By that time Bertrand felt a need to plug a mouth or arsehole with his own aching dick, and, once the third man had gratified himself in Bertrand's hot, slack back passage and shot his load up there, Bertrand struggled off the circular bed to find himself a willing bottom who wasn't already taking it hard from both ends, his aching thighs trembling as he pushed himself upright, spunk sliding from his well-fucked hole as he started to wander around the room.

The champagne, the joints, the endless supply of willing sex partners, all these things began to make Bertrand's head spin as he moved from man to man, and from men to men. At one point he was fucking one upturned ebony butt while fisting another that straddled it, at the same time as squatting down on a thick, pale candle to its base for the entertainment of onlookers, feeling its length slip well past the sphincter at the top of his rectum and up into his guts and loving that feeling. At another he was dripping wax over the kicking oversize cock of a muscular yellow-skinned man while sitting on his face and being deeply eaten out.

Perhaps most extremely, a beefy, well-hung and very dark man had gripped his shoulders and fucked him excitingly hard, come up his arse with a hoarse gasp, then kept his cock up Bertrand and pissed up inside him. Bertrand had gasped too, in shock and perverse excitement as the distension of his rectum caused by the flood of hot urine almost pushed him to climax himself. The man had then insisted that Bertrand squat over his face and allow the hot piss and jism to flood out back into the man's open mouth while the man wanked himself roughly to a second and equally violent orgasm within minutes of the first.

Bertrand had also sucked off several men while squatting on a champagne bottle, gradually dilating his anal ring wider and wider, until finally Auguste had found him and led him to the circular bed, tied him face down on it and fisted him vigorously. It was the first time Bertrand had taken a hand up his arse, but he found it intensely exciting, and came explosively without touching his own cock as Auguste rammed his balled fist back and forth inside Bertrand's well-stretched and well-greased anal cavity. Then Auguste completed their performance by fucking Bertrand himself. Still tied face down, Bertrand was by then so totally slack and exhausted he was quite happy for Auguste to use his hole to entertain the others and come up him, which the bowler-hatted youth did after several minutes' vigorous poling of Bertrand's greasy, wide anal opening, during which he held Bertrand's smooth, firm buttocks open to ensure he gave him the deepest penetration possible with his nine-inch dick, and fucking Bertrand back to semi-erection.

After being untied and let up from the bed, Bertrand had wandered around and sucked a few more men off, something that normally gave him great pleasure. But Auguste's hand had satisfied him anally, which was what really mattered to him, and shortly after the second man came in his mouth with a grunt and a flood of hot, salty jism, Bertrand had slipped away into one of the unoccupied alcoves with a joint and a glass of rum. He needed to get his breath back, and wanted to give his bruised orifices a bit of time to recover from the battering they'd received, while still being able to carry on watching the show.

It was here that Bertrand was introduced to the *bokor* Jean Lamartine, the last place in the world he would have expected to be reminded of that other side of the quest for forbidden knowledge and experience that had made him leave Croix-Le-Bois for Solaville in the first place; the last place he had expected a door to be opened into the night world of sorcery and *les mortes*, the dead.

Bertrand closed his eyes briefly as he lay back on the purple velvet cushions and toked on the joint. He was totally exhausted; every muscle in his lean young body ached. His throat ached. His cock ached. His arsehole ached and throbbed as if he'd just given birth from it. These feelings were good, but they were also the product of being fucked so senseless he really couldn't take any more for the moment. The yielding velvet was so comfortable under his buttocks and against his muscular, sinewy back. All he really wanted or needed was a few minutes on his own to pull himself together. Then he could decide what he wanted to do next, and with whom. He half wanted to get dressed and leave, but another part of him said, 'But where would you rather be than here?' and to that Bertrand had no answer. He was just hoping that his host, Valris Saint Jacques, wouldn't notice his temporary absence and think he lacked stamina or commitment to sex with men, when he became aware that someone had sat down next to him.

'Oh, man, I am spent,' he declared out loud, not opening his eyes. 'My arse is fucked slack, my throat is so bruised I must soothe it with rum. If you want, you can sit on my face and I will eat you out, man. My tongue is still willing. But otherwise –'

'No, man,' a velvety male voice said. 'It is not fucking I want. Not right now. I too am satisfied. No, I want to talk to you.'

The voice was unfamiliar, and something in its tone made Bertrand open his eyes and drag himself upright.

'What do you want to talk to me about, man?' he asked, suddenly aware that the joint and the drink had dulled his normally sharp mind. For no apparent reason the man's manner was making him uneasy. The unease was intuitive, and Bertrand had learned to trust his intuitions. 'Who are you anyway, man?' he asked, suspicion etching itself across his handsome features.

'I am Jean Lamartine,' the man sitting next to him said amiably, smiling as if he had not seen that Bertrand distrusted him, extending his hand for Bertrand to shake. 'And you, I know, are Bertrand Laverre.'

Bertrand nodded, trying to place a name he had certainly heard before, and not, at first, thinking it unusual that Jean Lamartine should know the surname he had never told to anyone in Solaville.

Jean Lamartine was the dark-skinned man with the shaved head and body who had been pushing his big, beefy, hairless arse down on to Auguste's fist when Bertrand first came into the room. Close to, Bertrand could see he was older than he had seemed at a distance – maybe a shade under forty. He had dark, almost black eyes, no eyebrows at all, and full, pouting and rather arrogant lips under a wide, very flat nose. The overall effect was slightly strange-looking but curiously sexual and provocative. The sapphire in one small, neat ear twinkled as Jean Lamartine moved his head as he talked, and one front tooth was a block of gold. His body was curvy but not fat, and his depilated and aubergine-dark skin was flawless. He dragged on a filterless cigarette, then passed it to Bertrand.

'You have an accommodating arse, man,' Bertrand said, taking the cigarette from Jean Lamartine, drawing on it and returning it to him.

'I need a fist for real satisfaction,' the shaven-headed man said with a shrug. His skull was shiny with sweat, and glinted darkly in the candlelight. Bertrand glanced down at his shaved crotch, which was also gleaming. His large, circumcised cock jutted forward at half-mast above big, loosely hanging balls. 'I think you do, too,' he added. 'Valris was most impressed with the show you and Auguste put on.'

'So you know Valris well?' Bertrand asked, trying to peg Jean Lamartine as to rank and social class: he didn't seem like a hustler, but then again he obviously wasn't upper class.

'I know all his secrets,' Jean Lamartine said casually, gazing out across the warm, stuffy room where men were still sucking and fucking and being sucked and fucked, his eye caught by a pretty black youth squirming his big booty down on to two greasy cocks at the same time, while his mouth was simultaneously plugged by a standing yellow-skinned man with a taste for rough face fucking who was gripping his shaved head with both hands and ploughing his throat.

Jean Lamartine's reply both surprised and unnerved Bertrand, and he let the conversation drop for a moment and joined in watching the two stiff dick shafts slowly slip up the squatting young man's stretched and greasy anal ring to the root.

'That boy has the *esprit* of a bitch,' Jean Lamartine said with a laugh, watching the ebony youth's cock kick between his thighs as he sat down fully on the two erections beneath him to their bases. 'When he's not getting himself fucked, he always has two or three love balls the size of billiard balls up his arse to keep himself feeling full. And I should know, man,' Jean Lamartine added. 'He borrowed them from me!' He laughed again, and Bertrand wasn't sure if he was joking or not.

'What does Valris enjoy?' Bertrand asked, the display pushing his thoughts back towards sex.

'Ah,' Jean Lamartine replied. 'Perhaps that is something that should only be seen and never told, man.'

'Is it a secret, then, man?'

'Not like his other secrets,' Jean Lamartine said teasingly.

'So tell me, man,' Bertrand said. 'I mean, why not tell me? You've seen me take cock, get spanked and take a hand up me, man. Can I be shocked? Can I speak of it? To who? Or perhaps you don't know.'

'I know.'

'Well then, man?'

'Valris likes – well, Valris is a voyeur,' Jean Lamartine said, relenting, and arching what would have been an eyebrow if he hadn't shaved it off. 'He gets great pleasure out of arranging these parties and watching the guests perform together. But that isn't his real turn-on.'

'Well?'

'He needs it rough, man. Very rough.' Jean Lamartine took a last drag and stubbed out his cigarette in a brass ashtray inlaid with topaz.

'How rough is very rough?'

'Have you been inside that room over there?' Jean Lamartine gestured towards a doorway that led off into shadow next to the pulleys and hanging chains.

Bertrand shook his head. 'No, man,' he said, intrigued.

'In that room is a gymnasium. There are weights, there is a boxing ring, a pommel horse, all things of that sort. But one thing is missing.'

'What, man?' Bertrand's voice betrayed his eager curiosity, and his dick stirred between his legs in profane anticipation.

'A punchbag.'

'I don't understand, man. So?'

'Valris Saint Jacques has his arms tied up to a chain above his head so he cannot shield his body in any way. His trousers and briefs are pulled down to his ankles. Then two or three tough, hard-bodied young men who he has spoken to before, and who understand exactly what is needed of them, put on boxing gloves and spar. He watches them box lightly with each other, working up a sweat, his excitement and anticipation building, his cock stiff-stiff, until at a particular moment a signal is given and first one, then the others say, "Man, that's enough sparring. I need to work out with the punchbag." And then they come over to him and work out with him like he was the bag. Not hitting his face, of course. But he loves it in the gut especially. Man, when a punch lands hard in his stomach you see his cock buck and drip! And when he wants to come he will order them to punch or knee him in the balls, or kick him in the balls with the flats of their feet from behind with his legs open. A good one between his legs and he comes without touching his cock.'

'Fuck me, man,' Bertrand said, genuinely disconcerted. 'That is heavy-heavy.' He thought for a moment. 'But he cannot do that often?' he said. 'It would be too injurious.'

'In between he just fucks or sucks or is fucked in the usual way like all of us, man,' Jean Lamartine said. 'But he is never really satisfied by normal loving. Without pain, there is no release for him. Of course there is a reason, but I do not know it. I will get a drink,' he added abruptly, pushing himself to his feet. 'And return in a moment. Then we will talk.'

Jean Lamartine wandered off in search of alcohol. The moment his back was turned, Auguste, naked apart from the bowler hat that was still on his head, only now at an even steeper angle, came up to Bertrand, his considerable dick wagging at half-mast.

'Do you know who you were talking to?' he asked anxiously and in a low voice, looking round to make sure Jean Lamartine wasn't coming back.

'Jean Lamartine,' Bertrand said easily. 'He praised our performance. Man, you fisted me! I can't believe you just greased my hole and got your hand right up me! When my arsehole sucked shut round your wrist I wanted to scream I felt so full. Man, it was amazing! And when you started to ram it back and forth –'

'Do you know who Jean Lamartine *is*?' Auguste repeated earnestly, cutting across Bertrand's rhapsodising.

'A slack black hole,' Bertrand replied shortly, annoyed at being cut off in mid-flow. 'A horny bitch. Slacker than me.'

'He's high up in the Zoboyo, man,' Auguste whispered sharply. 'And he's a *bokor*. A big-time *bokor*.'

Without another word, Auguste turned away and hurried back into the throng of coupling, sucking and fucking men. As he did so, Bertrand noticed that Auguste had lost his hard-on for the first time that evening.

'Whiskey on ice,' Jean Lamartine said, handing Bertrand a glass and sitting back down next to him. 'Drink.' He had reappeared next to Bertrand as silently as a cat.

Now he knew Jean Lamartine was a *bokor*, Bertrand felt an

extreme reluctance to drink from the proferred glass, immediately fearful of being poisoned, of having his *gros-bon-ange* captured and his body made into a zombie. It wouldn't involve any difficulty on the *bokor*'s part to explain away his sudden disappearance. After all, who would even really notice that he had gone? And to anyone who did notice, he would be just another young man who hadn't been able to stand the pace of the city, and had gone back a failure to whatever nameless village he had come from in the first place.

'Come,' Jean Lamartine said, as if reading Bertrand's thoughts, taking the glass from his wood-stiff fingers, sipping it and returning it. 'We are all friends here, are we not?' Bertrand smiled sheepishly and took a sip too.

'So you wanted to speak to me, *maître*?' he said hesitantly, avoiding the shaven-headed man's eyes.

'Yes, man,' Jean Lamartine nodded. 'So you know who I am, then?' he went on, having noted that Bertrand was now addressing him formally.

'I've heard a little about who you might be, *maître*,' Bertrand said carefully. 'But I do not *know*. This is the city, and there are so many rumours passing back and forth about so many things at every hour of the day and night that I only believe for sure what I see with my own eyes.'

'And you are curious – to see?'

'I am curious, *maître*, I admit it,' Bertrand confessed. 'And I want to see *everything*. Not just this –' He gestured towards the still-occupied circular bed, where a light-skinned young man sat on the back of a face-down, muscular man with a long plait and pumped a large, thick candle in and out of his upturned arsehole. 'But to gain *true* knowledge.'

'True knowledge of what, Bertrand Laverre?'

'Of how to gain power over the Mysteries, *maître bokor*.'

'Do not speak my title so loudly,' Jean Lamartine said coolly, shooting Bertrand a warning glance. 'Not even here.'

'Forgive me, *maître*,' Bertrand replied, nodding. As Jean Lamartine's glittering black eyes met his a sudden thrill came running up from behind the younger man's balls and coursed up through his chest to the top of his head, an intoxicating mixture of dread and anticipation that made his scalp prickle as if there was thunder in the air.

That evening had ended inconclusively, just before the eruption of a purple dawn shot through with scarlet, with Jean Lamartine disappearing into one of the side rooms Bertrand had not entered, locking the door behind him, and not emerging again. Bertrand had left Valris Saint Jacques's apartments sexually sated, but intellectually and spiritually hungry. He was determined not to let this chance for forbidden knowledge slip away from him. Even so, he knew better than to try to seek Jean Lamartine out: you do not impose on a *bokor*, especially if he is also an influential member of a secret society.

A week later an invitation to an anonymous house in a newish suburb on the eastern outskirts of Solaville had reached Bertrand through another street-corner boy, and it was there that his initiation into the world of the Zoboyo and sorcery had properly begun.

Black magic and crime are inevitably intertwined, since the former often requires elements that only the latter can provide, above all through grave-robbing. It was for this reason – to prevent graves being plundered – as well as to demonstrate reverence for the dead, that the bereaved raised heavy marble vaults above their loved ones' resting places or, if marble was too costly, then concrete would be used to fill and seal the tombs. For who, after all, likes to think of the skull or bones of his father, mother, brother or sister or grandparent gracing a *bokor*'s altar?

It was well known that both criminal violence and sorcery were routinely used by certain factions of the powerful in Solaville to intimidate their opponents. And even those so-called educated men who were sceptical of the power of the *lwa* and the power of the *bokor* to use them for baleful purposes feared the subtle poisons the Zoboyo were reputed to be able to insinuate into any bottle or bag or can of foodstuff, and feared the monstrous humiliation of zombification.

Within a short time Bertrand had become involved in all these activities: he had robbed graves under the vast yellow moon in the breathless night. He had injected unnamed poisons through the corks of old wine bottles in dusty cellars with stolen hospital needles. He had been part of a masked gang of youths terrorising suburban neighbourhoods with machetes to ensure they voted the right way at elections. And gradually he had won Jean Lamartine's confidence and been initiated into the rites of sorcery.

About a year after first leaving, he had returned briefly to Croix-Le-Bois on a mission for the Zoboyo, pouring a slow-acting poison down the well of a farmer in Sous-L'Eau who had reneged on a debt to Jean Lamartine. As an action it had been easy: no more than inverting a small green glass phial into the dark, clean water below. He had not seen the farmer, Pierre Mejeune, that day, although of course he knew him well enough by sight, and he did not see him die, although he stayed in Croix-Le-Bois long enough to hear the news of his passing in an agony of stomach cramps and coughing up blood.

Bertrand had planned to stay on longer in Croix-Le-Bois, as he enjoyed flaunting his new wealth in the faces of the villagers he imagined had previously disparaged and disliked him, but he found himself feeling uneasy after Pierre Mejeune's death. This unease was the product of both the conscience that Bertrand had thought up until then he didn't have, and something else: he had begun to be afraid that the *oungan* of Croix-Le-Bois, Ti-Charles, knew exactly what he had done, and how, and was contriving forces to punish him.

For the *lwa* know all.

So Bertrand had returned to Solaville sooner than he had planned, his worth as a member of the Zoboyo proved by his murderous act. He had been unnerved to discover on his return that Jean Lamartine already knew all the details of the farmer's death, and in this way was reminded that the Zoboyo had many invisible tentacles snaking out all over the island.

Jean Lamartine hated all *oungans*, as they offered their communities of believers both the spiritual and moral guidance and protection of the *lwa*. Also, through their affinity with and service to the *lwa*, they could impede, fight and even overcome the schemings of the *bokors* who sought to use the power of *Les Mystères* against them and their followers for reasons of self-aggrandisement and other, more evidently evil, purposes. Moreover, unlike *oungans* like Ti-Charles, men like Jean Lamartine had to walk in constant fear and vigilance, for that power, that channelling of all that was dark in the *lwa*, was waiting to turn on any *bokor* who failed to keep control of it.

Bertrand climbed the split, uneven marble steps that led up to the once-imposing front door of the Sonnelier mansion, which now stood permanently ajar. His mouth was parched. This meeting with Lamartine was supposed to be the final stage of his initiation into becoming a *bokor* himself, a step that was frightening, exciting and irrevocable. So far Lamartine had been a willing teacher, but Bertrand's mind was filled with the suspicion that the *bokor* would hold something back at this, the last moment, or demand something dreadful or impossible of him as the price of his final step into knowledge.

Inside the house it was cooler, if airless and dark: decaying shutters and curtains worn sear by the passing years covered the windows, through which occasional chinks of light glinted in like broken glass on velvet. The floorboards were rotten and treacherous underfoot, but Bertrand had been here many times now, and he was able to choose a path across them towards the east wing of the house that barely made them creak. Outside he could hear the sound of digging, and he shuddered at the repetitive sound of hoe on hard, dusty soil.

He made his way up a narrow old servants' staircase to the first floor and a suite of rooms that was less delapidated than the rest, rooms that Lamartine had made his own. He knocked three times on the black-lacquered door to the suite in firm, even strokes before entering.

Inside all was absolutely dark.

'*Maître*?' Bertrand called hesitantly. The darkness had a breathing quality. Panic immediately rose in the young man's chest.

There was a rasping sound to his right, and a match and then a candle sputtered into light. Jean Lamartine was standing before him, face macabrely lit from below. He wore a black double-breasted suit and a flame red, open-necked silk shirt. His face was shiny and impassive and his black eyes glittered like shards of jet. He said nothing, but gestured for Bertrand to follow him into an inner room behind him.

The room they now entered had perhaps once been a master bedroom. It was large, and high-ceilinged; a dusty, unlit chandelier hung from a dull brass chain high up above their heads. None of the original furniture remained, however, except a large cracked mirror above the mantelpiece of a fireplace that had erupted coal dust and soil over the hearth, in which weeds and suckers were struggling to grow without light. Heavy material had been nailed over the tall windows, totally shutting out the day outside.

In the middle of the room was a rectangular table draped with black cloth and lit with candles of the sort that were placed by mourners on the graves of loved ones or in the niches of their tombs. Next to it was a lidless coffin of dirty, unvarnished pine, over which a second black cloth had been draped, concealing its contents.

On the table sat six human skulls still caked with graveyard clay, grinning up at Bertrand with blank and unrevealing sockets. Other undoubtedly human bones were laid out in crosses before the skulls: femurs, tibias, ulnas, radii, the bones of a child's hand. In front of these were set a shovel and a pickaxe, also laid out crosswise. In the centre of the table was a wooden cross crudely painted in stripes of red and white. Around it a red feather boa was twined, in whorish parody of the *lwa* Damballah, who is represented by a serpent wrapped around a cross. Before it sat copper coins in a clay dish that had turned dull and green with age.

There were, however, no Voodoo symbols or sacred objects upon this table, or in fact anywhere in the room. Nor were any ritual words spoken, or obeisances made: this was not Voodoo, nor was it religious. It was necromancy: dealing with *les mortes*, the dead. Bertrand felt his skin crawl as he surveyed the table, and he struggled to fight down the panic that had cramped his gut earlier.

Jean Lamartine smiled at Bertrand, and in the candlelight his smile was mocking. 'But you have seen all these things before, my friend,' he said. 'Why do they trouble you now?'

Bertrand swallowed and tried to pull himself together, annoyed that his uneasiness was so apparent to the *bokor*. 'They do not trouble me, *maître*,' he said, forcing his voice to be steady. 'I am sweaty and dry-mouthed from the walk and the heat of the day, that is all.'

'Ah. But of course. Why *would* you be afraid, my grave-robber?'

'Well, *maître*?' Bertrand said, managing a little defiance now. 'I came as you asked me to.'

'Asked, man?' Jean Lamartine echoed. 'Ah, but it was not *I* who asked.'

The *bokor* turned away from Bertrand, bent over and pulled the black cloth off the draped and lidless coffin. At once a figure that had been lying within sat up mechanically: *there was a man inside the coffin.*

Bertrand inhaled sharply. The man's face was bloated, his sightless eyes concealed behind a pilot's smoked-glass goggles. His body was wrapped in a dirty grey winding-sheet and he stank of earth and decay. In the dim, flickering candlelight Bertrand could not be sure, but he felt a horrible certainty that he was now face to face with the zombie of the poisoned farmer Pierre Mejeune.

Bertrand fought an immediate and almost uncontrollable impulse to turn and run. What was he doing here? What had he become involved with? What had he turned into? But it was too late to run, too late to be afraid, and in any case it was fear that was holding him here, fear of the *bokor* Jean Lamartine, fear of the Zoboyo, and now fear of *les mortes*.

The mouth of the figure now sitting upright in the coffin began to move, at first soundlessly, then whispering hoarse, guttural sounds that Bertrand could neither clearly hear nor understand. The *bokor* leaned forward eagerly over the sitting figure and put his ear close to its lips and listened, nodding every so often and making small responsive grunts. Bertrand could only watch this macabre conversation, and sweat.

After several long minutes Lamartine stood upright. The zombie seemed to have stopped speaking. The *bokor* made a gesture with his left hand and it sank back into its coffin. The *bokor* stooped to pick up the black cloth from the floor and cover the coffin again. Then he turned to face Bertrand. His face was impassive but his black eyes glinted.

Bertrand ran his tongue over his dry, chapped lips. 'Well, *maître*?' he asked, after a silence that had seemed interminable.

'You must kill Ti-Charles, the *oungan* of Croix-Le-Bois,' Jean Lamartine said, malicious excitement clearly audible in his voice. 'That is the price *les mortes* demand.'

Five

'Kill Ti-Charles?' Bertrand echoed.

Jean Lamartine nodded. 'Today. Before the festival of the *mange-lwa* is completed, so that the *lwa* will be displeased with his *oufo*, with his temple, and will not aid his congregation.'

'Man,' Bertrand said, mopping his sweaty forehead and shaking his head. 'Man, that is too much.'

'Bertrand Laverre, you cannot go just breaking your obligations to the dead,' the *bokor* said, shaking his head too. 'They will collect your debt to them. But you know this, man. You do not need me to tell you. You must do what they ask of you.'

'But how?' Bertrand said, still wavering, but unable to reply to the truth of Lamartine's statement.

'With this.'

And Lamartine produced a small blue bottle from his jacket pocket. He held it out to Bertrand with a steady hand and, after a long, hesitant pause, Bertrand took it from him and placed it carefully in his inside pocket.

'But how, man?'

'Say you have come back to him. Say you want to take part in the festival. He will want to accept you, man. He will want to believe he did not fail you. Then you must find your moment.'

'And if I don't, *maître*?'

'Then you must take his place with your hoe in the cane fields outside.'

Bertrand shuddered, chilled in the stifling heat of the day.

'Ti-Charles! Ti-Charles!' Antoine shouted as he dashed in through the gates of the brightly whitewashed *oufo*, his butter-brown skin shiny and running with sweat, his slick black hair tousled, his large eyes wide. '*Maître* Ti-Charles!'

Petro and Sauveur broke off their drumming at the sound of the young man's raised voice, immediately realising Antoine had something urgent to tell their *oungan*, and the *ounsis*, the handsome young male initiates practising their dances in tight white breeches and red headscarves, all came to a worried standstill as Antoine hurried past them and crossed over to the peristyle, where Ti-Charles was on his knees before the *poteau-mitain*, the sacred pole that is the ritual conduit for the *lwa*.

Ti-Charles got to his feet as Antoine hurried up to him: he had just been completing a *veve* for Baron Limba and Baron Lundi, his *met-tête-lwa*, and the spirits to whom the *oufo* was consecrated.

'The military are coming, *Maître* Ti-Charles,' Antoine burst out. 'I saw their truck from the top of the east bluff with the cedar grove crowning it, down at the crossroads. They searched the ground as if they were suspicious some ritual might have been performed there, but found nothing.'

Ti-Charles nodded tensely. At least they did not find my offering to Ezulie, he thought. 'Could you see how many soldiers there were, man?' he asked Antoine. 'And how many trucks?'

'One truck, which then drove on towards Sous-L'Eau,' Antoine said. 'I saw at least three soldiers dismount and head into the banana plantations towards Croix-Le-Bois, but there may have been others that I did not see. They had rifles and radios.'

Ti-Charles nodded again. Behind him, having been disturbed by Antoine's shouting and the sudden cessation of the drumming, Sudra and Faustin came out of Ti-Charles's anteroom to see what was going on. Seeing it was Antoine who was talking with Ti-Charles, they stopped where they were, and stood a little distance away, looking on in slightly awkward silence. While waiting for

Ti-Charles to speak, Antoine glanced over at them, and became immediately aware that there was something between the two darker-skinned men that hadn't been there before. It was revealed in their postures, in the way they leaned slightly inwards towards each other so that their bare shoulders bumped casually and their hands brushed as one or the other raised a cigarette or bottle of lemonade to his lips. Antoine raised an eyebrow at their new-found ease and familiarity, but thought no more about it at that moment: he himself had moved on, after all, and other, more important matters were pressing on all of them as they were all *serviteurs* of the *lwa*.

Sauveur and Petro came over to join Antoine and their *oungan*, leaving their drums resting in the blue shade of the *oufo*'s outer wall, and looking worried: an army raid would mean the temple being torched at the least, and at the worst arrests, beatings and even shooting of the faithful.

Ti-Charles gestured to Sudra to join him and Antoine as well, and the constable stepped forward quickly, Faustin joining him. 'Soldiers have been sent to disrupt the *mange-lwa*,' Ti-Charles said. 'Both here and in Sous-L'Eau. Not many, but enough, and of course they are armed.'

'We must warn the *serviteurs* of Sous-L'Eau,' Sudra said. '*Maître*, I was told nothing of this. Perhaps it is suspected at Arbrerouge that I also serve the *lwa*.'

'It cannot be helped now, man,' Ti-Charles said. 'And you have forstalled intrusions and disruptions many times before, so don't blame yourself: most likely the decision was made from Solaville and was part of some policy to appease the Church or the Americans.' He shrugged.

'Still, I can ride to Sous-L'Eau, Ti-Charles. There may be something I can do to help them there.'

'How long since you saw the truck depart the crossroads, Antoine?' Ti-Charles asked the light-skinned young man, whose chest was heaving less violently now as he slowly caught his breath.

'Perhaps half an hour, *maître*.'

Ti-Charles thought for a long moment. 'I think it is better you do not go, Sudra. They will have reached Sous-L'Eau by now. If you arrive there and are seen speaking with people, suspicion will be cast on you, and the soldiers will also suspect that we here in Croix-Le-Bois have seen them arrive, and will radio to their comrades both to take care and perhaps to attack more quickly, which will give us no time to make any preparations. Also, if you go directly to their *oufo*, as you would have to to get ahead of the military truck, you might even bring the soldiers to it by accident through the dust your motorbike raises.'

Sudra nodded, his eyes glowing with the need to defend his faith and his fellow believers. 'What should we do, then, Ti-Charles, man?' he asked.

'I have an idea, *maître*,' Antoine said quickly, before Ti-Charles could speak.

'Yes, Antoine?' the *oungan* asked.

'If Sudra will give me a ride back to the village, I can speak with my friends among the fishermen who are not out on the ocean today and we can waylay the soldiers.'

'And how will you do that, man?' Sudra interrupted. 'With cutlass and machete? There would be drastic reprisals.'

Antoine shook his head. 'With our eyes and our lips and our willing bodies,' he said, flashing Sudra a bright white smile. 'With our arses and cocks. And there would be no reprisals for giving pleasure so freely.'

'You and . . . Henri Biassou?' Ti-Charles said slowly, trying not to let a selfish desire for the handsome young fisherman to whom he was so attracted distract him from authorising what needed to be done.

'Henri is not so free and easy,' Antoine said with a shrug. 'No, I will ask Ti-Coyo and Bossuet, who are without inhibitions, and any other man of the village who is available and willing.'

'That is a good plan,' Ti-Charles said. 'Or at least it is the best we have. If it can be pulled together in time. Sudra, will you take Antoine back to Croix-Le-Bois on your motorbike right now?'

Sudra shot Antoine a look, plainly unhappy with his enthusiasm for pleasuring the unknown soldiers, then let go of his anger and nodded to Ti-Charles. 'Of course, *maître*,' he replied. 'But then I think I should still ride over to Sous-L'Eau and pass out some sort of warning there.'

'Yes, perhaps you are right about that, man,' Ti-Charles said. 'You should go. But take this.' He lifted a *wanga* packet from where it hung around his neck on a leather cord. Sudra bent forward so Ti-Charles could put it over his head. 'It will protect you from harm. It is a charm against bullets and poison.'

'Thank you, *maître*.' Sudra felt a warmth where the cloth bag rested between the smooth dark domes of his hairless chest that was more than the transferred heat from Ti-Charles's body.

'But do not go to the *oufo* at Sous-L'Eau, Sudra,' Ti-Charles continued. 'Just to the village. Warn people there if you can, and then return here. But remember that this time you will have to *walk* the path here from Croix-Le-Bois.'

'Yes,' Sudra replied. 'I will go to the mechanic in Sous-L'Eau. He is a *serviteur* and a busy and respected man in the village. He will be able to pass the message on without arousing suspicion.'

Ti-Charles nodded. 'Good, man. Go now,' he said, speaking to both Sudra and the waiting Antoine. 'We have no time at all.'

'Yes, man,' Sudra said. Impulsively, he turned and kissed Faustin softly and quickly on the lips, making the shorter man dimple and flush, then hurried off after Antoine towards the entrance to the *oufo*, where his Harley Davidson was standing cooling under the shade of a silkwood tree.

'Should we continue with our practising, man?' Sauveur asked Ti-Charles, after the roar of the motorbike had faded away into the distance.

'No, man,' Ti-Charles said. 'We must avoid doing anything to bring the soldiers in this direction until Antoine has at least had a chance to gather some of the men of the village together and go in search of them. Then you can start the drumming once more.'

'I would have gone, man,' Sauveur said, his eyes hooded blackly by the bright sun overhead. 'My *met-tête-lwa*, Ogoun Feraille, sent me a strange dream last night that was a half-warning, I think, although I did not understand it until I heard what Antoine had to say just now.'

'What was your dream?'

'I was hammering a cutlass blade on the forge, but I was fearful of finishing it, because I suspected that whoever was buying it from me would, for some reason I could not guess, harm me with it. But there was a flaw in the metal and it cracked along its length as I beat it with my hammer. I was ashamed of my poor craftsmanship but relieved that as a weapon it could not be used against me. And then I was holding my dick in my fist and it was large, larger even than it really is.' Sauveur laughed. 'And before me a soldier all in green lay face down with his arse in the air and his rifle discarded at his side, his arsehole shiny with grease as if he wished me to fuck him. And I fully intended to fuck him, but then I woke up.'

'That is certainly a hopeful dream, man,' Ti-Charles said. 'But in any case you could not have ridden with Sudra and Antoine on the motorbike, and, since we do not know exactly where the soldiers are, you can't set out from here on foot and intercept them and turn your dream into reality.'

'You were pleased when Antoine said that Henri Biassou was not likely to join the others in distracting the soldiers,' Sauveur said, changing the subject.

'Henri is courageous and a true *serviteur*,' Ti-Charles said. 'If he feels it is his duty, then I will be proud of him for doing what needs to be done.'

'But you hope not.'

Ti-Charles inclined his head in agreement. 'But it is as the *lwa* will,' he said. 'Come, let us continue with the preparations.'

The Harley Davidson roared throatily as it bounced and churned its way along the narrow red-clay path leading from the *oufo* back to Croix-Le-Bois. Sudra had put on his crash helmet and dark glasses to give himself some protection from the whipping twigs and leaves of the orange and lemon trees that overhung it. Antoine had to bury his face in Sudra's broad back to protect himself as he gripped Sudra tight around the waist. Pangs of nostalgic regret for what couldn't be mingled with in Antoine's chest with excitement at the idea that he would be permitted to serve *Les Mystères* in a way that suited him so well, so soon after the realisation that he was Ezulie's spirit groom.

Sudra and Antoine reached the village in a little over ten minutes, pulling up in a long pink dusty swirl in the small square in front of a row of fruit-and-vegetable stalls. Three tethered black goats, one with red ribbons knotted around its horns, were drinking from a low tin trough set in the shade to one side of the square.

One of the *ounsis* from the *oufo*, Marcus, a pretty, cheeky, freckle-faced young man with a broad grin and a close crop, long legs and a firm butt that was the admiration of many a man in the village, was buying a few choice items brought in from Arbre-rouge that could not be obtained locally, so that the *lwa* would be offered the most fragrant and delicious food the villagers could afford, and so propitiated most favourably. Right now he was in search of saffron strands and cardamom pods from India, and chocolates from Belgium or France.

Unless the *lwa* possessed a *serviteur*, they did not physically eat the food that was offered on the altars – this was consumed by the believers afterwards. But they did eat it spiritually, taking its energy and leaving it curiously without substance or virtue, so food eaten once offered gave little pleasure to whoever consumed it. It was not, however, entirely worthless, and in a society so dominated by poverty, and where so many lived barely beyond subsistence level, it would have been unthinkable to waste it by just throwing it away.

'Pierre Leduc!' Sudra called, throwing out a lean, muscular leg to brace the bike but not dismounting, and keeping the engine running.

'Yes, Constable!' Pierre called back, smiling flirtatiously at the policeman, whom he had always fancied, looking, as he did, so fine as he sped from village to village in his tight black leather trousers on his gleaming Harley Davidson.

'I'm looking for Ti-Coyo and Bossuet, man. Have you seen them?'

'What do you want them for?'

'Soldiers are coming to disrupt the *mange-lwa*,' Sudra explained briefly. 'We need some plucky fellows to distract them with their charms.'

'I will help, sir,' Pierre offered eagerly. 'I have charms too.'

'You certainly do, man,' Sudra said, smiling in his turn. 'Good. More is better as we must have someone to turn on everyone.'

'Ti-Coyo and Bossuet went to Bossuet's just a short while ago to finish mending some crab pots in his garden before the evening.'

'Is Henri Biassou there also?'

'No, he is at the beach, patching the hull of one of the boats that was split on coral.'

'Then we must do without him,' Sudra said. 'Come the instant you can to Bossuet's. By the time you arrive I should have spoken with him and Ti-Coyo and made plans.'

'Yes, sir,' Pierre said, as Sudra revved the Harley back into life and roared off up through the village to Bossuet's shack, Antoine holding on tight behind him.

Bossuet and Ti-Coyo were sitting on the porch of Bossuet's tin-roofed, pink-walled shack repairing wicker crab and lobster pots, drinking sorrel pop and looking out over Bossuet's pretty, flower-filled garden when Sudra and Antoine pulled up outside its gate. Bossuet waved to them with his gleaming chrome hook.

'Constable Sudra!' he called. 'Come and visit with us a while! Antoine Dieudonne! How are you, man?'

Ti-Coyo made a sharp gesture to Bossuet as Sudra opened the white-painted wrought-iron garden gate.

'He knows we've been fucking with Antoine,' the shorter, startlingly lean man with the explosive Afro of dreads whispered through his large smile to the darker, burlier friend sitting beside him. 'Man, we're in the shit now.'

'Why?' Bossuet whispered back, also still smiling in the direction of the two men coming up the garden path. 'Antoine was doing what he wanted. Maybe Sudra wants some too.'

'I don't think so, man. Shh –'

Sudra had reached the porch steps, with Antoine in tow. His

ruggedly handsome, battered face was hard. Antoine looked self-conscious behind him, avoiding everyone's eyes.

'You want some pop, Constable?' Ti-Coyo offered.

'I need a favour.'

Bossuet and Ti-Coyo looked at each other. 'What favour, man?' Bossuet asked. Then, after a beat: 'I'm sure we would both be delighted to oblige you.' Bossuet flicked a glance at Antoine, who blushed hotly. If Sudra noticed this, he ignored it.

'Soldiers are coming to disrupt the *mange-lwa*,' he said. 'Three, maybe more, all armed. We need men of heart and stamina to waylay them and distract them.'

Bossuet's expression altered, the flirtatiousness disappearing from his features. 'You don't need to say anything more, man,' he said, putting aside his crab pot immediately and getting to his feet. 'I am ready.'

'Me too, man,' Ti-Coyo said, his expression now equally serious. 'Will . . . Antoine be assisting us?' he asked hesitantly.

'Yes, man,' Sudra replied matter-of-factly, his own expression unreadable.

'And you?'

'I must go to Sous-L'Eau straightaway and try to warn the believers there. But Pierre Leduc will be here in a few minutes to help you. Antoine will tell you where he saw the soldiers, and where they seemed to be heading last.'

'You can leave us to make the plans, Sudra,' Antoine said, turning and smiling at the shaven-headed constable fondly, and touching him on the hip. 'We won't let you down, man, and you should go as soon as you can.'

Sudra nodded, and his expression softened. 'You know you may well miss the festival if you do this,' he said, addressing all of them.

'We all serve as we can, man,' Bossuet said. 'And, if we do not do this, there will be no festival to miss.'

Sudra nodded again. 'Good luck, then,' he said slightly breathlessly, his eyes suddenly moist and his voice catching in his throat. 'Be careful, all right?' And he turned away and hurried out through the gate.

The Harley roared into throaty life, and a moment later he was gone.

By the time Pierre Leduc arrived at Bossuet's home, the other three men were excitedly drawing up their plans, sketching out the local area with willow sticks in the red earth.

'So the soldiers must still be around *here*, man,' Ti-Coyo said, prodding at an area beyond one of the banana plantations that ran down from the crossroads towards the sea, as Pierre hurried up the garden path. '*There* is a ravine that they will have been forced to follow downwards to get around. And if they go *this* way they will quickly see they will be forced to take a long detour and come so near the village that they would be bound to be seen, and so lose their element of surprise.'

Pierre quickly shook hands with the other three, then squatted down to study the map.

'Yes,' Bossuet agreed. 'They cannot ford the stream any higher up the hillside than where you pointed: its banks are too steep and it is too fast-flowing. The track running alongside it is on our side, not theirs. If we take it, that should give us enough time to head them off if we take the slantwise path through the lemon groves.'

'Also they are cutting across country,' Antoine said. 'That is slower than following a path. And now the drumming has stopped, they cannot be exactly sure of where the *oufo* is, even if they have been given information. Unless one of them knows the area,' he concluded with a shrug. 'It is unlikely, but –'

'It is possible, man,' Ti-Coyo said. 'And that would be serious if it's so.'

'In any case we must set out immediately, man,' Antoine said. 'We will have no chance of success if we are trailing along behind the soldiers. They must come across us directly in their path, as if by accident.'

'But first we should take a moment to dress as provocatively as possible, and give ourselves the best chance of involving them with us,' Bossuet argued. 'And in any case you and Pierre must change out of your ritual clothes or we'll be arrested immediately as *serviteurs*.'

Antoine nodded in agreement. 'Yes, you're right,' he agreed. 'But there's no time to return home or traipse about the village borrowing things,' he added, his wide green eyes looking worried in his handsome, high-cheekboned face.

'My cabin is nearby,' Pierre interrupted, speaking for the first time. 'I have quite a few things that might be suitable, I think,' he added, blushing slightly, his golden-hazel eyes bright.

'To fit all of us?' Bossuet asked doubtfully. He was over six foot, with wide shoulders, a large chest and bull neck, and large, solid thighs. His fellow fisherman Ti-Coyo was lean, snake-hipped and under five foot six. Antoine was in between, though muscularly curvy and with a beefy butt and chest. Pierre was Antoine's height, but much slimmer, although his butt was almost as large as Antoine's.

'Well, I think there should be something there for everyone, man,' Pierre said to Bossuet. 'Sometimes the other *ounsis* and I, we have little parties at my cabin, those of us who enjoy dressing up a little, who enjoy our bodies in colourful or outrageous clothing. We are quite varied, so there are most sizes there, and all sorts of styles at the more provocative end of things.'

'So you are the host, man?' Bossuet asked teasingly, feeling his cock stirring in his breeches at the thought of the slender young man with the big, high buttocks trashily dressed.

'I suppose I began things,' Pierre replied, avoiding Bossuet's eyes shyly. 'I have always liked to be a bit . . . flamboyant in my personal life. Not just at festival times.'

'Well, let's go and find out what Pierre has for us,' Ti-Coyo said. 'Time is short and getting shorter. It's no use how attractive we look if we miss the soldiers because of fussing in front of the mirror.'

Despite his decisive words, the evidently expanding bulge of his very large cock within his tight breeches revealed that Ti-Coyo wasn't averse to looking as enticing as he could in the circumstances.

Pierre Leduc's cabin was only five minutes' walk away, and in the direction they would have had to go anyway to strike the river path. He led them inside his modest whitewashed home and went over to a large cedarwood trunk that sat next to an altar beneath a painting of a bull wearing a tricorn hat that was dedicated to Bossou, his *met-tête-lwa*. He dragged the trunk into the middle of the room and threw the lid back. It was filled almost to the top with bright, richly patterned fabrics of every colour, shade and type of material, making up a pile of clothing in which each item had only two things in common with any other: extreme tightness and extreme skimpiness.

'We must be quick,' Pierre said, pulling the clothing out of the trunk in a great bundle and strewing it across his narrow camp bed for the others to look over and pick through.

Fortunately, as Pierre had said, there was a good range of sizes and styles, and as each man burrowed in excitedly he quickly found himself something that he was happy to wear, that turned him on, and that would suit their common aim of beguiling the soldiers from Solaville.

'Let's go,' Pierre said once they had selected their outfits and changed into them. He shoved the discarded items back into the trunk and picked up his transistor radio, and they set off.

Within ten minutes the four men were hurrying down the lane outside Pierre's cabin, which led to the beginning of the river track, all of them half aroused and full of excited, uneasy anticipation at what they were going to attempt to do.

Bossuet had chosen a pair of skin-tight, wet-look, black PVC trunks with a zip that ran down over his bulging crotch, round between his legs and up between his large, blocky buttocks at the back, and a pair of black patent army boots. Around his flesh-and-bone upper arm – the left – he wore a studded black leather arm band and another one around his neck, and he shielded his eyes with mirrorised dark glasses. His steel right arm glinted brightly in the sunlight, and his smooth, dark, bodybuilt physique gleamed and rippled as he strode along the grass-bordered path.

Next to him Pierre had gone for a personal favourite of his, a one-piece, parakeet-green, sequined Lycra leotard that was scooped low under the arms but high around the neck. It hugged his smooth, slender torso and crotch, his flat stomach and narrow waist, and followed the lines of his high, large buttocks, and had a short zip at the back only. The leotard left his long, shapely, hairless, caramel-coloured and well-toned arms and legs appealingly bare. He wore a gold chain around one wrist and another around an ankle, and walked on long, elegant bare feet, switching his hips a little as he went, on his pretty, freckled face a boyish expression of pleasure in his own daring at being seen in public dressed that way. He also wore a little lip gloss on his full, soft lips, just to add to their sensual appeal. Bossuet found himself glancing round at Pierre's highly inviting butt as they walked along, imagining getting on his knees and eating it out, then fucking Pierre hard on all fours, as there was no question as to which role he preferred: the zip being only at the back of the leotard said everything that needed to be said on that subject.

Ti-Coyo was perhaps the least flamboyant of the four in what he took from Pierre's box, although he did eventually choose a pair of white, skin-tight breeches with a lace-up crotch that drew attention to his bulging endowment, a white furry bowler hat that he perched on top of his wild Afro of dreads, jazz-man sunglasses, an open white waistcoat and a high-set choker of cowries that rose and fell sensually with his larynx when he swallowed.

Antoine, perhaps becoming competitive with the fey and naturally flirtatious Pierre, had chosen the most outrageous things he could find in the trunk: very low-cut, gold-sequined bikini briefs that stretched over his narrow hips and flat stomach, barely containing his bulging crotch and covering the lower half of his beefy butt like a second skin, leaving the upper half of his smooth, sweet cinnamon globes exposed for all to see. He still had the thin gold chain that Sudra gave him around his firm waist. He wore supple and close-fitting gold-painted bike boots that rose to the tops of his calves, and gold-painted metal arm bands around both his upper arms. Over his eyes he wore a glittering golden-sequined eye mask. In the trunk he had also, to his great delight, found a barely used bottle of gold nail varnish, and had just made enough time to paint his nails with it before they had had to hurry out of Pierre's cabin in search of the soldiers.

The wild and liberating spirit of carnival filled the chests of the four men as they took the riverside path in their skimpy, glittering and provocatively colourful and revealing costumes, hips and bare shoulders jostling as they walked fast. They were the embodiment of carnival out of season, bringing chaos and disorder to the plans of the military and the government, hoping to turn them upside down.

The well-trodden track wound sharply uphill, following the gushing stream as it twisted and plunged in its dark, sheer-sided cleft among greeny-black, jutting rocks and moss-covered stones. The track was wide enough for the men to walk two abreast, and was pleasantly dappled by overhanging silkwood and tamarind trees that shaded higher up into great groves of laurels. Ti-Coyo, Bossuet, Antoine and Pierre soon found themselves wishing that they could turn aside from their mission and idle by the cool, running water for a while. But, if they couldn't do that, at least they could refresh themselves as they went.

After they had gone on for nearly two miles, the four *serviteurs* reached a stretch of the small river that ran wide and spread out over a shallow bed of sand and gravel, almost making a flat pond. The boys of the village sometimes came to catch crayfish here, and it was the one place where the stream was readily fordable. Ti-Coyo hurried forward and checked the soft yellow sand quickly for marks.

'No one has crossed here,' he said with certainty.

'Good,' said Bossuet.

The path carried on following the stream upriver, but a second, less well-trodden path branched off it, winding away westish through the laurel groves in roughly the direction of the *oufo*. There was no doubt that, once they had forded the stream, the soldiers would follow that path for some way before once again trying to cut across country. So Bossuet and the others took it, glancing backwards to make sure that there was no sight of the government troops behind them yet.

There didn't seem to be.

They walked more easily now, knowing they were ahead of

the military. The track started to meander among the laurel groves and become overgrown.

'What about here?' Antoine suggested after a while, gesturing around him.

Bossuet shook his head. 'We should find a grove a little way off what's left of the path, man: it will be more believable that we came up here to be on our own together that way.'

'But then won't they miss us, man?' Antoine asked, wrinkling his brow.

'No, man,' Ti-Coyo said. 'Because we have Pierre's radio. If we play it quietly they will hear it and come to us, like birds lured from the trees.'

'And all we have to do until then,' said Antoine, a playful half-smile on his lips, 'is act with each other as if we didn't know we were going to be interrupted. Do you think we'll be able to manage that, man?' he asked Ti-Coyo.

'I think so, man,' Ti-Coyo said, gripping Antoine's shoulder and shaking it.

The others laughed softly as they turned off the track and ambled into the shade of the laurel trees.

The four soldiers, now hot and sticky from the heat of the sun beating down on their heads, stumbled their way down a crumbling bank of dusty red earth, their rifles slung over their shoulders. They had been following the zigzagging course of the steep-banked stream for several miles, in search of a fording place. Now finally they had reached one: here the stream ran broad and crystal-clear over orange and yellow gravel, and was so shallow that it would barely cover their boots to the ankle. They came to a stop at the water's edge, and looked across. On the opposite bank was the path that had constantly teased them by running along smoothly parallel to the stream while they had had to struggle along laboriously on their side through a tangle of underbrush and thrusting, dusty roots, their sergeant leading the way, hacking grumpily and sweatily through vines and suckers and obstructing branches with his machete.

None of their tempers were good, in fact, and there had been a fair amount of cursing as they had struggled along on the wrong bank. Also, the distant drumming that they had heard faintly when they disembarked at the crossroads in the banana plantation had stopped over an hour earlier, which made them suspect that they might have been noticed by the believers despite their speedy arrival and slipping under cover.

However, it now seemed that their luck might be turning: opposite the point where the stream ran wide enough to ford, they could all see a track running off into great groves of laurels and tamarind trees. It was well trodden and fairly straight, and even seemed to be going in almost exactly the right direction. The prospect of not having to struggle along for a little immediately lifted their spirits.

Private Dany Dutilleul slipped his dull-green metal helmet off, bent forward and scooped up some of the clear, cool stream water and poured it over his shaved head. A handsome, dark-skinned, clean-shaven and rangy young lad of twenty-one, he wore a tight grey-green T-shirt that clung to his compact chest and flat belly, and butt-hugging camouflage trousers tucked into dusty black army boots. He screwed up his eyes as he surveyed the tangle of greenery on the opposite bank, shading them with the palm of his hand.

What were they doing this for? he wondered, seeing nothing but trees and the occasional bright, flashing movements of birds on their branches. He had joined the army to defend his country against invasion, and now here he was taking part in an action that he knew had something to do with buttering up the American general and his troops stationed in Solaville. Their aircraft carrier sat outside the capital's harbour like some great grey cliff that had been pushed up out of the sea. It loomed dull and dangerous over the colourful fishing boats, shops, bars and houses around the harbour, like the emissary of some great imperial power, which is exactly what it was. Dany Dutilleul didn't know much about politics, but he was no fool either: there was no military value in this mission.

My grandmother was a *mambo*, he thought to himself, remembering the bright-eyed old woman in richly embroidered shawls with her wise, wizened, mahogany-brown face and delicate hands. Priestess to a small village. She got on with everyone, helped people. Healed. Advised. Mended broken hearts. She even got on with the Catholic priest until word came from Solaville that Voodoo was outlawed. That priest brought the military to her *oufo* and helped burn it to the ground. My mother and father had left for Arbrerouge by then. Perhaps it was being in town, perhaps it was in response to the oppression of those times, but neither my father nor my mother brought me up with the beliefs they must have surely had. I was sent to a Catholic school and encouraged to disparage Voodoo. I joined the army to fight for my country, and here I am, doing what was done to my grandmother all over again, what was done to my parents, who veiled their beliefs. To me. To our country.

Dany Dutilleul had already sworn to himself that he would not fire a single shot against the *serviteurs* when he and his fellow soldiers found them, except in defence of his own life, or the lives of his comrades.

Beside Dany stood his good friend Private Valentine Dumonde. He was shorter than Dany and lighter-skinned, and had a pumped physique that was the product of many hours in the army gym inspired by the regimes of the American bodybuilder Charles Atlas. He was twenty-five years old. His face was round and boyish. His eyes were hazel, he had a close-clipped moustache, and his hair was cut close to his scalp. He showed off his beefy café-au-lait musculature by wearing a tight-fitting, dull-green mesh vest that enhanced his smooth, well-defined curves and left his bulging arms bare. His skin was now sheened with sweat, and he too scooped up water with his helmet, but drank before tipping it over his head, watching the opposite bank more warily than Dany.

Valentine had spent some years in the United States when he was a teenager, and so he felt less affinity for the land of his birth and early years than the others, who had never left it. Also, the countryside was an alien place to him, and he found Voodoo beliefs and practices threatening, both because they seemed to make his people look primitive to the outside world and because, much deeper down, he feared that his own lack of sympathy for Voodoo, derived as it was from the religious practices of Africa, revealed some lack in himself as a descendant of African slaves. And that gave him a certain uneven anger towards it.

Still, he wished he hadn't been chosen for this mission: it didn't seem to him that there was anything to gain by terrorising or threatening Voodoo believers. Fear does not make people lose their beliefs, it only makes them conceal them, he reflected.

Also, Valentine knew perfectly well that the truth was that the vast majority of people on the island believed in the *lwa* and honoured their ancestors to some extent, and since from America he had brought back a particular notion of freedom and democracy for all – despite the looming grey symbol of United States imperialism in the Solaville harbour – he saw no reason not to continue allowing people to believe whatever they wanted to.

In addition and paradoxically, while in America Valentine had for the first time in his life experienced racism, and so, like Dany, he was unwilling to be part of the persecution of Voodoo if it was, as seemed quite likely, part of some United States-appeasing policy of the government in Solaville.

Dany and Valentine began to ford the stream. The other two soldiers stepped forward into the quickly moving water just behind them. Their names were Sergeant Jestin Guillaume and Private Obry Laverne.

The sergeant was a dark, smooth, stocky man with a tough manner at odds with his neat, pretty features and large, melancholy eyes. His camouflage fatigues stretched tightly over his high, large and dynamically muscular butt, and the loose green army vest he was wearing with them broke over his large, perky globes invitingly. It was rumoured that it was Jestin's skill with that well-built booty that had got him promoted to sergeant, rather than his military excellence, but he was in fact a fair officer who treated the men under him well, and was shrewd and practical in the field: one time Dany Dutilleul had slipped and broken his ankle on a training exercise, and Sergeant Jestin had bound and splinted the wound with such deft lightness of touch that Dany had barely felt it.

Obry Laverne was the tallest of the four men: six foot four and lankily muscular, with a long, handsome, clean-shaven face, flawless mid-brown skin, wide greeny-gold eyes, full lips and an immaculate box-cut fade. His dull-green army fatigues were tight around his narrow hips, emphasising his bulging crotch and neat, firm buttocks. His chest was flatly muscled, with dark, protuberant nipples that he showed off by leaving his flak jacket unzipped, and his bare arms were smooth and strong. He was ambitious to make sergeant, and a strong believer in following orders, and so was perhaps the least well liked of the four, although when drunk on imported American beer he would offer – and give – blow jobs with considerable expertise, and, in his greed for cock, he would go down on anyone, regardless of rank, which endeared him considerably to his fellow privates.

Sergeant Jestin Guillaume, by contrast, was well known to love being fucked, but felt it would interfere with platoon morale if he gave it up for the men under him. While he – like just about everyone else on the base – had let Obry suck his good-sized cock to explosion several times, he generally kept his romantic and sexual life away from the camp dormitories where the soldiers slept and relaxed. Jestin preferred to ride into the local town for his adventures and release, often returning to camp bow-legged after weekends on leave, laughing about having got himself 'fucked senseless' by numerous well-hung local men, and telling tall tales about their endowments and insatiable appetites for screwing his slack, juicy chocolate star.

Dany and Valentine, on the other hand, conducted affairs with other privates, and occasionally even officers, both commissioned and noncommissioned. They had been lovers for a while, just after basic training, but were now easy-going companions in the hunt for cocks, arses and hearts, sometimes even sharing their usually eager conquests with each other, often at the same time.

The four soldiers forded the stream, barely getting their feet wet, and set off at once down the track leading into the laurel and tamarind groves. They moved as silently as possible, and with the minimum of talk, believing that, despite the delay in crossing the stream and the silencing of the drums, they still might have the advantage of surprise. Having had to hack their way through the tangle on the other bank, being able to follow a straight, clear path for a while was a relief to all of them, and they immediately began to feel more cheerful. The shade from the trees was cooling, and the birdsong melodious, and the sense of being on a military mission began to slide from their minds as they ambled easily along the grassy track, not much able to care whether they found the suspected *oufo* or not.

'Man, we should've brought a picnic lunch,' Dany murmured to Valentine, shooting him a smile. Valentine nodded his agreement and grinned back at him. Obry overheard Dany's remark and laughed softly as a breeze stirred the leaves above them gently.

Jestin looked round sharply at Dany and the others, irritated by their inattentive casualness. He gestured to the three privates to unsling their rifles, attach bayonets, and advance in a more military fashion, so that they would be ready to face possible ambush and attack. Wordlessly, Dany, Valentine and Obry did so at once, their features setting into military mode, aware that the verdure and the blue sky were being dangerously beguiling and seductive and that, whether they believed in the power of the *lwa* or not, they were entering their realm, and it was a realm where many things may not be as they seemed.

After they had followed it for a little over a mile, the track began to peter out among the laurel groves, and Jestin signalled to the others to come to a halt while he decided what their best way forward would be. They had been approaching the *oufo* from the northeast initially, assuming his information had been correct in the first place, and now he reckoned they were pretty much exactly due east of it, and that it was perhaps another mile and a half away. He consulted his compass, glanced round at the lie of the land, and decided to head due east, even though what there was of the track started to curve northwards beyond the grove they were now standing in. While Jestin thought, Dany drank from his water canister, then passed it to Valentine and Obry. Then he offered it to his sergeant.

'Thank you, Private,' Jestin said, taking a deep swig. 'We will go directly east now,' he continued, wiping the back of a hand across his mouth and returning Dany's flask back to him.

'Can you hear something, Sergeant?' Valentine interrupted abruptly.

'What, man?'

'I think it is music.'

The four men listened intently, and indeed they could hear music playing faintly some way off. It was *rara* music, played by a band well-known on the island, and so they realised that they must be listening to a radio.

'Which direction is it coming from?' asked Jestin, screwing up his dark, pretty features in concentration as he tried to catch hold of the elusive sound.

'Shh,' said Obry, turning his head left and right. Then after a moment: 'That way.' He pointed downhill to the left, towards a dell where the laurels grew more thickly.

Jestin glanced round at Dany and Valentine for confirmation. They nodded agreement. The sergeant nodded too, then, touching his fingers to his lips, gestured that the other men should follow him, and led the way off the track and down into the dell, rifle at the ready.

They had to move with great care among the laurels to avoid disturbing the tangle of parched, brittle undergrowth, since the slightest creak or crack might give their presence away to whoever was listening to the radio and give him or her a chance to slip away unseen, so their progress was slow and tortuous. At the same time a sense of unease began to descend on the four soldiers: the radio was a modern invention, it was true, but they all began to have the sense that they were being lured on by its sound like characters in a folk tale.

As they neared the centre of the dell, they became aware of other sounds as well as the music, sounds of breathing, soft gasps and repressed, whispered laughter. In this place, and on this mission, the sounds seemed eerie and unnerving, the laughter perhaps that of one or more *Legbas*, the trickster *lwa* of the Voodoo pantheon riding their followers and turning them to strange and disquieting activities in secluded places.

There seemed to be an open space in the centre of the dell that was latticed with shadows from the overhanging laurel branches, the sunlight strewn across it like a handful of diamonds or a shimmering, shifting glitter-ball as a sudden breath of wind stirred the laurel leaves above. It was an effect that was heightened, almost artificial, which perfectly suited the entirely unexpected activity that was going on in the glade: outrageously clad and beautiful men performing sexually with each other, to the rhythmic accompaniment of the *rara* music that was playing on the small portable transistor that sat on the soft, emerald-green grass nearby.

Ti-Coyo, Antoine, Bossuet and Pierre had prepared their trap well: the four soldiers were barely able to contain their gasps of surprise as they peered into the glade from their hiding places in the dense, dark foliage, and they were immediately, on a profound level, disarmed by the four scantily clad villagers before them.

Pierre, in his figure-hugging green leotard, stood behind the darker, bulkier Bossuet, reaching round the shaven-headed muscleman's spreading back with well-shaped cinnamon-brown arms and caressing the great ebony domes of Bossuet's chest, teasing the well-built, one-armed man's clamp-trained nipples with long, eager fingers. Bossuet groaned as Pierre's nails bit into his tits, and ground his large, solid, arse in its tight black patent trunks against Pierre's bulging crotch to the music on the radio. Pierre then sank to his knees behind Bossuet and began kissing Bossuet's blocky buttocks with his soft, full lips, stroking his smooth, bodybuilt thighs as he did so, his own erection jutting out obviously within his leotard, stretching the green, sequined material and staining it where his swollen cock head was oozing pre-come.

After a while, he reached up between Bossuet's legs and unzipped him smoothly from the front to the back. Bossuet's large, thick, stiff cock popped free from the constraining black leather as the zip slid over its constricted shaft, and wagged heavily above his swinging balls in the warm air. Pierre reached up and gripped Bossuet's balls firmly and tugged on them. Bossuet leaned forward responsively, bent over and pushed his large, shaved, plain-chocolate-brown arse back towards Pierre's handsome young face, offering it up invitingly. Pierre leaned forward, opened his mouth and began to tongue Bossuet's puckering anal star, teasing the shaven-headed man's sphincter with his probing tongue tip, pushing his own butt out provocatively as he did so, the globes of his glutes curving invitingly inside his skin-tight, green-sequined one-piece, the gold chain glinting provocatively on his ankle as he pushed his head forward and began to tongue-fuck the dark-skinned muscleman bent over in front of him with ardent relish.

While this was going on, Antoine and Ti-Coyo were dancing sensually to the *rara* rhythms, grinding their crotches together, sliding their large, rigid erections over each other through thin layers of tight fabric, caressing each other's muscular butt and kissing hotly. The gold ring in Ti-Coyo's small, dark, stiff nipple glinted in the flickering sunlight as he writhed against Antoine. Then Ti-Coyo brought the palm of his hand down on to Antoine's smooth, brown, half-displayed buttocks with a sharp crack, making Antoine gasp and shiver and moan excitedly into Ti-Coyo's hot mouth.

Then, to the delight of the concealed watching soldiers, Ti-Coyo pushed his hand down the back of Antoine's low-cut golden briefs and brazenly began to finger-fuck his arsehole, visibly pushing two fingers up the beefy, lighter-skinned young man's butt to the knuckle without meeting any resistance. In fact, Antoine even reached back and pulled his large, café-au-lait buttocks open with both hands to give Ti-Coyo's probing fingers greater access to his much-used anal canal.

Ti-Coyo pumped his fingers back and forth in Antoine's arsehole for a while, keeping his mouth firmly on Antoine's. Then he withdrew his hand from the back of Antoine's briefs, broke off the kiss and spoke.

'I'd like to see you eat Pierre out, man,' he said throatily, with a broad, white, gap-toothed smile. 'Get your tongue up his arse.'

Smiling too, Antoine turned immediately and sank on to all fours behind the kneeling Pierre, unzipping the back of the slenderer youth's green one-piece where it rose up between his

143

buttocks, to expose his arsehole. Pierre responsively pushed his high, muscular arse back as he was unzipped behind, his throbbingly stiff cock and full balls still constrained by the tight Lycra of the one-piece, eager to make his butthole available to Antoine, eager to be tongue-fucked as he pushed his tongue up Bossuet's chocolate star. Pierre groaned in pleasure as Antoine ran his long, firm tongue up between Pierre's buttocks, before pressing its tip firmly against his quivering and receptive anal opening.

At the same time as Antoine began to tongue-fuck Pierre, Ti-Coyo went round in front of Bossuet, who was still bent over while he was being rimmed, now bracing his large, muscular torso up with a thickly sculpted arm ending in a large, splayed hand, and a metal one whose hooks pushed into the turf they stood upon, and pushing his beefy mocha arse back firmly on to Pierre's face. Ti-Coyo positioned himself so his bulging crotch was inches from Bossuet's handsome-ugly, shining face, unlaced the front of his tight black-and-white shorts and tugged his thick, eleven-inch cock out before the muscleman's dark, lust-dulled eyes.

'Suck it,' Ti-Coyo instructed Bossuet, placing one hand on the beefily built, dark-skinned man's slickly shaven head and feeding his outsize erection into Bossuet's open mouth with the other, inhaling slightly at the sensual thrill of Bossuet's lips against the smooth, hot dome of his glans.

Bossuet didn't need any encouragement to pleasure Ti-Coyo's cock with his mouth. He kissed his swollen glans, then slowly stretched his full lips to take it into the warm wetness beyond. Gradually he moved his open mouth down on Ti-Coyo's mammoth erection until it was pressing against the back of his throat. Then, with greedy gulps, he began to swallow Ti-Coyo's bulging crown down towards his oesophagus with greedy eagerness. Ti-Coyo let his head fall back, and gasped, pushing his shorts down to free his balls and expose his high, neat, muscular arse as Bossuet took the shorter, Afro-dreaded man's beer-can-thick dick down his throat to the root, the sinews in his neck standing proud as he did so, his neck seeming to swell outwards as he dragged in breath around the rigid pole of throbbing manhood that was blocking his windpipe so excitingly.

'Oh, yeah, man, you know how to suck a cock!' he grunted throatily. 'You know how to please a man! Oh, yes!'

Out of the corner of his eye Ti-Coyo could see the bright and shining eyes of the four soldiers watching him and his friends through the dark-green laurel leaves that formed a glossy wall around the glade. He caressed his own nipples to add to his performance, tugging on the gold ring that pierced the right one, groaning as he did so, and rubbed a hand over his lean, flatly muscled chest and taut, trembling belly.

'Oh, man,' Ti-Coyo moaned in a throaty, inviting voice that he raised to make sure that all the watching soldiers would hear it. 'This is so hot, so sexy, but still I wish there were more men here. I could be taking it up the arse while you suck me off, Bossuet, and someone could be fucking Antoine's arse. Look how inviting it is! And I would like to suck a cock, too. And I know you need more than a couple of dicks up you to satisfy you, Bossuet, and you could be sucked and fucked at the same time, man. Oh, man, I wish . . . I wish . . .' he repeated, letting his voice trail off, then gasped suddenly as Bossuet swallowed his cock head again.

In the bushes Dany and Valentine glanced at each other: they needed no encouragement to throw their rifles aside and go and make come true the fantasy the narrow-hipped, bushy-haired, lean-bodied, rather good-looking and exceptionally well-endowed man with the close-cut goatee being enthusiastically blown had just expressed. They looked round at their comrade Obry, expecting him to guess what they had in mind, shake his head angrily and insist that protocol be followed and arrests be made. But Obry was watching the scene before them with such intentness that his eagerness to join in was in no doubt, and he was even rubbing his constricted crotch in excited anticipation of some all-male sexual action.

Then Dany and Valentine looked at Jestin. Their sergeant too was obviously excited by what he was seeing, but was clearly being torn between his duty to his commander, despite the mission being one for which he saw little or no military justification, and the call of his body and his heart.

'We could say we never found the *oufo*,' Dany whispered breathlessly, a little afraid to even suggest such a dereliction of duty. He tried to make his remark sound as if he had just spoken a thought out loud without realising it, while making sure it was loud and clear enough for the sergeant and Obry to hear his words. Dany shot another glance at Obry to gauge his reaction, and saw to his pleasure that Obry was also looking imploringly to Jestin to join the beautiful, gaily clad men in the glade.

'We could say there was no *oufo*,' Obry said quietly.

'Why should we not do this?' Valentine asked in a low voice. 'Looking for the *oufo*, it is all about pleasing the Americans, not about defending our island.'

Jestin said nothing, just kept on looking ahead, wavering. He adjusted his stiff cock in his tight camouflage trousers, but kept a grip on his rifle as he did so.

'I bet that man would fuck you good with that thing, Sarge,' Obry said teasingly to the sergeant. 'I bet he'd give it to you hard.'

Jestin shot Obry a glance but didn't reply. He just stood up slowly and placed his rifle carefully down on the ground. He had made his decision. His three men did the same. Then, as one, they took a deep breath and stepped out of the shadows and into the dappled light.

To the soldiers it all seemed like an unbelievable, beautiful dream: breaking off only momentarily from what they were doing, the four near-naked men in the glade looked round at them with warm eyes and welcoming smiles. They did not question the soldiers' presence or their purpose in being there, or why or how long they had been watching. They asked nothing of the men in khaki and camouflage, just gestured for them to come forward and join in the action, briefly introduced themselves and received the soldiers' names in turn, and then resumed their greedy sucking and enthusiastic rimming.

Excitement overcoming them, the soldiers quickly shucked off their heavy boots, their uniforms, until they were all but naked and their pulsing erections bobbed and their balls hung free. Satisfying some quirk in himself, the lean, leggy, mid-brown Obry put his boots back on once he had stripped, and for some reason the dark, slim, lanky young Dany kept his helmet on, perhaps a gesture towards the carnival spirit of dressing up for sex. The most immediately exhibitionist of the four, Valentine was the keenest to undress completely and display every inch of his finely honed, honey-brown physique for the visual pleasure of those around him.

Jestin was the keenest to throw himself into the sex once he had removed his clothing, keeping on only a dull-green belt he pulled tight around his firm, waspy waist, and in among all the other titillations of the day, the three privates were perhaps especially curious to see their dark-skinned, shaven-headed, pretty-featured and big-bootied sergeant in action with other men, to see if he would display the trampy love for cock up his arse that he bragged of repeatedly back in the barracks.

Jestin walked naked over to Ti-Coyo, his veiny, curving, cut, heavily ridged cock wagging in front of his close-cropped crotch, and smiled at the shorter, hard-bodied man with the goatee and tangled explosion of dreaded hair. Then he confidently ran a hand down Ti-Coyo's smooth, firm, sweaty and well-muscled back as the bent-over Bossuet gurgled and gagged repeatedly on Ti-Coyo's eleven-inch pole while having his arse eaten out by Pierre.

Jestin reached across Ti-Coyo's flat, muscular chest and tugged gently on his gold nipple-ring. Ti-Coyo met his enquiring gaze with hazy, dark-gold eyes, his full, ruddy lips parted to reveal large, white teeth.

'What would give you pleasure, man?' Ti-Coyo asked Jestin, keeping his eyes on the sergeant's, challenging the dark-skinned man with the appealingly large and beefy butt.

'I need that cock up my big brown arse, man,' Jestin answered breathlessly. 'I love being fucked. I *need* to be fucked.'

'There is Vaseline in the jar by the radio,' Ti-Coyo said, Jestin's enthusiasm making him smile. 'Why not get one of your comrades to grease you up and get you ready for a big stiff cock up your hole?'

Overhearing this, Bossuet pulled his mouth off Ti-Coyo's rigid, throbbing gristly enormity with a great sucking gasp, pre-come falling in sticky, clear strands from his full, shiny, well-defined lips. He looked round at the other three soldiers, who hung back, suddenly bashful.

'Hey!' he called to them. 'Why are you fellows standing about? I want my dick sucked while I'm being eaten out. I want one of you men on his knees sucking my cock,' he ordered throatily. 'I want lips round my ebony pole *now*!'

The demand broke through the three soldiers' inhibitions, and Dany immediately hurried forward to oblige Bossuet, sliding on to his knees on the soft, lush grass and slipping under the arch made by the tall, dark, thickset bodybuilder's arms, his bulging chest and his ridged stomach, and pushed his face between Bossuet's massively curving, braced and sinewy thighs, kissing Bossuet's satiny ballsac, lapping Bossuet's balls with his tongue, kissing and licking his way up Bossuet's stiffly curving shaft, then taking Bossuet's glistening, swollen cock head into his mouth. This made the beefily muscular man arched above him gasp with pleasure around Ti-Coyo's rigid endowment, which was once again pumping in and out of his mouth and throat. Bossuet's throbbing, hot rigidity immediately flooded Dany's mouth with bittersweet pre-come.

Meanwhile Valentine moved round behind Antoine and sank on to his knees between the masked youth's legs. He pulled Antoine's gold bikini briefs down at the back, exposing his firm, muscular demerara-brown globes in all their lust-arousing perfection. Antoine responsively pushed his arse back, making it as available as possible for Valentine's pleasure.

Valentine turned to look for the lubricant Ti-Coyo had mentioned: Jestin had already found it in the shadow of the transistor and embedded his long, dark fingers in it. He withdrew them, stickily coated with the petroleum jelly, and tossed the jar to Valentine for his use.

'Normally I pregrease for action, man,' Jestin said with a half-smile, not caring now that he was letting the military hierarchy collapse by revealing his personal quirks to his subordinates.

'Because you never know where or when some good action may come your way. But for a cock that big –' he gestured to Ti-Coyo's shiny hard-on as it slid in and out of Bossuet's open mouth, making the one-armed bodybuilder's throat bulge '– I need some extra to help me take it.'

Ti-Coyo gestured to Jestin. 'Come back over here, man,' he ordered. 'Face away, bend over and spread in front of me. Brace yourself up on your hands and feet and give me your arse, man. Give it to me fully.'

Jestin quickly pushed two Vaseline-covered fingers up his own anal sphincter to get it ready, and went over to Ti-Coyo. He turned away from him, bent over and assumed the position that the wild-haired, hard-bodied, café-au-lait-skinned man had asked him to, bracing himself up with both firmly muscled mocha arms and pushing his buttocks up as high as he could for Ti-Coyo to take charge of.

Ti-Coyo looked down at Jestin's smooth, dark, freely offered butt and felt excitement rise in his achingly stiff erection as Bossuet carried on pumping his mouth on it with almost professional relish, the shaven-headed muscleman's excitement mounting in his own tingling, throbbing shaft as the kneeling Dany sucked him off greedily and Antoine rimmed him deeply.

Without warning or preparation, Ti-Coyo pushed three fingers straight into Jestin's greasy, upturned arsehole to the knuckle. Jestin gasped excitedly as the bunched fingers slithered into his somewhat prepared rectum, his cock bucked and dripped pre-come, and he almost came spontaneously.

'Oh, *man*, you've opened me up!' he exclaimed hoarsely. 'Man, you know how to work a man's arse and that's the truth!'

'That's just my fingers, man,' Ti-Coyo replied, working them back and forth roughly in Jestin's well-lubricated anal ring, dilating it, relaxing it. 'My dick will open you all the way up till you're full to bursting up there.'

'Plug me with your dick, man,' Jestin gasped. 'I'm begging you. Give me the whole length of it up my arse.'

By way of a response, Ti-Coyo withdrew his hand from Jestin's backside for a moment, making Jestin moan disappointedly, then pushed four greasy fingers firmly into Jestin's upturned, shiny chocolate star. Jestin groaned, and moved his big, muscular butt from side to side to accommodate them up his back passage to the knuckle. It was an effort, but he managed it.

While Jestin was wriggling his arse back on to Ti-Coyo's fingers, Valentine greased his own eight-inch rigidity, gasping as he masturbated himself slowly with a Vaseline-slickened fist. He gazed down at Antoine's invitingly offered booty, its milk-chocolate, flawless smoothness framed by the gold chain round Antoine's firm waist and the stretched gold material Valentine had pulled down to the middle of his thighs, a masterpiece of sexual invitation. Antoine's waist was supple and narrow, and his back spread out in a muscular fan up to his shoulders. His head with its glossily conked hair was pressed hard against the kneeling Pierre's exposed caramel butt, as he continued to eat the slender youth out enthusiastically while Valentine caressed his own freely offered globes.

Valentine placed one hand in the small of Antoine's curving back, and with the other pointed his throbbing, rigid dick down towards Antoine's glossy, waiting hole. Valentine angled his hips forward, positioned his cock so its head was pressing slickly against the sphincter of the beefy young butter-brown man on all fours before him, and began to push it into Antoine's rectum.

Antoine gasped as he was penetrated anally by the muscular café-au-lait man kneeling behind him, but put up no resistance, and Valentine's cock slid up his arsehole to the root in one easy thrust. Valentine gasped too, excited by Antoine's ready yielding, his accommodating arsehole, and the smooth, hot feeling of the lining of his rectum against Valentine's cock head as he thrust deeply into Antoine's anal canal. Antoine broke off rimming Pierre for a moment and looked round at Valentine through his glittering gold eye mask.

'Fuck me hard, man!' he ordered. 'Use my arse for your pleasure!'

Valentine needed no urging on, and began to pound Antoine's upturned, butter-brown booty hard, excitement coursing through his groin and belly at the good feeling of Antoine's tight, greasy ring around his throbbing cock shaft, his lean, flat hips slapping rhythmically against Antoine's upturned demerara buttocks.

Obry had hung back a little, for some reason shyer than the others of throwing himself into the situation. His initial impulse had been to get round between either Jestin's or Dany's legs, get a hot, stiff cock in his mouth, and pump until he got a serving of the hot, sour, creamy jism he adored, but then his eye had been caught by the concave-convex-concave flexing of Valentine's high, smooth, muscular, light-brown booty as he pumped the arsehole of the youth before him on all fours hard. The desire to fuck Valentine while Valentine ploughed the youth filled Obry's mind like an artist's inspiration striking. Stepping forward lankily, naked except for his army boots, Obry knelt behind Valentine, between his sinew-corded calves, and ran a hand over the firm, shiny globes of his arse.

'I want to fuck you, man,' Obry said, his voice slightly tentative, a little fearful of rejection. 'You've got such a great arse, Valentine. I've always wanted to stick my cock up it.'

Valentine, now gleaming with sweat, slowed in his butt-fucking rhythm and glanced round at Obry, the expression on his face serious, his hazel eyes clouded. Obry's own long, handsome face became serious too: had he offended Valentine? Then Valentine's full lips split into a broad, white smile.

'So what are you waiting for, man?' he asked. 'The future is now.'

'The grease, man,' Obry replied, smiling too. 'I'm waiting for the grease, to make your ride easy.'

He reached between Valentine's hairless caramel thighs from behind and gripped the beefily muscular young man's large, pendulous balls. As he cupped Valentine's silky, hot, heavy scrotum, Obry's fingertips brushed the base of Valentine's stiff, slick shaft as it pumped in and out of Antoine's stretched, lubricated arsehole. 'Or are you so slack I can fuck you dry?' Obry added provocatively.

'Hey, even the sarge needs greasing, man,' Valentine said lightly, passing the Vaseline back to Obry.

'Only for four fingers,' Obry replied, smearing the petroleum jelly liberally over his long, rigid and smoothly curving erection. Valentine laughed at that, and resumed pumping Antoine's upturned butthole with renewed vigour, flexing his smooth, muscular buttocks for Obry's visual pleasure.

Obry pushed two greasy fingers up Valentine's arse as Valentine continued to fuck Antoine, who was now gasping throatily into Pierre's arse as he carried on tonguing his juicy man-pussy while being screwed hard by the muscle-bound soldier.

Antoine now pushed the gold-sequined briefs he was wearing down at the front as well as the back, freeing his own aching erection and balls. Then the conk-haired, buttery-brown and curvaceously muscular young man began to move his fist on his own throbbing shaft, finally giving himself some relief as Valentine's thick, wood-hard cock slid in and out of his now open and fully dilated arsehole. Pre-come ran freely in long sticky threads from Antoine's piss slit, making his fist sticky and slick and exciting, and his breathing was becoming laboured as Valentine's cock head rammed repeatedly against his prostate.

Valentine himself had taken Obry's two fingers up his anal star to the knuckles without resistance, so Obry quickly moved his lean hips into position behind the short, muscular, light-skinned man, gripping Valentine's waspy waist from behind with both hands. At first Obry just slid his large, greasy cock up and down between Valentine's big, firm buttocks, getting into the rhythm of the café-au-lait-skinned man's butt-fucking of Antoine, Obry's leanly muscular cinnamon hips moving back and forth in line with Valentine's curvier, more buttery ones.

Then Obry seized his moment, arching back and bringing his missile-like cock head down into position against Valentine's greasy sphincter. Without a pause he pushed his rigid cock right the way up Valentine's arse as his comrade carried on fucking the curvaceous young man on all fours in front of him.

'Oh, *yeah*, man!' Valentine grunted, not breaking his rhythm for an instant as Obry's rigidity filled his rectum to the internal sphincter at its top in one firm thrust. 'Oh, fuck me!'

Obry kept his cock deep in Valentine's rectum, matching Valentine's rhythm perfectly, doubling the short, bodybuilt young man's pleasure as he fucked and was fucked up the arse simultaneously, a perfection of ecstasy for Valentine Dumonde that he had never expected to find in any fancy house in Arbrerouge, let alone have freely given to him in a laurel grove two miles outside the Voodoo village of Croix-Le-Bois.

Pierre broke off rimming Bossuet to look round and see what was happening behind him. He was still wearing his stretchy green-sequined leotard; only his smooth, lanky brown arms and legs and delicious mocha arse were exposed, and Antoine was still tonguing his quivering, receptive hole. Pierre's erection throbbed against the constricting fabric of the figure-hugging one-piece as Antoine tongue-fucked him, soaking it dark with oozing pre-come, and excitement shot through his heaving chest as he saw that Antoine was being fucked by Valentine while Valentine was taking Obry's cock up his arse at the same time and with evident pleasure.

'I want cock up me too, man,' Pierre gasped to Antoine over one muscular, shiny and cinnamon-brown shoulder.

'Well bring your arse to my dick, Pierre, man,' Antoine demanded breathlessly, taking his hand off his own throbbing, aching, eight-inch erection. 'It's stiff and dripping and waiting for your tight, wet hole.' His conked hair was tumbled forward in a glossy mess over his forehead, and his pretty, boyish features were bloated with sexual ecstasy, his full lips parted to reveal his gold-framed front teeth, his eyes wild.

Pierre immediately wiggled his way backwards until his knees were positioned outside Antoine's knees, his large, muscular demerara buttocks were hovering invitingly just above Antoine's crotch, and Antoine's strong, muscular arms were positioned either side of his broad-shouldered, smooth back. Sweat dripped down from the curving domes of Antoine's smooth, well-built pectorals and protuberant nipples on to Pierre's wide, flat shoulders, and Antoine's slick, trembling belly pressing against Pierre's freely offered butt. His throbbing glans bumped thrillingly against the back of Pierre's swinging ballsac.

Antoine's expert rimming had relaxed and loosened Pierre's anal ring, and Antoine's achingly stiff dick was already lubricated and sticky with pre-come. He gripped its shaft with one hand as Pierre moved his buttocks backwards towards him, aiming its smooth, blood-hardened dome towards Pierre's glittering, hairless arsehole.

A shiver ran through Pierre's body as he felt Antoine's cock head pressed firmly against his sphincter, but he kept on pushing his buttocks backwards on to Antoine's hot, throbbing crown until it slowly slipped inside his anus.

The rigid shaft of Antoine's eight-inch cock was then driven all the way into Pierre's upturned arse in a series of rough, abrupt rabbit hops that made him gasp and cry out. These were the result of vigorous thrusts by Valentine of his cock into Antoine's backside that jolted Antoine forward, thrusts inspired in Valentine by Obry's rigidity being slammed up *his* arse to the root.

Pierre made sure to keep his own arse in place as Antoine began to fuck his greasy hole enthusiastically. Like Valentine, Antoine was now loving the good feeling of a stiff cock slamming in and out of his anal cavity behind him, while his own tool was gripped by the greedily elastic anal ring of another handsome young man on all fours in front of him. Pierre braced his whole body up as he was rammed vigorously up the arse, knowing that he was the anchor in this chain of butt-fucking, grunting loudly at each thrust into his anal canal, a thrust made all the more intense for Pierre by knowing that it was made with the momentum of all three of the muscular men behind him.

Meanwhile, Ti-Coyo had pulled his eleven-inch whanger out of Bossuet's mouth and pushed Jestin down on to all fours on the ground in front of him, keen to fuck the shaven-headed army sergeant's beefy arse. Ti-Coyo sank to his knees behind Jestin, between his open legs, gripped his stiff, hefty cock, and slapped its thick, saliva-shiny shaft against Jestin's large, plain-chocolate-dark, upturned butt.

'Move backwards, man,' Pierre gasped to Ti-Coyo as Antoine's greasy erection slid in and out of his upturned arsehole. 'Then I can tongue-fuck you while you give him your cock up his arse.'

Ti-Coyo nodded and did so, his face flushed, letting go of his outsize cock so he could grip Jestin round the waist with both hands and pull him back too. Jestin didn't resist, and soon Ti-Coyo's neat, high and very muscular buttocks were pressed firmly against Pierre's upturned face. Ti-Coyo grunted in pleasure as Pierre began to distractedly tongue his sweet, tight hole while Antoine's cock was slithering in and out of his well-lubricated chocolate star. At the same time as he pulled Jestin back, Ti-Coyo sat up and braced himself on his knees, so that Jestin could sit down on his thick rigidity and take its whole length up into his anal canal.

His own cock bucking between his legs, Jestin slowly did so, sinking the big, muscular globes of his arse down on to Ti-Coyo's stiff, hole-stretching thickness, opening up slowly to take its greasy length into his body, having to pause when he realised his rectum was full to capacity, then slowly squirming himself down further on to the lean, hard-bodied man's eleven-inch cock, allowing the dome of Ti-Coyo's glans to work its way into his intestines, a gratifying sense of chaotic fullness flooding outwards from his stretched anal canal and through his stomach and chest as he took Ti-Coyo's entire length up his back passage.

Slowly Ti-Coyo pushed Jestin forwards until he was back on all fours, leaning with him and finally bracing his lean, sinewy, coffee-brown arms either side of Jestin's smooth, gleaming ebony back. He opened his thighs, giving Pierre's tongue better access to his arsehole.

'I'm up you now, man,' Ti-Coyo said to Jestin hoarsely. 'You've got all eleven inches of my good sweet dick up your arse to the root. Now I'm going to fuck you with it until you beg me to stop. And then I'm going to fuck you some more.'

'Oh, yes, man, fuck me,' Jestin replied, pre-come dripping spontaneously from his own untouched cock head as it bobbed between his smooth, dark thighs. 'Oh, *yes*,' he repeated, as Ti-Coyo began to slither his massive shaft in and out of Jestin's slack, upturned arsehole.

'What about me, man?' Bossuet complained. True, Dany was still sucking him off, but now he was neither sucking cock himself, nor being rimmed: it didn't seem like enough. He looked down at the lean, dark young soldier kneeling before him. 'You like to fuck, man?' he asked hopefully.

'I'm more of a bitch in bed, man,' Dany replied, breaking off his cocksucking, his voice breathless, his full lips shiny with pre-come, his dark eyes bright with excitement, his own stiff cock jutting up from his crotch as he spoke, turned on just to be sucking dick.

Ti-Coyo turned his head. 'That doesn't matter, man,' he said hoarsely, addressing his words to Dany. 'He needs more than a dick, anyway.'

'I don't understand you, man,' Dany replied, kissing Bossuet's shiny cockhead.

'Have you ever put your hand up a man?' Ti-Coyo asked, keeping his hips moving regularly against Jestin's shining, ebony globes, each thrust in making the darker-skinned man on all fours before him arch his back up and gasp sharply as his anal canal was filled to bursting.

'It was the initiation ceremony at the camp I was trained at,' Dany replied, surprising his fellow soldiers, who didn't know this side of their comrade. 'I took a hand up my arse the first week I was there. I kind of enjoyed it. And afterwards I gave a fist to any other soldier who needed it. Soon I was the most popular fister in the barracks. They said it was because I had enthusiasm for it. And, because I had enjoyed taking a hand, I knew how to give it with pleasure.'

'Pass him the Vaseline, man,' Bossuet said to Antoine abruptly over his shoulder, interrupting Dany's monologue. 'Man,' he said to the pretty, dark-skinned and still-kneeling cocksucker, who was still wearing his metal army helmet, 'give me all you've got!'

Bossuet then went and lowered himself on to all fours next to Jestin, and pushed his blocky, bodybuilt butt up into the air. He would have been envious of the army sergeant alongside him who was being so vigorously poled by Ti-Coyo's throbbing weapon, but the prospect of a fist up his own arse more than compensated Bossuet for missing out on his fellow fisherman's rigid tool.

Dany pushed all his fingers into the half-used jar of Vaseline, coating them and pulling out a solid gobbet of the petroleum jelly at the same time. He then began to push his bunched fingers against Bossuet's shiny, shaved ebony hole, folding in his thumb as well. Bossuet's cock kicked and his balls clenched, then relaxed as his sphincter began to dilate to accommodate the intruding digits. Dany watched Bossuet open up for him with pleasure, and his own dick dripped pre-come as he felt Bossuet's anal ring relax and start to accommodate his four bunched fingers and thumb.

Bossuet braced himself up on his bodybuilt arm and his metal arm, his shaved head down, sinews standing out in his bullishly thick neck and spreading out across his broad, beefy shoulders. His fanning back tapered to a waspy waist. The deep mocha globes of his arse muscles stood magnificently proud, and he pushed them up and back towards Dany, eager to get a hand up his arse to the wrist.

When he had agreed to help distract the soldiers, the last thing Bossuet had expected was to receive the extreme anal gratification that he had previously been able to get only on his very occasional trips to Arbrerouge. Truly the *lwa* were smiling on All Saints' Day.

Bossuet shifted his arse from side to side and had to breathe in and out heavily as Dany's knuckles began to press against his stretched sphincter: this was the hard part, the widest part, and although he was slim and lanky, Dany's hand was large and broad, not easy for Bossuet to take. But, while its size made it harder for Bossuet to get it up him, he felt the added thrill of knowing how much fuller Dany's hand would make him feel once he did finally accept it.

Dany moved his bunched fingers backwards and forwards against Bossuet's sphincter, softening Bossuet's anal opening up, relaxing it, dilating it, massaging it. Then finally he pushed into it with assured firmness. Bossuet groaned and cried out sharply in alarm and ecstasy as Dany's hand dilated him fully, as Dany's knuckles stretched Bossuet's anal ring wide, stretched it achingly wide, stretched it ecstatically wide for one unbearable moment, and then Dany's whole fist slithered abruptly into his rectum, filling it immediately and making Bossuet's cock buck repeatedly as Dany began to move his hand back and forth inside Bossuet's body. Bossuet breathed hard, and his curved, ridged stomach pushed out as Dany increased his fisting rhythm.

Next to Bossuet and also on all fours, Jestin was moaning and groaning as Ti-Coyo fucked him hard from behind, slithering his enormous cock in and out of Jestin's upturned plain-chocolate butthole. The horny bottom's breathing got sharper and higher as Ti-Coyo slammed his hips against the sergeant's smooth brown globes with sharp smacking sounds, penetrating Jestin's anal cavity fully with each thrust. Jestin wasn't touching his own cock, but he felt the excitement building in it as he was fucked vigorously up the arse by Ti-Coyo. There was nothing Jestin could do to control the mounting excitement: any second he was going to come without touching his dick, just from having Ti-Coyo's massive whanger filling his anal canal and slamming itself repeatedly against his prostate.

'Oh, Jesus, oh, fuck, oh, fuck me!' Jestin yelled throatily, arching up, ecstasy slamming through from his rectum to his clenching balls, and hammering along the shaft of his bucking cock, come surging up his aching, rigid pole and flooding uncontrollably from the gaping piss slit in his crown in hot, white gouts as Ti-Coyo continued to plough his greasy hole, pumping it out of him by pumping Jestin's arse. 'Oh, fuck, oh Christ,' Jestin groaned, slumping forward, more jism spurting out of his kicking cock as Ti-Coyo rammed his bruised hole vigorously from behind. Jestin slumped face down on to the ground, now totally prone and sated, worn out by Ti-Coyo's vigorous shafting, but unable to deny Ti-Coyo his satisfaction, accepting that Ti-Coyo would need to keep on fucking his arse until he came himself.

Pierre, while thrusting his fist back and forth in Bossuet's upturned arse with an almost dispassionate efficiency, looked round at Ti-Coyo as he carried on fucking Jestin's now totally slack hole while Jestin lay face down on the grass, grunting quietly with each thrust into his bruised, used anal canal.

'Man, he's worn out,' Pierre observed to Ti-Coyo. 'His hole won't grip your cock shaft and give it pleasure. Why not fuck my arse, man? It's fresh and tight and ready to go.'

With a grunt, Ti-Coyo immediately pulled his stiff, greasy,

eleven-inch tool out of Jestin's backside. Jestin quivered, and exhaled thankfully. His slick, shiny anal opening gaped, however, so well fucked that it naturally relaxed dilated. He turned his sweaty, shaved head to watch Dany take Ti-Coyo's still-stiff tool up his arse.

For a moment Dany wondered if he'd done the right thing: now that he could see it outside Jestin's arse or Bossuet's mouth, Ti-Coyo's cock was more enormous than he'd realised, and his own arsehole was tight and hadn't been greased or rimmed, and his hips were narrow. Still, he'd taken a fist before at the army camp, he reasoned. Why should he have a problem with this?

In any case, Ti-Coyo didn't give him a moment to change his mind: he was so eager to reach his climax pounding a tight arse – and Dany was offering it to him – that he slipped straight round behind the kneeling youth, placed one hand on his narrow hips and, without a pause, pushed his greasy weapon, generously lubricated with Vaseline and pre-come, between Dany's small, high, muscular plain-chocolate buttocks and positioned its crown against Dany's tightly closed anal star, and began to push against it firmly.

To Ti-Coyo's gratification, Dany's well-trained arsehole opened instantly and obligingly, and Ti-Coyo's cock began to slide smoothly into the dark-skinned, slender youth's back passage. Ti-Coyo hadn't wanted to hurt Dany, of course, had in fact wanted only to give him pleasure, but his own need to come was now so intense that, if Dany hadn't yielded immediately, Ti-Coyo knew he could have been selfishly rough with him. As it was, Dany was clearly an experienced bottom who could take a decent length of cock and appreciate a passionate fucking, and Ti-Coyo was the well-endowed top to give him what he wanted. He gripped Dany's narrow hips with both hands and began to pump his arse vigorously, while Dany kept his balled fist moving back and forth roughly in Bossuet's arsehole, making the larger, body-built man with the steel arm grunt and groan loudly.

Meanwhile Obry, Valentine, Antoine and Pierre were building to a rhythmical multiple climax of their own with the proficiency and togetherness of a rowing team, their hips moving back and forth so that each man was as deeply penetrated as possible by each thrust forward, and each had the cock withdrawn out of his arse as far as was possible without its actually springing out of his slack, greasy hole with each pull back. Their chests began to heave as the four men moved their hips faster and faster. Their muscular brown bodies glistened with sweat, and their cocks began to grow in heaviness and their buttholes slacken as their rhythms built in speed and intensity.

It was Valentine, the light-skinned, bodybuilt soldier, who came first, with a throaty yell, his dick exploding deep in Antoine's accommodating rectum as Obry rabbit-fucked him up his arse. He was propelled towards his climax not only by the tightness of Antoine's greasy anal ring around his throbbing, aching cock shaft, but by the attentions of the lanky soldier who was positioned behind him, and was hammering himself towards a violent explosion in Valentine's anal canal. Obry gripped Valentine's waist tightly so that the short, muscular, butter-brown man in front of him couldn't escape from his greasily invading erection until after Obry had shot his load up Valentine's arsehole. Lean, flat chest heaving, Obry came with a loud shout, leaning his hips forward and thrusting his surging, spurting cock deep into Valentine's rectum, making Valentine cry out too, and his own still-hard manhood buck inside Antoine's arsehole in echo of this second explosion.

On all fours in front of Valentine, Antoine fucked his way towards his own climax in Pierre's back passage with the soldier's still-stiff dick and hot load of come up his arse, flexing his muscular demerara globes as he dicked the wriggling, excited Pierre eagerly, and gripping Valentine's dick with his own anal ring to make sure Valentine didn't pull it out before he had come.

Pierre responded to Antoine's increasingly rough pounding of his upturned caramel butt by wanking himself off vigorously through the fabric of his green-sequined leotard, gasping in a high voice as Antoine's rigid dick slammed in and out of his slack, greasy anal star, filling and evacuating his rectum over and over again. Antoine's heart hammered in his chest as he pumped his throbbing hard-on through Pierre's anal ring until he was past the point of no return, and he gripped Pierre's narrow hips and drove into his arsehole as hard as possible with a yell as he climaxed inside the youth's greasy back passage. With a gasp Pierre came too, almost simultaneously, pumping his fist on his cock through his leotard and shooting a thick, hot load into the green, sequined fabric as Antoine flooded his bruised anal cave with jism.

The four men collapsed forward in a sweaty, exhausted heap, thick, semi-stiff cocks still up slack, well-fucked arses, watching dazedly as Ti-Coyo pounded Dany's upturned butt as hard as he could while Dany dazedly but enthusiastically fisted Bossuet. Then suddenly Ti-Coyo was grunting hoarsely and gripping Dany's hips and forcing his cock right the way up Dany's back passage to the root as he came inside the lean young ebony-skinned man's body. Dany squealed excitedly and pushed his arse back greedily.

'Keep it up there, man,' he ordered Ti-Coyo breathlessly. 'Keep your cock right the way up my backside while I beat off.' He pumped his fist frantically on his own aching, dripping rigidity, while keeping his other hand moving vigorously inside Bossuet's rectum. Bossuet, too, was wanking himself off hard and fast. Within a minute and shouting out loudly, both Dany and Bossuet brought themselves to explosive orgasms, shooting great gouts of hot, white jism on to the lush green grass below them from pumping cock heads, sinews tensing across every muscle of their bodies, sweat pouring from their pores, both men achieving satisfaction at last.

Ti-Coyo gave Dany's butt a playful slap, then let his still-hard cock slide out of the dark-skinned young soldier's slack, juicy and thoroughly fucked hole with a slurping pop that made Dany gasp. Then Dany carefully withdrew his fist from Bossuet's well-worked rectum. Bossuet inhaled sharply as Dany's knuckles once again stretched him to his limits of anal elasticity, and then exhaled heavily with relief as Dany's hand slithered greasily out of his backside, leaving it gaping and satiated. The shaven-headed body-builder slumped forward on to the grass below him, every muscle aching, totally exhausted. Silence, stillness fell.

Time passed.

The sun glittered through the flickering leaves above the men, imparting a golden quality to the air as it moved slowly west, and light, pleasant music was playing quietly on the radio. All seemed totally peaceful, totally harmonious. No man was quite sure where his body ended and the bodies of the men next to him began, and the feeling was comfortable, and good. They were like a pride of muscular, recumbent Nubian lions, stretching and dozing in the shade through the passing heat of the day. Great green and yellow butterflies flitted drunkenly around the grove above the eight men, occasionally alighting briefly on a casually outstretched hand or a smooth shoulder to sun themselves, or rest their wings.

Sergeant Jestin drifted in and out of postcoital sleep, his shaved head resting on the dozing and face-down Bossuet's broad, warm mocha-brown back, Antoine's arm sprawled casually and intimately over his thigh. Something about the music on the radio was bothering Jestin, but he couldn't work out what it was. An undercurrent, an echo, a dissonance . . . Something. Did it matter? Perhaps the radio wasn't tuned in properly, although it had been before. Nobody else seemed to have noticed. Jestin pushed a heavily lidded eye open and squinted towards where it was sitting nearby. If he made just a little effort he could stretch out and reach it. He took a small breath and did so, grunting at the exertion.

Jestin pulled the radio to him and twiddled inattentively at one of the dials to fine-tune it. By mistake he chose the volume dial, and inadvertently turned the sound all the way down when he twisted it, clicking the radio off. But he could still hear music playing. Immediately he started upright. The undertone of drumming that he had been hearing all this time hadn't been on the radio at all: it was coming from the unseen *oufo* that lay nearby. The mission! Jestin thought, suddenly wide awake. And yet the stillness and tranquillity of the grove, and the easy intimacy of the seven other men stretched out somnolently on the dappled grass in careless embraces pulled at him powerfully.

'We have to go now,' Jestin said groggily, struggling to get to his feet. 'Right now.' He repeated, looking around for his discarded clothes.

'Why, man?' Ti-Coyo asked him languidly, running a hand

caressingly over the sergeant's beefy mocha butt. 'Why are you taking this sweet chocolate peach away from me, man? What are you hurrying off for?'

'Because it is our mission, man,' the army sergeant replied half-heartedly, enjoying the feeling of Ti-Coyo's hand on his buttocks, even more loath to leave now than he had been before. 'We have a mission to carry out.' Jestin glanced round at his men. Obry was asleep, curled up spoon-fashion with Valentine, whose forehead was leaning against Pierre's, the light-skinned boy also dozing, and with his face turned towards the sleeping bodybuilt soldier's. Dany's head rested peacefully on Ti-Coyo's smooth, caramel thigh, and he too had his eyes closed, although there was a tenseness about his body that suggested he heard every word Jestin was saying, and just did not want to obey his orders.

'Come lie back down with me and tell me about it, man,' Ti-Coyo said to the half-crouching Jestin, reaching out to the beefy, mocha-skinned sergeant. 'Come,' he repeated. He caught Jestin's hand and gently pulled him back down on to his knees. 'Curl up with me. Yes, man. Just like that.'

Unable to resist Ti-Coyo's invitation, Jestin lay down on his side on the cool, soft grass and snuggled his buttocks back into Ti-Coyo's crotch, feeling the warmth of Ti-Coyo's large, soft cock and hanging balls against them. Ti-Coyo wrapped his lean, muscular café-au-lait arms around the well-built, darker-skinned sergeant's waist, then slid them up to his chest. Jestin could feel Ti-Coyo's breath warm and regular on the back of his neck, and suddenly he felt that he belonged here, in this glade, with these men, more than he had ever belonged anywhere. Even the distant drumming made something leap in his chest, drew some response from deep inside him.

'We're supposed to go to the Voodoo temple round here and stop the ceremony and round up the ringleaders,' he said eventually, closing his eyes as he spoke.

'Why, man?' Ti-Coyo asked him.

'Orders.'

'Why were you ordered?'

Jestin shrugged his shoulders. 'I don't know, man,' he admitted. 'But that's the army. You give orders and you obey them.'

'Even bad orders?'

'You have to trust your superiors. You can't always see the whole picture,' Jestin said, keeping his eyes shut, not wanting to talk about the military or his mission at Croix-Le-Bois: it all seemed just depressing and pointless now.

'Have you ever been to a Voodoo ceremony, man?' Ti-Coyo asked him quietly, nipping the lobe of his ear with his teeth.

'No, man,' Jestin admitted, shaking his shaven head. 'Not at all.'

'Then don't let them turn you against what you don't even know, mister soldier,' Ti-Coyo said.

'I know, man,' Jestin said. 'I know . . .' His voice trailed off. The government line, the Church line faded from his mind. All he knew was that he belonged here more than he belonged anywhere else, and that the distant drumming was part of his belonging.

'I tell you what, man,' Ti-Coyo said, toying idly with one of Jestin's pert, plain-chocolate nipples, and trying to make his voice sound light and playful. 'I will make this deal with you: leave your guns and your bullets and your military ranks here, just as you left them when you stepped into this grove, just for this one evening and night, and come with us to the ceremony. Come with an open mind, a free mind. Watch, and judge for yourself how we deserve to be treated.'

'Then you are –'

'We are *serviteurs*, man,' Ti-Coyo said. 'We serve the *lwa* as we can.'

There was a catch in Ti-Coyo's voice. This, he knew, was the most dangerous moment: if he hadn't charmed and convinced Jestin sufficiently, the sergeant could still turn on him and his friends, rally his men round and arrest Ti-Coyo, Antoine, Bossuet and Pierre as Voodooists. 'Can you do that for us, man?' he asked Jestin quietly. 'Will you come with open hands and minds, and in good faith?'

Jestin twisted his head round to see if the other soldiers were taking in this unexpected conversation, this provocative invitation. They were, all three of them: Dany, Valentine and Obry watched their sergeant with dark and thoughtful eyes.

It was Dany who spoke first. 'Nobody would ever know that we'd been,' he said, looking down, a catch in his voice. 'Who would tell?'

'We could say our tip-off was no good,' Obry chimed in. 'That there wasn't an *oufo*. Or there wasn't a ceremony.'

'These men have only done us good, not harm,' Valentine added. 'How can we return harm for good?'

'The drums call all the way from Africa,' Ti-Coyo said. 'From Guinée. Don't you hear them, man? Don't you *feel* them?'

Jestin closed his eyes and snuggled down again to think: he *did* feel the drums, as if they were some other heartbeat that had always been part of him that he had always denied. Time stilled before he spoke, as if the trees were holding their breaths.

'Very well, man,' Jestin said eventually. 'We will leave our guns and our orders, and come.'

Dany, Obry and Valentine exhaled in relief and smiled to each other, even laughed softly, tension passing from their weary muscles as the burden of serving an unjust regime was lifted from their shoulders. Ti-Coyo, elated that neither he nor his friends would now have to miss the most important festival of the year, craned forward and kissed Jestin on the temple, making the shaven-headed sergeant smile too.

'We will have to return to the village before we can go to the *mange-lwa*, so we can change into more appropriate clothing,' Ti-Coyo said. 'Both us and yourselves. But not yet, man,' he added, hugging Jestin to him, and the sergeant felt Ti-Coyo's manhood stir against his muscular buttocks. 'There is plenty of time for us to be close for a little while yet. And after the ceremonies,' he continued teasingly, 'perhaps we can be close again.'

Six

The sun had sunk below the mountain tops, and the sky was turning a pale silvery blue as dusk fell. The full moon was a ghostly, absolutely still disc suspended high and faint above the blackening silhouettes of the jutting peaks. A sensation of anticipation filled the motionless air, a sensation so intense it was as if it was boiling up from the earth like steam after a tropical storm.

Dressed in their best and most colourful clothes, the people of the village of Croix-Le-Bois, led by two handsome young *ounsis* wearing only clean, tight white breeches and red headscarves, made their way in silence along the secluded red-clay path that led from the village to their *oufo*. No drumming was now audible from within its unseen, whitewashed walls.

The two young adepts held up large flags on poles as they moved in slow, measured steps along the track just ahead of the rest of the villagers. A sudden slight breeze, over as quickly as it had begun, caught the brightly coloured material the flags were made of and set their sequins shimmering in the draining light. These two leading flags symbolised, and were embroidered with the name of, the society of believers in Croix-Le-Bois: La Société des Serviteurs de Baron Lundi et de Baron Limba.

Behind them the villagers carried other highly decorated flags on poles representing the various *lwa* of the temple – Legba, the

166

opener of the way and spirit of the crossroads, Ezulie, the spirit of love, Azaka, guardian of farmers, Ogoun, *lwa* of war and the forge – but the flags displayed most prominently were those dedicated to the *Ghedes*, the *lwa* of the dead. And it was the *Ghedes* who were to be honoured above all the other Mysteries tonight. Chief among the family of *Ghedes* was Baron Samedi, and also to be most honoured alongside him were the *massissi* lovers Barons Limba and Lundi, to whom the *oufo* and Ti-Charles, its *oungan*, were dedicated.

Earlier in the afternoon, after sending Sudra and Antoine off on Sudra's Harley Davidson to distract the intruding soldiers and warn the nearby village of Sous-L'Eau that their *mange-lwa* ceremony was also in danger of being disrupted, Ti-Charles had made time to go down to the village cemetery and wait attendance on the bereaved, and those who wished to speak with their dead ancestors.

The graves had been carefully tended, the weeds pulled, the stones whitened with chalk or whitewash, and flowers and votive candles put in place. The spirits, or *gros-bon-anges*, of the departed were elsewhere, contained in *govi*, heart-shaped clay pots, either in family shrines in the homes of the relatives, or in Ti-Charles's shrine at the *oufo*, where they could be kept under the young *oungan*'s protection. Despite this, the custom was that if you wanted to contact a dead relative on All Saints' Day, you came to the cemetery to do so. Perhaps it was so that the spirit could see that his or her grave or tomb had been well tended, that his or her memory had been materially honoured.

Ti-Charles had gone to the small, closely crowded ceremony wearing sunglasses with a lens missing, and a top hat, and plugged his nostrils with balls of cotton as if he was a corpse prepared for burial, because there he knew he was to be ridden – possessed – by Baron Samedi, the chief *lwa* of the *Ghedes*. There he had been taken, and had spoken to the gathered faithful as the Baron, passing on messages, advice and instructions from *les mortes*, the dead, to the living. The Baron had left him an hour or so later, so far as he could judge from the movement of the sun across the sky between before he lost his consciousness, his *gros-bon-ange*, and after he had regained it. Those who had come to the graveyard to hear him, or rather to hear Baron Samedi, seemed on the whole content with whatever advice he had chosen to give them, although as always one or two grumbled about the expensiveness of the sacrifices the *Ghedes* had demanded to put things right between themselves and their deceased relative.

For in Voodoo the dead are in constant dialogue with the living, and the spirit world is the mirror of the living world – always present. The living energise the spirits, *les mortes* and *Les Mystères*, and the spirits empower the living, filling their lives with meaning in a world where nothing happens without chance, nothing happens for no reason. And, if that world is demanding, it is at least a world where action can always be taken, where no one is truly powerless.

Baron Samedi, as well as the chief *lwa* of the dead, is also the guardian of children: who better to guard them from the harms of the world than one who understands *les mortes* and the myriad ways they pass through the surface of the cosmic mirror so well?

As always, Ti-Charles could remember nothing he had done or said while possessed by the Baron. The *lwa* had not ridden him violently, as if understanding that the *oungan* had much to do and see over tonight, but still Ti-Charles had been left feeling for the moment as drained and exhausted as if he had been dancing all night, and had had to sit in the cooling green shade of a spreading cypress tree for a while beside the blindingly white tombs, recovering his stamina.

The villagers had offered him refreshments, and after a while he felt well enough to walk, and had returned to the *oufo* at an easy pace. When he got back there, he found that Sauveur had completed all the necessary preparations, and that all he, Ti-Charles, had to do, was wait for the arrival of the procession when dusk fell.

Ti-Charles couldn't help but feel tense, however: he didn't yet know the outcome of Antoine's attempts to waylay the soldiers. Perhaps it had failed, and they would still appear to disrupt things and make arrests. Perhaps Antoine and whoever he had gathered together to help him had already been arrested. And, even if that wasn't the case, there was still Antoine's spirit wedding to Ezulie to be confirmed, and then there was the matter of Ti-Charles's own prayers to Ezulie, and to his *met-tête-lwa* Limba and Lundi concerning his sweetheart, the handsome young fisherman Henri Biassou.

The procession of villagers reached the gates of the *oufo* to find the first lamps had been lit against the deepening night and set welcomingly in alcoves on either side of them. The air was filled with the sound of chirruping cicadas. No one spoke. The villagers had brought with them offerings for the *lwa*: cooked foods, live speckled brown-and-white chickens, a black goat with red ribbons tied to its polished horns that broke the stillness of the night by bleating. One of the *ounsis* stepped forward and knocked on the *oufo*'s gates, then stepped back.

Almost immediately the gates swung open and Sauveur stepped out, flanked by two more handsome young *serviteurs* dressed in tight white breeches, this time wearing white headscarves. The dark-skinned, sinew-corded older man, whose braided hair was pulled back into a long pigtail, was dressed all in red for the ceremony: he wore a red bandana round his neck, a red mesh vest and tight red denim shorts. Embroidered *wanga* packets hung around his neck. In his right hand he held a cutlass. His dark eyes glinted brightly as he looked from one handsome young flag-bearer facing him to the other.

The older of the two young *serviteurs* began to sing in a strong, soaring voice: 'Baron Lundi, *na salue drapeau-là*. Baron Lundi, we salute you with these flags, Baron Limba, we salute you with these flags.' As he sang out, naming the various *lwa* honoured at the temple, he and his fellow *serviteur* held out the flagpoles to the two young men facing them, who stepped forward, took the flags from them, then stepped back. Sauveur held out his cutlass. The two young men flanking him held out the flagpoles they had been given at the same angle, imitating his pose. Then the three men went through a ritual drill that made the cutlass glint in the lamplight and set the sequined and embroidered banners floating on the still air. A sheen broke out on their skins as they made the required movements, faces set in concentration.

Abruptly, they turned and went back inside the *oufo*. The procession of villagers followed them inside silently, already being drawn into a state of religious awe by the ritual greeting. Entering the compound this evening was not the same as entering it on any normal evening: tonight the *lwa* would come from Guinée to be fed and to ride, and *les mortes*, the spirits of the dead, would be made manifest. The villagers lined the whitewashed inner walls with the flags on their poles and made their way past various huts and shrines and sacred *mapu* trees over to the peristyle, the area where the ceremony was to be performed. It had no sides, but a light roof of banana leaves had been constructed overhead, supported by long, slender poles, and from which oil lamps hung, lighting the space brightly and warmly. In the centre of the peristyle stood the elaborate and brightly painted *poteau-mitain* post.

Around the post some offerings had already been placed during the course of the day, as well as various ritual objects and the visual props of the various *lwa* – sunglasses and a top hat for the *Ghede*, a pipe and a *macoute*, a straw sack for Azaka, among other things – for when they came to ride the *serviteurs*, and Ti-Charles had also marked out some of the *veves* the *mange-lwa* service required with flour and coffee grounds on the smooth, compacted earth. Others he would mark out during the course of the ceremony, as was usual. As the festival proceeded the *veves* would be danced over by the *serviteurs* and obliterated, their work of invitation done.

On the white plaster walls of the compound that ran around the edges of the peristyle more lasting large and elaborate *veves* had been inscribed by Ti-Charles and other believers, along with various written sayings, and colourful paintings of the *lwa* themselves – often in the form of Catholic saints – shone bright and clear in the lamplight as if they contained some strange internal radiance.

Slipping in behind the last of the villagers, a straw hat with a wide brim shadowing his face, was a light-skinned young man dressed in dull colours. He was sweaty and seemed nervous, his eyes darting around the *oufo* and settling nowhere. He carried a heart-shaped box of chocolates in one hand and a bottle of cane liquor in the other.

The young man was Bertrand Laverre, and he knew he was playing a very dangerous game in coming to the *oufo* the way he was doing, as so many of the villagers knew him from before he had gone away, and would remember his face. If they recognised him and dragged him in front of Ti-Charles, not only would his chance of poisoning the *oungan* be lost, but, more than that, Ti-Charles would know instantly what he intended, for the *lwa* would tell the priest what was in his former *ounsi*'s mind, and Ti-Charles would have Bertrand exposed as a dealer in sorcery and poison. And then perhaps the minds of the villagers would be turned back to the unexpected death of the farmer Pierre Mejeune and the police would be called. And Bertrand knew that the constable, Sudra, was a Voodoo *serviteur* and a personal friend of Ti-Charles, and that a man could be hanged if found guilty of even attempting to poison another, particularly if the poisoning was to be done with the intention of turning the victim into a zombie: there the system of justice imported from Enlightenment France combined with the anxieties of the Voodoo believer to bring the full harshness of the law down on the wrongdoer.

If he had had any choice, Bertrand would have turned and slipped quietly away. But he knew that even if he renounced the quest for power and knowledge he could not escape the reaches of the *bokor* or the Zoboyo by simply recanting. Jean Lamartine would claim him. And, even if the *bokor* and his associates didn't reach Bertrand physically, they could always reach him psychically and magically – send some malevolent little *baka* scratching at the back door of wherever he was staying late one night, some dwarfish creature with sharp claws and teeth that was thirsty for blood.

So Bertrand hung at the back of the group of villagers with his hat pulled low, hoping that everyone would be too engrossed in the ceremony and their own hopes of being ridden by the *lwa* or having their questions answered and problems solved by *Les Mystères* to notice him slip the poison into the glazed clay basin from which Ti-Charles habitually refreshed himself during the course of the night-long ceremony.

Ti-Charles, meanwhile, sat quietly waiting in the elaborately painted chair that had belonged to his mentor, and that had been placed to one side of the *poteau-mitain*, dressed in clean white breeches that hugged his thighs, and with an embroidered red headscarf tied carefully around his head, his dreadlocks carefully tied back inside it. His smooth, bare chest rose and fell, his pretty features set. In his lap rested his *asson*, the sacred gourd rattle with the mesh of beads and snakeskin vertebrae around it that symbolised his status as the *oungan* of Croix-Le-Bois. He would be using the *asson* to direct and set the tempo of the service.

Sauveur entered the peristyle backwards, swivelling his body in one direction, then another until he had reached roughly its centre.

Up until then Ti-Charles had been rapidly scanning the crowd for a sight of Henri Biassou. He was pleased to see him at the front of the gathered villagers, looking as handsome as he had ever looked in white breeches that hugged his thighs and crotch, a blouson-sleeved white shirt open to the waist that showed off the domes of his chest, and a necklace of cowries tight around his throat. His straw hat was pushed back on his shaved head, which was wrapped in a flawlessly white bandana, his skin glowing, his eyes bright, his full lips glossy . . . Ti-Charles's dick stirred in his own breeches, and he forced his attention back to Sauveur, returning himself to the moment, and to his duty of service to the community of the living and the dead, and to the *lwa*.

The well-muscled blacksmith turned to each of the four cardinal points and marked them as crosses in the impacted red earth of the floor of the peristyle with deft, muscular movements. These points mark the lines of intersection of the planes of the living and the spirit world, and energise the forces that will bring them together for the ceremony. Then, as the villagers and the gathered *ounsis* looked on, Sauveur saluted the *poteau-mitain*, the three waiting drums that would be played tonight, and finally Ti-Charles.

Sauveur came forward, brandishing the cutlass as if he was going to attack the young *oungan*. Ti-Charles got to his feet, holding up his *asson* to block the blow. It was a stylised, theatrical and symbolic duel, where each man repeatedly blocked the other's attack, then tried to press his advantage. The villagers and *ounsis* looked on, fascinated as they were always fascinated, although the outcome was never in doubt: the fascination and the excitement came out of seeing the playing out in stylised form of everything that made their lives meaningful – life against death, belief against chaos, wisdom and knowledge winning out over violence and darkness.

Finally Ti-Charles and his *asson* prevailed over Sauveur and his cutlass, and the broader, more muscular man sank to his knees, embedding the sword's tip in the ground as he did so, and kissed the hard, smooth earth at Ti-Charles's feet. The two *ounsis* who had stood with Sauveur at the entrance stepped forward – still bearing their flags – and, kneeling beside him, kissed the ground too.

Ti-Charles pulled the tops of the flagpoles they were holding towards him and kissed them. Then he bent forward and kissed the hilt of Sauveur's sword, a symbolic gesture: that Ti-Charles could both control the powerful forces of the spirit world and dedicate himself to the principle of service to the community and the *lwa*; that he was not proud, and did not hunger for power over others.

Ti-Charles returned to his seat. The two *ounsis* went and placed the flags against the wall with the others. Sauveur carefully put the cutlass aside and went and sat behind his drum, next to Petro. A certain tension passed from his body: now his role was purely that of musician. But, before he could begin to play, there were certain rituals that Ti-Charles had to perform.

The *oungan* began to move his *asson*, building up a fast hissing rhythm. He began with a quickly muttered litany of the Catholic saints, following with an invocation of the Trinity and Christian prayers to the Almighty. The *ounsis* responded with fast 'amens' after each prayer. To an onlooker who was not a believer, this might have seemed a strange element of the service – almost a parody – but to the believer the Christian god was just one of the manifestations of the primal cosmic force that it was appropriate to honour. To Ti-Charles and his fellow *serviteurs* there was no necessary spiritual conflict between Catholicism and Voodoo; indeed the pantheon of saints – whose function it was to intercede with a Supreme Being who was remote – mirrored the role of the *lwa* for the believer. In any case, in a universe filled with capricious forces, it was always better to be on the safe side and make sure that each was honoured in its own way.

Ti-Charles then invoked the Voodoo Trinity, *les mortes, Les Mystères et les marassa*, that is the ancestors, the *lwa* and the divine twins who are the progenitors of humanity and embody cosmic totality. As he spoke, he took a jug of water and lifted it towards each of the cardinal points. His eyes were dark and remote as he stared into the endless night beyond the *oufo*'s walls, a night peopled with innumerable invisible spirits, *Les Mystères*, the *lwa*. Then he bore the jug over to each of the four open walls of the peristyle and poured welcoming libations there. He trickled thin lines of water from these points of entry to the base of the *poteau-mitain*, for the *lwa* are led into the sacred space on water, from Guinée, the Watery Place below. As he did this he chanted an invocation to Legba:

'Papa Legba, *ouvri bayè-a pou mwen*, Papa Legba, open the gate for me, so I can go through. When I return I will honour the *lwa*.'

He passed the jug to one of the *ounsis*, and the handsome young man immediately began to repeat the ritual pourings. Ti-Charles bent and picked up a flat dish of ash, lifting that to the cardinal points too. This was the ash with which he would mark out the other *veves* the service required that he had not completed earlier. Behind him, Sauveur and Petro sat patiently behind their drums, the large a*soto* and the smaller *manman*. A third drummer, another of the temple's adepts, sat next to them behind the smallest of the three drums used in the *Kongo* rituals. Another *ounsi* held a double bell, the other essential instrument for the festival.

'*Oungan*, draw a *veve* for me,' the rest of the *ounsis* chanted, starting to clap their hands in time, to encourage their *oungan* in his work.

With deft strokes Ti-Charles poured fluid lines to mark the twin *veves* of the male *lwa* who were homosexual lovers and to whom the temple was dedicated, Baron Limba and Baron Lundi. As he worked he chanted imprecations in the secret language of *Les Mystères*, the long-ago language of Guinée. The patterns he made for these two *lwa* had a warm simplicity that was born of Ti-Charles's sincere affection for them, and the part they had played in his life. They were his *met-tête-lwa*, his guides and guardians, and he was intimately bonded with them by half a lifetime of service.

He stared down at the spaces between the pale-blue interweaving lines as if he was looking through a doorway into the earth, and what lay beneath it: Guinée. As he worked he chanted invocations to the other *lwa* as well, and each time he named a *Mystère* that was of particular importance to one of the adepts, the young man would come forward and kiss the ground before the *poteau-mitain*.

One of the *ounsis*, lifting the jug of water high above his head, carried it over to the villagers and saluted them with it, particularly the fisherman Henri Biassou, as Ti-Charles had instructed him earlier. But all of them were ritually welcomed in this manner.

It was at this point that Antoine, Bossuet, Pierre and Ti-Coyo arrived with the four soldiers. The gates of the *oufo* stood open, for the temple was open to any respectful visitor, and no part of the ceremony was secret in the sense of being shameful or concealed, although the language in which Ti-Charles spoke to the *lwa* was understood by himself and *Les Mystères* alone. The four *serviteurs* had changed out of their carnival finery into white shirts and breeches, and red headscarves, and they had found similar clothing for the four soldiers, who hung back uneasily in the entrance, not certain how they would be received by the people whose ceremony they had been sent out to disrupt.

Pierre immediately went to join the other *ounsis* while Antoine, Bossuet and Ti-Coyo looked back and beckoned the soldiers forward, leading them by the hand until they were all lined up before Ti-Charles. The young *oungan* stood and put the dish of ash to one side. Moving his *asson* fast he walked up and down before Dany, Valentine, Jestin and Obry, studying each man carefully with dark, shrewd eyes that seemed to the four soldiers when they spoke of it afterwards to reach somewhere deep inside them. He sent the *asson* hissing out towards them repeatedly, as if trying to make them flinch and test their nerve. Then suddenly he laughed a loud, clear laugh and gestured for the water jug to be brought to him. With deft ritual movements he lifted it high above the head of each of the soldiers, and then saluted Bossuet, Antoine and Ti-Coyo in the same fashion. The three *serviteurs* knelt and kissed the ground before him, then sat back on their heels.

'You are welcome,' Ti-Charles said to them. He turned to the soldiers, who were looking uncertainly at each other: were *they* expected to kneel? 'You also are welcome guests,' he said with a smile. Then he passed the jug back to an *ounsi* – Pierre this time hurrying forward to take it from him – and turned back to completing the *veves*.

He finished marking out the elaborate patterns on the floor of the peristyle, praying to the *lwa* as he did so, then knelt back on his haunches, flourishing his *asson* in the direction of the waiting Sauveur and Petro with a prolonged rattle. The drums burst into responsive life, their pounding beats matching and then rapidly superseding the handclaps of the *ounsis* while at the same time being punctuated by the harsh, repetitive clang of a double bell wielded muscularly and with assurance by a fit young adept who stood stripped to the waist beside them. As the music peaked in volume and intensity Ti-Charles struck the ground three times with his *asson*, flamboyant, stylised blows. And then, abruptly, there was silence.

The *lwa* had been welcomed. Contact had been made.

Ti-Charles got to his feet and went back to his seat and sat down. There was a heavy, palpitant expectancy hanging in the air. In the distance the throaty roar of a motorbike engine became faintly audible above the cicada song: Sudra was returning from Sous-L'Eau. Ti-Charles noticed Faustin among the villagers shooting an excited look in the direction of the sound, along the path to Croix-Le-Bois, up which Sudra would certainly be speeding in a couple of minutes' time. Faustin was wearing a gold-coloured shirt and tight black trousers that hugged his crotch and butt, and looked glossily handsome. In one hand he held a small bottle of perfume, a gift no doubt for his *met-tête-lwa*, Ezulie, goddess of love. It glinted in the lamplight. Ti-Charles found himself wishing the shaven-headed, lovestruck Faustin well in his quest to win the battered, handsome constable's heart.

Bertrand Laverre turned away from Faustin sharply, adjusting the angle of his broad-brimmed straw hat to conceal his face from him as Faustin looked round in the direction of the *oufo*'s gates. If Faustin saw Bertrand there and recognised him, he would know immediately that Bertrand was up to no good, and the aspirant *bokor* would almost certainly be done for. Or would I? Bertrand asked himself, suddenly thoughtful. After all, Faustin had consulted the *bokor* in the old Sonnelier house, and that was not a fact he would want broadcast to the rest of the village, or to his * oungan*. Perhaps he could be counted on to keep quiet even if he did recognise Bertrand. Perhaps he could even be pressed into helping Bertrand in his mission as the price of Bertrand's silence . . .

But no, not for this. Buying a charm to beguile a sweetheart was one thing; cold-blooded, premeditated murder was another.

Murder. Bertrand was sweating profusely. The small bottle of poison hung on a leather loop loosely around his left wrist, the glass warm and smooth against his pulse. How much did he want to become a *bokor* if it really came to it? Enough to do this? Yes. Oh, yes. To transform the world and bend it to his will excited him more than transforming himself through rapport with the *lwa*, sorcery setting itself against Voodoo as religion.

The silence stretched and solidified unbearably.

It was broken after what had been only a couple of minutes, but had felt like hours to everyone there, by Ti-Charles ringing a handbell sharply. The waiting crowd exhaled in one audible gasp of relief and the drumming began again immediately, quickly building in intensity, sweat breaking out on the foreheads of the three drummers as they pounded the taut skins of the elaborately painted and ritually consecrated drums with supple, fast-moving palms, generating elaborate, crisscrossing rhythms.

The *ounsis* began to dance, turning this way and that in formation with each other, following the music with carefully rehearsed but passionately vigorous movements, raising their voices in harmonic response to Ti-Charles's throaty calling out, sweat breaking out on their dark, bare torsos as they danced around the elaborate *poteau-mitain* through which the *lwa* would be conducted to the feast, obliterating the *veves* Ti-Charles had laid out so carefully earlier on with the soles of their stamping feet. They were all young men. It was unusual for the initiates of an *oufo* to be exclusively male, but the villagers of Croix-Le-Bois understood that Ti-Charles, their *oungan*, was *massissi*, was attracted to the same sex, and had been married to both Baron Limba and Baron Lundi when he was seventeen. He was now twenty-five, and, since he was a good priest and a healer, no one had any objection to his choice of initiates. Besides, if his choices had been wrong, would not the *lwa* have spoken and made it clear? Instead they blessed their *serviteurs* with their wisdom and good fortune: Croix-Le-Bois was peaceful, and, although life was hard, all were good-hearted, and none went hungry there.

The villagers now began to dance, too, moving forward with their offerings and mingling with the *ounsis* in the peristyle, advancing to the sacred post and placing gifts and platters of food at its base, the ingredients carefully chosen to please the *lwa* each villager hoped to consult, or gain favours from, or be ridden by. There was brandy and unrefined sugar for Azaka, the *lwa* of farming; there were black cockerels for the *Ghedes*; a red cockerel for Ogoun Feraille, *lwa* of blacksmiths; and Henri Biassou came forward with a bottle of champagne for Agwe, the spirit of the ocean, pumping his muscular thighs and narrow hips as he popped the cork and poured the frothing, guttering contents over the base of the *poteau-mitain* among the other offerings, the luxurious froth echoing sea foam as it guttered over the red earth, darkening it.

'*Maître* Agwe, with your sea-green eyes, keep us safe upon the sea,' Henri repeated as he offered the libation to his *met-tête-lwa*. 'Keep us safe and fill our nets.'

The offerings made, the tempo of the drumming increased, and the singing of the initiates built in intensity, as did the dancing of both *ounsis* and villagers, and the still air warmed. Now all the focus was on dance, on shifting the rhythms of the *serviteurs* until they came in harmony with the rhythms of the cosmos, brought the two sides of the mirror together in exact symmetry, and the *lwa* could arrive and feast. Sometimes this happened almost instantaneously, sometimes it took many hours.

It was up to Ti-Charles to set the tempo with his *asson*, to orchestrate the drumming, bell-ringing, chanting and dancing to produce the desired result. Sweat began to run down his temples and his bare, smooth chest as he swayed his butt from side to side and speeded things up. This reaching for harmony was entirely intuitive, based on feeling and practice and openness to the whims and ways of *Les Mystères*.

Sudra arrived, leaving his Harley Davidson outside the *oufo* and coming in on foot. He bore with him an embroidered fuschia-pink silk square, which he dedicated to Ezulie and placed at the foot of the *poteau-mitain* with a modest flourish, bobbing his shaven head as he did so. Then he went and found Faustin, who was dancing nervously among the other villagers, and kissed the shorter man confidently on the mouth. Then the two men danced together, hips grinding, eyes meeting eyes, lips parting breathlessly in their excited discovering of each other.

After he had made this deep connection with Faustin, Sudra kissed him lightly, broke off their embrace, and went over to Ti-Charles, who had temporarily retaken his seat. Sudra kissed the ground at Ti-Charles's feet, and then quickly told the *oungan* his news: he had managed to reach Sous-L'Eau in time to warn the *oungan* there that the military were on their way to break up the village's festival – passing the army truck on his way where it had fortuitously bounced into a ditch, and was being laboriously dragged out of it by the sweaty, irritated-looking soldiers who had been riding inside it. The believers of Sous-L'Eau had therefore been forced to postpone their service, but at least there had been no arrests or vandalisation of the *oufo*, and the already

179

tired soldiers would all be bogged down in their search for a ceremony that, since it wasn't happening, couldn't be found.

All this Sudra told to Ti-Charles without Ti-Charles once breaking the rhythm he was setting for the drummers with his *asson*. The *oungan* just nodded, feeling sympathy for the faithful of Sous-L'Eau, and gratitude for the protection the *lwa* had extended to his own *oufo* through the attention and dedication of his *serviteurs* Antoine, Ti-Coyo, Bossuet and Pierre, who now danced passionately with the rest of them.

After an initial period of unease, the four soldiers whom Antoine and his friends had brought to the *mange-lwa* began to join in with the dancing, moving only a little at first, uncertain of what was appropriate, not wanting in some unknown way to give offence, but then gradually they became freer in their movements, and warmer, and more a part of what was going on and, as they did so, they found themselves slipping slowly from being mere onlookers to becoming genuine participants. The feeling was not unpleasant.

The intensity of the atmosphere increased, the drumming filling the air until it was solid with sound, the dancing building frenziedly, building, building in the crystallised blood heat until the blood was pounding through the veins, the ears of everyone there. The trees, the stones, the earth and all animal and vegetative life became suddenly acutely sentient; everything became compellingly interlocked, connected, and energy came flooding down from the sky and up from the ground into the brightly painted *poteau-mitain* around which the *ounsis* and the villagers danced ecstatically.

The lanky, dark-skinned and slightly fey young private Dany Dutilleul had become completely caught up in the ceremony by this point, shiny with sweat and exuberant as he threw his lean body around to the passionate, consuming pounding of the drums. To the shock of his comrades also dancing sweatily and excitedly alongside him, he suddenly arched up on tiptoe, eyes rolling up into the back of his head, and started to fall backwards.

Immediately two *ounsis*, one of them Pierre, were on either side of him. They caught hold of the young soldier and spun him rapidly around three times, then lowered him carefully on to the ground.

'What is happening, man?' Sergeant Jestin asked Pierre worriedly, having to shout above the din of drums and clanging bells.

'He is being ridden by one of the *lwa*,' Pierre said. 'He is their horse. It is a great privilege for one new to *Les Mystères*.'

'Which one rides him?' Jestin asked, aware of his own ignorance of the Voodoo mysteries and their powers and natures, their dangerous reality.

'We shall see who rides, man,' Ti-Charles said, coming up quickly with his hissing *asson* to where Dany writhed and convulsed on the ground: the minute he had seen the young man that evening, Ti-Charles had known the *lwa* would favour him. He passed the *asson* over Dany's body several times in quick succession, and Dany became still. Then, eyes still rolled up in his head, he got to his feet and started to sway rhythmically towards the *poteau-mitain*. As he danced, moving his narrow hips and shaking his big butt invitingly, he let his white blouson shirt slip off one shoulder. Then he glanced back over this bare shoulder at Ti-Charles and the other soldiers and smiled flirtatiously at them, his dark eyes now normal, if somehow shallower than usual.

'Ezulie, the *lwa* of love, *maître*,' Pierre said to Ti-Charles.

Ti-Charles nodded, keeping his *asson* moving to keep control of the tempo of the ceremony, even though he had great trust in the ability and sensitivity of his drummers, particularly Sauveur. He moved back under the banana-leaf roof of the peristyle and took his seat again, watching the possessed young man carefully.

Dany made his way to the *poteau-mitain* and helped himself to a roast chicken leg. Then he took a bottle of perfume that a worshipper had left there – Faustin, in fact – and dabbed it on his wrists and just under his jawline on either side of his neck. He turned with a light, pretty and uninhibited laugh. The villagers and *ounsis* kept dancing, but their attention was all on their doubly unexpected visitor.

Still dancing and swaying his hips, Dany made his way Antoine. The two men moved together, hip to hip, grinding their pelvises against each other, erections clearly visible in their over to breeches. Dany kissed Antoine hotly on the mouth, then tipped his head back, stretching his sinewy, sinuous throat.

'I need you in my marriage bed,' the young soldier said, gazing up at the woven roof of the peristyle, and everyone present knew immediately that it was Ezulie who was speaking, not Dany. 'I need you to make your vows to me as you promised you would.'

'I will make those vows, Ezulie,' Antoine said breathlessly.

'You will make for me a room here in the *oufo* and drape it with fine things,' Dany-Ezulie said, his head still tilted back. 'You will sleep in that room in my bed every Thursday night, and on that day you will be intimate with no one. On other days you may do as you please – but with men only.' Here Dany's voice was sharp. 'No women. And you must save your heart for me.'

'I have no desire for women and my heart was always saved for you, Ezulie,' Antoine said with sincerity. 'How soon must I make these vows?'

'Before the end of the year,' Dany said. Then he turned and looked intently at Sudra and Faustin, who naturally had been watching his performance with Antoine with great interest. Dany's eyes sparkled.

'Love each other,' Dany said to the two breathlessly waiting men. Then his eyes rolled up in his head again and he slumped to the ground, unconscious, half held up by Pierre and another *ounsi*. The two of them carried the delirious young soldier off to one of a number of straw pallets that had been set up beside the peristyle for just such a purpose. One stayed by him, holding his hand as he drifted out of the possessed state.

It was while all this had been going on that Bertrand Laverre had seized his chance: while Ti-Charles had been examining Dany, the would-be *bokor* had stolen round behind the *oungan*'s chair, and emptied the small bottle of poison into the basin of water that had been placed beside it for Ti-Charles to refresh himself from as the *mange-lwa* proceeded. Then Bertrand backed away quickly and slid round behind one of the groups of villagers watching Dany.

I should leave immediately, Bertrand thought, his heart hammering in his chest, his eyes darting around at the other people in the peristyle, his mouth cotton-dry. Although Dany's possession had provided him with the ideal opportunity to poison Ti-Charles's drinking water, the fact that the *lwa* were arriving at the *oufo* put Bertrand in great danger of being exposed: nothing is hidden from *Les Mystères*, and who could tell which arriving spirit might choose to expose him to the wrath and judgement of the community?

Still the drums held Bertrand, and, besides, it would be very hard to leave now without being noticed. He would have to wait for some other event to enable him to slip away unseen – provided it was before Ti-Charles took a drink from the water in the bowl.

And yet, and yet . . . Looking at Ti-Charles – the handsome, dark-skinned and lean-bodied young *oungan* of Croix-Le-Bois, in his tight white breeches, the now darkly stained red headscarf covering his dreads, his bright, wise brown eyes and his large, handsome-pretty features – moving his *asson*, guiding the *serviteurs*, channelling the *lwa*, Bertrand wavered. Why had he left all this? What had he gained by abandoning his devotion to the *lwa* to serve the ends of power and sorcery? There was something good here that he had not found in Solaville, or with the Zoboyo, something that only having gone away allowed him really, finally, to see. Suddenly he felt like Jean Lamartine's fool, realising that he had been the plaything of the *bokor* for all this time, and nothing more. Jean Lamartine would never tell Bertrand all his secrets. Why had he ever expected him to? Instead he would bind Bertrand to him ever more tightly by threatening to expose the dark things that Bertrand had done to please him, the shameful things no one would want known that they had done. Bertrand would be as helpless as the zombies that toiled in the canefields around the old Sonnelier house.

But perhaps Ti-Charles could protect him. Not from being shamed, of course, if Jean Lamartine chose to broadcast what Bertrand had done around the neighbourhood, but from the wrath of the *bokor* – from malign spells and curses, and from *baka* and malevolently directed *lwa*. Yes, Ti-Charles *could* do that, Bertrand knew: he was a true servant of *Les Mystères*. But would he? For Bertrand? Perhaps. Just perhaps . . . The thought of being free of Jean Lamartine soared up through the light-skinned young man's chest and he felt fearful and empowered at the same instant. He knew that if he was going to do anything to set himself free, now was the moment. He felt *les invisibles* crowding all around him, pressing in on him.

Looking round in search of Ti-Charles, Bertrand saw that he was seated in his ceremonial chair again. He seemed incredibly beautiful to Bertrand then, his skin as shiny and flawless as carved jet. Ti-Charles looked down beside him and picked up a cup, which he dipped into the bowl of water next to the chair. The pounding of the drums moved to a new level of intensity and the chanting rose up to fill the compressed dome of the sky.

Seven

Bertrand leaped forward and, with the rapidity of a snake striking, dashed the cup from Ti-Charles's hand, sending it flying across the peristyle. The drumming stopped abruptly as everyone looked round in surprise, and the chanting of the *ounsis* faltered and fell silent.

The young man in the broad-brimmed straw hat spun round with wild eyes like a hunted animal at bay. A susurrus of recognition passed through the villagers: *Bertrand Laverre*. For a second it looked as if he was going to try to run, and most likely no one would have tried to stop him, since why he had done what he had done was still unclear. Instead, after a moment, he dropped to his knees before Ti-Charles, and kissed the ground at the *oungan*'s feet. He remained bent over there until Ti-Charles touched his shoulder and gestured to him to squat back on his heels so they could speak.

A hubbub of conversation was breaking out now among the villagers and some of the *ounsis*. Ti-Charles gestured for them to be quiet, and brought his gaze to bear on Bertrand.

'*Maître*, give me your protection, I beg you,' Bertrand said in a hoarse, fear-filled voice, looking up at Ti-Charles with wide, frightened eyes.

'From what, Bertrand Laverre?'

'From the *bokor* in the old plantation house.'

'And why do you most especially need protection?'

Bertrand looked down at the ground. 'Because I have had dealings with him, *maître*,' he said in a tremulous voice. There were gasps from the people watching the conversation.

'I know,' Ti-Charles said softly.

Bertrand was surprised for a moment. How? But then he thought, From Faustin, of course.

Ti-Charles exhaled thoughtfully. Then he took a *wanga* packet from around his own neck, removed Bertrand's broad-brimmed straw hat, and put the charm on its leather thong over Bertrand's inclined head. Bertrand tucked it inside his shirt wordlessly. Reaching down for a rum bottle that sat next to the poisoned basin of water, Ti-Charles took a swig from it, and blew a mist of the cooling alcohol over Bertrand's now upturned face. Something passed between them.

'You know what you have to do, man,' he said to the kneeling youth.

'Yes, *maître*,' Bertrand replied. 'But then – can I be forgiven?'

'There are many debts you must repay, to *les mortes* and *Les Mystères*, as well as to the living,' Ti-Charles said, shrugging. 'I don't know. I'll help you, man, so long as you're serving and not dealing.' He twisted round in his chair and tipped the poisoned contents of the bowl by him out on to the ground. 'Now go.'

Bertrand struggled to his feet. 'Yes, *maître*,' he said, bowing to Ti-Charles tightly. Then he turned and, without meeting the eyes of anyone else there, hurried bareheaded out of the *oufo*, pausing only to catch up an oil lamp as he went: the night was dark now, and he had another need for it.

The villagers and *ounsis* watched him go, staring after him until the light of his lamp was swallowed by the trees. Then Ti-Charles gestured to Sauveur with his *asson* and the drummer started to build up the rhythms again, more quickly this time, re-establishing contact with the waiting *lwa*.

The heat within the peristyle increased until all the dancing *serviteurs* were sweating heavily, and the air was musky with their scent. The pounding drumbeats pulled at them, connecting them viscerally with the earth and tugging them upwards towards the spiritual at the same time. Around Ti-Charles one *ounsi*, then another, became possessed, and was spun and helped to the ground by his fellows. Ti-Charles left his chair and went over to the 'horses' to make sure they were not being ridden too hard, or had been entered by uninvited *lwa*. Satisfied, he returned to his seat. The air grew heavier and heavier and the sound of the drumming, punctuated by the sharp clacks of the double bell, denser and denser. In a loud, throaty voice Ti-Charles called out, 'Baron Lundi, Baron Limba, come! Come!' And the *ounsis* responded, echoing his words in strong chorus: 'Baron Lundi, Baron Limba, come!'

Holding the oil lantern up before him to light his way, Bertrand Laverre hurried along the path that led away from the *oufo* towards Croix-Le-Bois. Conflicting thoughts circled and bumped around his head like the large yellow-white moths that were gathering thickly around the lantern's light, and he was sweating profusely. Fear was uppermost in his mind, but offsetting that was a determination to try somehow to make things right, to get off the path he had found himself on, and make reparations for the wrong he had done to so many people, and to *Les Mystères*.

Bertrand's fear had two sides: on the one hand there was his concern at the physical harm Jean Lamartine and the Zoboyo would try to do him when they realised he had deserted and betrayed them – and who was to say they did not have some agent at the *oufo* unknown to him, observing his actions, that they did not already know of his betrayal? – and on the other was his dread of the power of sorcery and the wrath of the *lwa* he had sought to control.

These fears fused in the single threat that Jean Lamartine had made to him in the old plantation house: 'If you do not kill Ti-Charles, it will be you who labours in the cane fields by night.' *Zombification*. He did not want his soul, his *gros-bon-ange*, captured by Jean Lamartine and his body set to toil in endless, brainless slavery.

Bertrand fingered the *wanga* packet that hung around his neck.

187

It gave him some reassurance, but still, how did the old saying go? 'The *oungan* may give you a protective charm but he won't tell you to lie down in the middle of the road to prove that it works.' And wasn't that exactly what he was going to do now?

Too late to change his mind: there was no escape from his destiny. Bertrand's chest was cramped with anxiety, and his sense of rising dread was heightened by the alarmingly flickering shadows the lamplight cast through the trees and undergrowth. The shifting, fluid black shapes set the light-skinned young man imagining that scuttling *baka* had already been dispatched by the *bokor* in the old Sonnelier house to torture, maim or murder him. Sometimes the light felt more like a beacon betraying his position to his enemy, than a help on his way. Still, it speeded his journey and so he kept it lit, although he knew he would have to snuff it out once he came within sight of the plantation house and, if he was wise, sometime before then.

Despite his fears, Ti-Charles's forgiveness had given Bertrand some heart, and made him realise that escape from his situation was possible, and it was the knowledge of that possibility that gave him the courage to keep on going, even though he was alone and weaponless.

Soon he reached the place where a narrower, slightly over-grown track branched off the main path to the east. Little used for many years, it arched through orange and laurel groves across the steeply rising slopes above the village, and headed off slantwise in the direction of the Sonnelier estate in the next valley. He took it after a momentary hesitation, his heart hammering in his chest.

Bertrand's mind was curiously blank concerning what he intended to do when he reached the old plantation house. Confront Jean Lamartine? What would that mean? What could it achieve, if he was honest about it? What would he have to do in order to confront him? Would it come to violence? Would he have to try to kill the *bokor*? If it came to that, it was more likely that the *bokor* would kill *him*: Bertrand knew from personal experience that Jean Lamartine was capable of killing given the slightest provocation, and apparently without the slightest prick of conscience or remorse afterwards. But, even if Bertrand somehow got the better of him, what would he do then? Liberate the trapped souls and the toiling zombies? Perhaps gain some upper hand by means of which he could threaten the *bokor* and force him to leave the inhabitants of Croix-Le-Bois alone without having to kill him?

What if there were other members of the Zoboyo there?

He set his face, and extinguished the lamp.

Immediately, he became aware of the star-filled night sky above him. He stopped for a moment and listened intently. Very faintly he could hear the distant drumming from inside the *oufo*, and the ringing of handbells. The sound of it gave him heart, somehow: perhaps now he was renouncing sorcery, the *lwa* would aid him, or at least not obstruct him in what he was trying to do.

'Cousin Azaka, you are my *met-tête-lwa*, you are my inheritance,' Bertrand prayed softly. 'My father was a farmer, my grandfather was a farmer, and they honoured you, Azaka. I ignored their wishes and your guidance because I thought I saw something in the city that was more wonderful than your simple wisdom. And now I have discovered that what I saw was gaudy and false in heart. So forgive me, Cousin Azaka. From today I will honour you, if I survive. I will give you corn and brandy –'

Something touched Bertrand's bare foot and he looked down with a start. A small lizard, pale green in the starlight, darted in front of him, its long tail flicking dryly over his toes. The lizard was a mabouya, which is a symbol of Azaka's. It disappeared into the shadows of the grass by the path.

For the first time since he had set off, Bertrand felt a surge of real hope.

Soon he was passing through the severely neglected outlying cane fields that fringed the Sonnelier estate. The path ran straight here, walled in by the cane on either side, and disappearing into inky obscurity in either direction. A slight breeze off the sea set the dry cane leaves whispering, and Bertrand felt his nerve draining away again. A strong sense that he was being watched came over him, even though the plantation house was not yet in view. Every sense – hearing, sight, touch, even smell – was heightened out here, and he became intensely aware of the thudding of his own blood against his eardrums.

Then, very faintly and some way off ahead of him, he heard the sound of hoes tilling soil. This meant that Jean Lamartine, at least, was certainly in. Bertrand moved forward with determination, and a few minutes later took a curving, grass-grown path that brought him within sight of the old Sonnelier mansion, its vastly rising and decaying black bulk no longer energised for him with secrets and intoxicating mysteries, only heavy with dread and horror. He could hear slow, methodical digging on either side of him now, getting closer. How many are out there now? he wondered. Repressing a shudder, he kept on going, and soon the unseen toilers were left behind him, although the grandly porticoed front of the mouldering plantation house loomed larger and larger ahead.

Normally Bertrand would have walked up the drive and approached the sagging front doors of the delapidated mansion quite openly, but not tonight: tonight he slipped off the broadening, weedy gravel path as soon as he could, taking cover in a small walled orchard that abutted the family cemetery plot on the west side of the house. The leafy branches of the unpruned apple and pear trees formed a thick tangle of rough black limbs overhead that no eye could easily penetrate. The wall nearest to the house was tumbledown, so Bertrand had no trouble climbing through it into the little family graveyard beyond.

The stones in the small cemetery had tilted with time, their surfaces eaten away by lichen and the sun and wind and rain: no one honoured these dead. No one claimed their souls back from the watery place *là-bas*. They were not fed and they had no wisdom to give. No strength. The Sonneliers were silenced for ever, and that was just.

Bertrand made his way forward, using the ornately carved slabs and slanting, angel-surmounted vaults as shelter from the staring black windows of the house. Soon he was pressed up against the peeling clapboard of the long wall of the west wing. He knew he could reach the front doors from where he was without being seen by any watcher within. Not that there was any particular reason to believe that anyone would be watching, but still . . . It was just possible that Jean Lamartine might be keeping a lookout for him, to hear that Bertrand had carried out his orders successfully.

Keeping his back pressed against the west wall of the house, Bertrand slid along it in the direction of the front doors. He had to duck down repeatedly under the sills of the tall windows that looked out westwards from the spacious, lofty and once-glittering salon within. One window towards the end of the wall, rather smaller than the rest, gaped permanently open now, its glass gone, its shutters fallen, its frame termite-devoured and collapsed. To increase his chance of surprising the *bokor* and whoever else might be in the house, Bertrand decided to clamber in through this window rather than enter by the front door, as he had initially planned.

Holding his breath and taking great care, Bertrand swung himself over the sill and into the unlit room beyond. He had been in this room many times and knew it well, even in the dark, but somehow tonight it was different: tonight it was a battleground.

He moved as noiselessly as possible across the rotting floorboards, feeling his way carefully with bare feet, and crossed to the passage leading to the servants' stairs. This was now the only way up to the first floor, the main staircase in all its sweeping, balustraded glory having long since collapsed in a heap of rubble into the marble-floored hall below. A minute later Bertrand was standing outside the door that led into the *bokor's* suite of rooms. He stifled the impulse to knock, to seek permission to enter from this man he feared so intensely. His heart was hammering in his chest as he gripped the brass doorknob in his sweaty hand and began to turn it as slowly as he could.

It had been oiled, and it turned silently. He exhaled with relief.

Bertrand pushed the door open an inch at a time. It squeaked on its hinges, but not loudly. He squeezed through the gap and found himself in a small anteroom into which a little starlight filtered through a grimy skylight high above. The entrance to the larger room beyond, where Bertrand knew the *bokor* had set up his altar, had a heavy black cloth hung across it, and no door.

Holding his breath, Bertrand lifted the curtain carefully and peered through.

A lit oil lamp and a row of candles burned among the human skulls and bones, shovels, crosses and other objects on the altar. The coffin from which the *bokor* had produced the zombified body of the farmer Bertrand had poisoned was gone. The tall windows were all hung with black drapes that shut out sun, moon and stars. At the back of the room was a shrine made up of twine-wound dolls hung upside down, inverted crosses, human skulls, and a number of clay pots and sealed bottles containing the stolen spirits of the zombies who toiled outside, and perhaps other spirits as well. The room smelled of candlewax and stale blood. From somewhere in the darkness beyond the glow of light Bertrand could hear panting and moaning.

Curious, he pushed the curtain aside and stepped into the room, still taking care to move as silently as possible. Peering into the shadows the candlelight failed to disperse, he became aware of a low camp bed in an alcove on which two figures were moving. Keeping out of the light himself, Bertrand moved forward around the edge of the room to get a closer look at what was going on.

There were two men on the bed, naked and sweaty, both face down, one on top of the other, fucking him. The man fucking was the *bokor* Jean Lamartine. The man being fucked was Bertrand's friend Auguste. Auguste, who had warned him against Jean Lamartine and the Zoboyo. Bertrand's jaw dropped and he had to cover his mouth with his hand to stifle his gasp of surprise. Although he was otherwise nude, Auguste's bowler hat was still glued firmly on to his shaved head as he pushed his beefy brown arse up and back for the *bokor*'s pleasure.

'Fuck my arse, *maître*!' Auguste gasped. 'Fuck my arse and tell me your secrets! I give you my body, *maître*. Give me your knowledge. Take me and ride me and give me power!'

Jean Lamartine pumped his greasy cock in and out of Auguste's curvaceous, upturned arse with muscular enthusiasm, bracing himself up on the shorter, younger man's broad shoulders with both hands. Auguste grunted sharply with each rough thrust of the *bokor*'s throbbing rigidity into his aching anal cavity.

'Yes, *maître*! Yes, *maître*! Yes, *maître*! Use me, *Maître* Lamartine,' he begged breathlessly.

'You love my cock, Auguste? You love my cock up your arse?' Jean Lamartine demanded hoarsely, slamming his hips against the firm chocolate-brown globes of Auguste's arse so hard the slapping of flesh against flesh sounded like a whip crack, his cock head ramming deep into Auguste's back passage.

'Oh, yes, *maître*,' Auguste groaned throatily, his eyes screwed shut, his face being pushed into a black silk pillow by the force of Jean Lamartine's hands on his shoulders. 'Give me your secrets, *maître*,' he moaned. 'Tell me the dark things you know –'

Anger flushed up through Bertrand then, both at Auguste, his supposed friend, and at the sight of the *bokor* taking advantage of another foolish young man to whom he would never give his secret knowledge: why should he? He was getting everything he wanted from Auguste without doing so, just as he had taken everything he wanted from Bertrand already. Bertrand stepped forward, silhouetted by the light of the candles and the oil lamp on the altar, casting a deepening shadow over the two men on the camp bed.

'He will never tell you, man,' he said to Auguste, his voice loud but strangled. 'He will use you and make you do terrible things, but he will never tell you.'

Auguste looked round, confused and alarmed by Bertrand's sudden appearance, not recognising him at first. Jean Lamartine's cock was pushed all the way up his arse, his own throbbing dick was rammed painfully into the thin mattress, and waves of ecstasy were ebbing and flowing through his aching, suddenly terribly vulnerable body as he squinted up at Bertrand.

But, if Auguste was paralysed with shock and surprise, the *bokor* was not. His eyes fixed on Bertrand's, naked and gleaming he slid backwards off Auguste's back in a single, sinuous movement, his stiff, greasy dick springing out of the younger man's slack, well-fucked arsehole with a softly audible pop as he did so. Shaven-headed and -bodied and slick with sweat and curvaceously muscular, Jean Lamartine moved as fast as a snake, bending down and twisting round to snatch up a machete from the tangled pile

193

of his and Auguste's discarded clothes that Bertrand hadn't noticed in the dark. Bertrand's eyes widened: he had no weapon.

'Ah,' Jean Lamartine exhaled, brandishing the heavy, rusty blade in Bertrand's direction, his wide eyes dark and flat and lightless, his large teeth bared ferally. 'So you're betraying me, man?' He tilted his head in a grotesque parody of a beguiling look and pulled his blade arm back. His mouth was twisted up into a grotesque smile. 'You're plotting treachery against me? Against *me*?'

'I want to be free of you, man.' Bertrand's voice caught in his throat as he groped for defiance.

'Too late!' the *bokor* snarled. And he rushed at Bertrand, slashing at him with the machete with frenzied malevolence. Bertrand stumbled back in alarm, tripped and half fell against the altar behind him, scattering and snuffing out candles and clattering, shattering skulls. Bertrand's hand closed around the handle of one of the shovels that had been laid out crossways on the altar, and he brought it up fast to fend off Jean Lamartine's machete blade as the *bokor* brought it down towards Bertrand's head.

Metal clanged flatly against metal as Bertrand defended himself, struggling to his feet as the *bokor* chopped at him repeatedly. Behind him, Auguste, eyes wide with fear, was pulling on a pair of tight black leather shorts cut very low on the hips, and wriggling his feet into a pair of patent-leather army boots.

Keep an eye on him, Bertrand thought.

Jean Lamartine then brought the machete down on Bertrand's shovel so hard that it snapped the end clean off. But that strike was his undoing: the momentum of his swing sent him stumbling forward, his shaved head thumping into Bertrand's bare chest. Bertrand twisted round fast and shoved the overbalanced *bokor* face down on to the floor. The machete went skittering out of his hand and into the shadows. Jean Lamartine darted after it, but in doing so opened himself to being hit repeatedly over the head by Bertrand with the handle of his shovel.

Blood ran down over the *bokor*'s scalp as Bertrand got two good cracks in, but he had his blade again, and he turned as quickly as ever, jumping to his feet. His face, lit from below by the oil lamp, looked skull-like and macabre as blood libated it.

Cousin Azaka, *aidez-moi*, Bertrand thought alarmedly. Azaka, help me now. He gripped the handle end of the broken shovel tightly in his fist and jabbed at Jean Lamartine as the *bokor* advanced on him, the machete held back, looking to strike the killer blow. Bertrand circled backwards, keeping away from him, glancing around the room for something that might help him, that might make a better weapon, making sure that Auguste wasn't about to attack him from behind.

'There's nowhere to run to, Bertrand Laverre,' the *bokor* said, smiling a malignant smile. 'Run out of this room, and wherever you go, the Zoboyo will be waiting,' he hissed, crouching to spring. 'You will end your days in the canefields outside –'

Just as Jean Lamartine was about to throw himself forward, Auguste stepped over to the altar, caught up the still-burning oil lamp and flung it with all the strength he could at the shrine that stood in the corner of the room. The lamp shattered and exploded in a ball of fire, and a burning carpet of spreading oil ran out from it in all directions.

'No!' The *bokor* turned in horror, then turned on Auguste in a rage, waving the machete at him. 'Another traitor,' he said in a low, ugly voice. 'I will cut you to ribbons and feed you to my *baka*!' Weaponless and bug-eyed, Auguste cowered back.

Bertrand seized his moment, rushing forward and slamming into the *bokor* with the weight of his whole body, sending Jean Lamartine's machete flying, and sending the man himself stagger-ing back into the furiously burning shrine. The elaborately piled and displayed objects collapsed inwards under his weight and he disappeared from sight, a writhing, struggling, shrieking darkness at its heart.

Bertrand and Auguste watched the scene in horror. As they stood there, sparks flying upwards from the flaming shrine began to catch on the hanging black fabric that covered the windows. All the wood in the place was severely dessicated and the floorboards were crackling and popping already. Smoke from the rapidly growing fire was billowing up towards the ceiling.

'Come on, man,' Bertrand said, catching Auguste's hand, and they hurried from the room and down the servants' stairs. There was no need for care or silence now. A few seconds later they were running down the cracked marble steps at the front of the old mansion and on to the broad sweep of its once-elegant carriageway. Never letting go of each other's hand, the two young men kept on running.

Only once they were a mile away or more did they stop and look back.

The Sonnelier place was going up like a tinderbox, the west side lit up red and orange, flames streaming from the windows, the east side belching thick black smoke in preparation for combustion. An intense sense of freedom welled up inside Bertrand's chest as he watched the *bokor*'s residence burn.

After some time he turned and looked at Auguste.

'Why did you do that, man?' he asked him. 'I thought that you were going to attack me, and that I was truly done for.'

Auguste's face was impassive. He was still gazing at the fire. 'Someone dear to me,' he began awkwardly, his voice catching in his throat. 'He died. And I heard, later on, that he had been poisoned. That he had been made into a zombie by Jean Lamartine.'

Auguste looked at Bertrand then. 'I had to find out where he was, man. Where the *bokor* was keeping his *gros-bon-ange*. So I could set it free. And the only way I could do that was pretend I wanted to become his student. Like you, only you were not pretending.'

Bertrand looked down, ashamed. 'I have learned better since, man.'

Auguste shrugged. 'That is something.' He exhaled. 'It was only tonight that he consented to show me where he kept all the spirits he had imprisoned. He thought that keeping them here, far from Solaville, they would not be discovered by his enemies.'

'So you threw the oil?'

'Yes. I think now my friend is free.'

Hand in hand, they watched the mansion burn. A slight breeze fanned the flames. When the east wing had collapsed in on itself in a fiery heap of rubble, they turned away from the sight and began to walk slowly back towards the *oufo* of Croix-Le-Bois.

Back at the *oufo*, and totally unaware of what was going on at the old Sonnelier place, the drumming and chanting in the peristyle built in intensity like waves of solid sound crashing against the shore of the believers' psyches as they honoured the *lwa*. Sauveur and Petro ran with sweat, their every muscle aching as they pounded their palms on the taut leather drum skins, building the rhythms that brought the physical and spirit worlds into harmony and permitted contact and interpenetration at the deepest, profoundest level. The double bell clacked insistently, and the rhythms were pierced and pointed up by the sudden, repeated ringing of a handbell as those *serviteurs* being ridden by *Les Mystères* writhed on the ground, transported to a place beyond ecstasy as the *lwa* honoured them.

Ti-Charles hurried about the peristyle, watching over the possessed, making sure they did not injure themselves as the *lwa* took charge of them, observing them to see which spirit they were manifesting by their speech and actions, and by which props they chose to symbolise that manifestation – a crutch for Legba, say, or a *macoute* straw sack for Azaka – as well as making sure that only invited *lwa* arrived and rode, tactfully dismissing any that were uninvited with promises that they would be honoured at a future date. At the same time he kept the tempo of the service building both musically and psychologically. Ti-Charles turned to face the *poteau-mitain* in the middle of the peristyle and threw his arms wide.

'Baron Lundi, come! Baron Limba, come!' he called out in a loud, throaty voice, shaking his *asson* so fast it was a hissing orangey-red blur in his hand.

Now Ti-Charles's sweetheart Henri Biassou was dancing before the richly painted *poteau-mitain*, undulating his lean, narrow hips against it, his head tilting backwards, his lips parted, his eyes closed, totally caught up in the music, in the ecstatic, transcendental moment.

'Baron Lundi, Baron Limba, come! Come!' the handsome

young *ounsis* responded passionately, tossing their heads and pounding their bare feet on the impacted earth as the villagers danced among them, sweat streaming down their bodies.

And suddenly the spirit was moving into Henri Biassou; he tossed his head back, eyes rolling, pelvis thrusting, *gros-bon-ange* displaced, every sinew in his dark, lean, muscular body straining as he arched up on the balls of his feet and began to fall slowly backwards. But the *hounsis* were there to catch him before he could fall to the ground and injure himself, bearing him upright and away from the centre of the peristyle, kicking and convulsing, cock thrusting to visible instant erectness in his breeches, straw hat tumbling off his shaved, white-headscarfed skull.

Ti-Charles jumped to his feet excitedly, and was about to hurry forward, both to make sure that Henri wasn't being harmed by the *lwa* that had entered him, and out of strong curiosity about which *lwa* it was. But, before Ti-Charles could make his way through the dancing *serviteurs* to where Henri lay moving restlessly, the muscular fisherman had jumped up and strode over to the *poteau-mitain*. From its base he took certain ritual garments, the clothing appropriate to the *lwa* that was riding him, and pulled them on. Then a moment later Henri was dancing forward, wearing an undertaker's battered black top hat, dark glasses with a lens missing fom one eye, and a purple neckerchief tied around his sinew-corded neck, his torso mocha-brown and hard and defined, glossy with sweat, small nipples erect on the domes of his chest, waist liquid. And he came forward and took Ti-Charles's hand as he had before at other ceremonies and led the young *oungan* into the heart of the dancing throng, and Ti-Charles shook his *asson* above the two of them like a benison as the two men ground their crotches together, each straddling the other's thigh, rigid cocks erect and straining against the tight white cotton of their breeches. Ti-Charles gazed into Henri's one mirror lens and saw his own large eyes, his own full lips slightly parted with desire. Henri's other eye was shallow as glass, unreadable.

'Who are you?' Ti-Charles whispered under the pounding of the drums, his voice throaty with fear and desire.

'Baron Samedi,' Henri said in a hoarse, nasal voice. And he threw back his head and laughed a full, rasping laugh, reaching out with strong fingers for Ti-Charles's flatly muscled chest and gripping one of Ti-Charles's protuberant, bullet-shaped nipples brazenly in front of the entire village. 'My *massissi* brother *Ghedes* sent me, so I come. And I want you.'

'Are you mocking me?' Ti-Charles asked breathlessly, arsehole clenching and unclenching, dick shaft aching, glans throbbing, knowing all too well the *lwa*'s reputation for practical jokes and provocative behaviour.

'No, man. I do not mock you. I give you what you want.' And Henri slid a hand down the back of Ti-Charles's tight white shorts in front of the whole celebrating village, pressing a long, strong finger against Ti-Charles's receptive sphincter. 'I want to mount you human-wise through the one you desire, the one you love. Ezulie sent me. Lundi sent me. Limba sent me. And tonight, man, tonight I must ride manstyle.'

The heat of Henri's body, the scent of cocoa butter on his smooth skin mingling with the background scents of the offerings of the food, of oil lamps and candles, eucalyptus and orange blossom, all intertwined sensually in Ti-Charles's nose. He was powerless to resist the needs of the *lwa*, and anyway they were his own needs also.

'Ride me, Baron,' he whispered breathlessly in Henri's ear.

'Come with me to my *kay-mystère*, man,' Baron Samedi said in answer. Then he swung the heavily erect and unresisting young *oungan* up into his arms and carried him through the parting crowd of initiates and villagers. Ti-Charles no longer cared: let them all see he was *massissi* without dispute. It was nothing they didn't already know. The drumming rose to a new height of intensity and the most senior of the *hounsis* stepped forward and led a fresh chant as Baron Samedi pushed the elaborately patterned black curtain at the entrance to his shrine aside with one elbow and carried Ti-Charles inside.

Within the *kay-mystère* the air was heavy, thick and still, scented with candle wax and heated to blood warmth by the the many candles that lit the interior of the small, whitewashed hut. There was a strange intensity of energy in there, like the pre-storm build-up of static before a violent downpour, even though the sky outside was clear. Baron Samedi laid Ti-Charles down gently in front of his altar, before plates of rice and goat curry, bottles of spirits, *wanga* packets, mirrors, candles, dolls wrapped in twine and hung upside down, the skeletons of snakes and a human skull.

Baron Samedi kissed Ti-Charles on the mouth, the taint of cigar smoke on his breath, pushing his strong, muscular tongue between Ti-Charles's full lips, the top hat still pushed down on the white bandana wrapped around his shaven, sweaty head, the sunglasses still covering one of his eyes, the other unrevealing. Ti-Charles wrapped his arms around the mounted Henri's strong, broad, well-muscled back, sliding his pink palms over smooth, hot, mocha-dark skin, sucking on Baron Samedi's probing tongue, gasping muffledly as the possessed Henri slid his hand down over Ti-Charles's lean, trembling stomach and began to massage his erection firmly through his skin-tight cotton breeches. Ti-Charles opened his thighs to give Baron Samedi's roving hand greater access to his balls and round between his legs to his buttocks and arsehole.

Tentatively – shy both of the young fisherman and the *lwa* possessing him – Ti-Charles slipped one hand round from Baron Samedi's broad back to his muscular chest, fumbling for a small, stiff nipple. Finding it, he elicited a groan of pleasure from the top-hatted young man bending over him, and he moved his hand down over Henri's ridged stomach and began to explore his full and rigid crotch.

Suddenly desperate to suck the possessed fisherman's cock, Ti-Charles broke the kiss and turned his head so it was pushed into Henri's bulging crotch. Baron Samedi arched back and pushed the bulky lump made by his his rigid dick and balls into Ti-Charles's face. Ti-Charles nuzzled the stiffness behind the well-washed fabric like a cat trying to get itself stroked, then pulled eagerly at the buttons of Henri's flies with nervous, fumbling fingers, getting them open, then tugging the tight breeches down over the mounted Henri's large, muscular butt and down over his smooth, well-shaped thighs to his knees. Baron Samedi's large, stiff, veiny cock sprang up, the dark, satiny foreskin sliding back to reveal its glistening, lighter-brown head. In its piss slit a drop of pre-come glittered like a diamond.

Ti-Charles extended his trembling tongue and licked the salty drop from the opening in Baron Samedi's bulging glans. It tasted more intense than any man juice he had ever tasted before, and he felt a strange, ecstatic energy pass through him as he closed his mouth over Baron Samedi's crown and slid his lips down over his stiff, veiny shaft, swallowing Henri's cock head down his throat as he gagged all nine hot, hard inches down and pressed his full lips into the tight, sparse coils of pubic hair at its base. The ridden fisherman gripped Ti-Charles's head with strong fingers and began to fuck the young *oungan*'s face rhythmically. Ti-Charles's heart began to pound excitedly as Baron Samedi took control of him and filled his throat with his stiff, thick and throbbing cock, another form of possession.

And yet even as Ti-Charles gratefully swallowed Baron Samedi's large, rigid and pulsing cock down past his tonsils over and over again, the face-fucking rhythm mirroring the muffled rhythms of the drummers outside the *kay-mystère*, even as Ti-Charles gasped and gurgled in pleasure as Baron Samedi massaged and kneaded his bulging crotch vigorously while fucking his throat, the young priest wondered if this was the *lwa*'s joke: to give him Henri and not, to mischievously fuck him with the knowledge of the whole village through the one man the *Mystère* would know Ti-Charles could not refuse. And yet surely the other Barons, his *met-tête-lwa*, would not permit it?

Ezulie, I will give you much honour, he thought, opening his throat and tilting his head back so that Baron Samedi could slide his cock further down towards the young *oungan*'s stomach with each firm thrust of his lean hips. I will build a shrine for you next to the shrines of Baron Lundi and Baron Limba in my *oufo*.

Henri slid round on top of Ti-Charles and pushed his strong, smooth, muscular thighs in between Ti-Charles's darker, leaner and open ones. Ti-Charles stared into his own face reflected in Baron Samedi's sunglasses lens, pretty, boyish features bloated by excitement. Henri's other eye was closed. Phallic *Ghede*, one-eyed, as the dick has one eye.

Henri's skin was hot against Ti-Charles's now, and Ti-Charles knew he had no power to refuse the possessed fisherman anything. Henri slid his hands firmly down Ti-Charles's body and pulled his breeches down and off in one confident movement. Ti-Charles's large erection sprang up and slapped against his flat, trembling belly, making him gasp, and the warm air felt cool around his heavy, hanging ballsac, between his thighs.

'Fuck me, Baron Samedi,' Ti-Charles begged the young fisherman astride him breathlessly. 'Fill me with life in defiance of death. Give me your cock, your seed. Fuck my arse. Come up me. Give me your manhood, your energy.'

Sweat running glistening down the sides of his shaved head, top hat still firmly in place, the now otherwise naked Baron Samedi reached around to the piled offerings at the foot of the altar. Next to a bottle of rum was a small pot of chicken fat, offered up by one of the shrine's supplicants earlier that day. Baron Samedi pushed long fingers into it, coating them with the thick, waxy grease. Ti-Charles opened his long, muscular, cocoa-brown legs receptively, then threw them wide, rolling back on the altar's base so that his legs and buttocks were up in the air and spread, and his receptive arsehole was made as available as possible to the horny Baron's fingers and his large, stiff dick, Ti-Charles longing for deep, profound penetration into his body, into his psyche, and into his anal cavity.

'Oh, yes, oh, yes,' Ti-Charles moaned, closing his eyes in pleasure, letting his head fall back over the edge of the altar base as Baron Samedi boldly pushed two fingers into his brazenly offered arsehole straight to the knuckle, making the young *oungan* grunt, and his own stiff dick buck between his legs. Baron Samedi worked a third finger in alongside his first and second fingers with casual insistence, and Ti-Charles was surprised to find he could take it easily, as if his body was yielding to the possessed Henri on some deeper level than just being fucked by the hot and heavily aroused young fisherman, opening itself more profoundly to the mounting *lwa* within him.

'Ride me,' Ti-Charles begged Henri-Samedi. 'Mount me through this man and ride me.'

With a wide grin and a coarse laugh, Baron Samedi nodded and slid his long fingers out of Ti-Charles's now open arsehole, dipping them into the small pot and greasing up his large, rigid erection with confident strokes. The watching Ti-Charles hooked his leanly muscled arms up and under his thighs, raising his lower back, pulling his arsehole up as high and spreading it as wide open for the Baron as physically possible in the constricted space, his heels knocking things over on the cluttered altar as he did so.

Baron Samedi knelt on one knee and guided his large cock head towards Ti-Charles's waiting, well-greased anal star. Ti-Charles groaned as he felt its smooth, hot, egglike curve push against his now accommodating sphincter, then gasped sharply as the Baron slid his crown in past Ti-Charles's still-tight anal ring and pushed his throbbingly rigid nine-inch shaft all the way up Ti-Charles's arsehole. Ti-Charles's stiff dick kicked between his legs, and pre-come beaded at its head, but he didn't try to grip it to give himself some manual relief as Baron Samedi began to fuck him with long, deep, passionate strokes. Instead he gave himself up to the total anality of the experience, to the ecstasy of being fucked, penetrated, filled so completely on every level, by the large and throbbing cock of the riding *lwa*.

Ezulie, give me this man. Limba, Lundi, give me this man.

Baron Samedi's smooth cock head rammed repeatedly against the sphincter deep inside Ti-Charles at the top of his rectum and punched against his prostate, each firm thrust pushing increasingly milky drops of pre-come out of the now gaping piss slit of the young *oungan*'s throbbing, aching erection. Ti-Charles lowered his arms so he could brace himself up on his elbows and push his large, muscular buttocks back on to Baron Samedi's thrusting dick in rhythmic response to the *lwa*'s hard fucking of his arse, and force the thick, pulsing rigidity as far up himself as possible with each thrust.

Outside, the drums pounded and Ti-Charles felt the tug on his spirit as he was opened up on every level at once – musically, spiritually, sexually, emotionally. He groped for his *asson* and began to caress his sweaty skin with it, letting the gourd's roughly netted, knotted surface tease his rising chest, his large, protruding nipples. Ti-Charles felt as if his whole body was melting from the inside out, from his guts outwards, as if the lining of his arse had become the skin wrapping the *lwa*'s large and rigid pole as it rammed in and out of his backside, possessed by spirit and man together.

And Baron Samedi's voice was hoarse and loud and ribald: 'Keep your arse up in the air so I can fuck it deep, man. Kick stars with your heels and open your back door wide. Spread like Limba when Lundi takes him from behind. Open to your rider, man. Let me mount you and ride you deep-deep-deep.'

And Baron Samedi rammed his great thick dick up Ti-Charles's arse with all the muscular strength he had until Ti-Charles was gasping high and fast and hard and losing control of himself in ecstasy, time dissolving into one eternal, unbearably exciting moment. Ti-Charles's cock was heavy and pulsing against his trembling belly, his balls clenched tight, Baron Samedi hooking the uncontrollably turned-on young *oungan*'s smooth, long legs up to his shoulders, then twisting Ti-Charles around so he was fucking him on his side, then from behind. He was stretching Ti-Charles inside, adding to the young priest's ecstasy as Baron Samedi shoved his large hard-on into Ti-Charles's rectum from every possible angle, even swivelling its rigidity inside the young *oungan* to really totally open up his anal passage to the pleasure of being thoroughly and totally fucked.

Without withdrawing his wood-hard nine-inch cock from Ti-Charles for a moment, Baron Samedi rolled the *oungan* back round on to his back again, hooked the young man's knees over his broad shoulders and began to fuck him with hard, deep strokes that rammed up against Ti-Charles's prostate with practised assurance over and over again: the *lwa* was an expert butt-fucker, and Ti-Charles's achingly stiff dick bucked uncontrollably with each thrust as he threw his lean arms up over his face, his chest heaving, every muscle in his body trembling, all control finally thrown away as pre-come ran from his cock head down his grooved belly and towards his heaving chest as freely as water.

'Oh, yeah, fuck me, man, fuck me,' Ti-Charles gasped, pushing his buttocks back on to Baron Samedi's crotch with small thrusts, his heart hammering, his lungs compressed. 'I'm open to you, *maître*, totally open. You're filling me till I'm bursting with your cock –'

Baron Samedi's top hat tumbled from his head as he fucked Ti-Charles as hard as he could, his lean hips slapping sharply against the globes of Ti-Charles's buttocks. Now wearing a white bandana around his shaved scalp, he laughed hoarsely, tossing his head back as he pushed all the way into Ti-Charles, then swivelled his erection around vigorously inside Ti-Charles's rectum, making the young *oungan* grunt and gasp and beg for release even as he prayed for his arse-fucking never to finish.

And then, strangely, just as he seemed to be hammering his way towards a climax, the Baron's posture, his manner, even his breathing changed in some strange and subtle way. He slowed the pumping of his lean hips against Ti-Charles's upturned butt. Ti-Charles, confused by the change, opened his eyes and looked up and saw that the face now gazing down at him was different somehow – younger, more innocent. It was no longer knowing or mocking in its expression. His cock, however, seemed if anything somehow suddenly larger, stiffer and hotter inside Ti-Charles's bruised and aching rectum. Rather than being alarming to the passive young priest, the feeling was good.

His large erection still buried to the root in Ti-Charles's arsehole, the young fisherman now rotated his pelvis more gently, as if he was suddenly less concerned with his own gratification, and more concerned with the pleasure of the man beneath him. Shaking his head in confusion, he reached up with one hand and took the sunglasses from his face, as if wondering how they had got there.

To his shock, alarm and excitement, Ti-Charles found himself staring up not into the opaque eyes of Baron Samedi, but into the soft, deep, dark eyes of the startled young fisherman, Henri Biassou. They were open wide and totally present, their pupils dilated to the limit with – what? Annoyance? Surprise? Fear? Or even – could it be – desire?

Henri bent forward carefully and kissed Ti-Charles on the mouth, and his breath tasted sweet. A new sort of excitement coursing through him, Ti-Charles wrapped his arms around Henri's broad back and began to squirm his big, muscular buttocks as the horny young fisherman began to move his hips rapidly back and forth against the heavily aroused passive *oungan*'s upturned and freely offered greasy anal star. Each man was suddenly eager to give the other the most pleasure he possibly could.

'You want me, man?' Ti-Charles asked breathlessly, staring up into Henri's handsome, shining brown face as the leanly muscled young fisherman broke their kiss so he could lean back and brace himself up with his strong, muscular arms and fuck the *oungan* more deeply and more fluidly with his stiff, aching cock.

'I always wanted you, man,' Henri replied as he slid his throbbingly stiff, nine-inch pole in and out of Ti-Charles's slack, juicy, open arsehole. 'More than the biggest catch of fish. More than the most brightly painted fishing boat. But I was afraid. I was just a fisherman with no big plans. Why should you want me? I would never have dared to do this in a thousand years. And then suddenly I am here and my cock is inside your body and your body tells me you want me and your eyes tell me you want me –'

'I wanted you from the first moment you came to the *oufo*,' Ti-Charles replied breathlessly, trying to keep his eyes on Henri's as Henri fucked him with increasing rapidity and passion, but finally having to let his head fall back and yield to the ecstasy the young fisherman's large, stiff dick was producing in his rectum. Henri rammed deep into Ti-Charles, thrusting up into his anal canal hard, giving his lover his whole rigid length with each insertion. Then Henri pumped his cock in and out of Ti-Charles's hot, smooth rectum rapidly, thrusting himself towards a climax inside Ti-Charles's arsehole, each push in making Ti-Charles's own throbbing hard-on heavier, ramming the spunk out of his balls. And, inch by uncontrollable, untouched inch along its shaft, Henri literally fucked the come out of Ti-Charles's aching dick as, with hoarse, loud gasps that were almost bellows, he exploded inside the young *oungan*'s anal passage, flooding it with hot white jism, the pressure of his climax making Ti-Charles explode with a loud, sharp cry, too, come spattering thick and white up the length of his trembling belly and arching torso, drops landing on his chest, in his clavicle, one even hitting his chin, so great was the force of his excitement.

Carefully they lowered their aching bodies to the ground, swivelling around awkwardly so as to make sure that Henri's still-hard cock stayed pushed up Ti-Charles's slack and warmly accommodating arsehole. They stayed like that, lying on their sides like spoons, Henri inside Ti-Charles's body, his strong, muscular arms wrapped around the darker-skinned young *oungan*, for some time, there at the base of the altar of the *Ghedes*, listening to the service continuing outside.

'The *lwa* are satisfied, yes, man?' Henri said eventually, hugging Ti-Charles to him, his voice soft and grainy in Ti-Charles's ear.

'The *lwa* are never satisfied,' Ti-Charles replied. 'But tonight we have honoured them.'

'If it is what the *lwa* will, I will honour them in this way every night,' Henri whispered, leaning round from behind Ti-Charles and smiling playfully. Ti-Charles turned his head and the two young men kissed softly on the lips.

'It is what the *lwa* will,' Ti-Charles replied, smiling too.

After a little while they dressed, and returned to the service, hand in hand, wreathed in the first flush of love. Sauveur, who had been keeping the ceremony going without Ti-Charles, owing to the flair and confidence of his drumming, gave his *oungan* a warm, wide smile when he saw him emerge from Baron Samedi's *kay-mystère* holding Henri Biassou's hand, and even the often dour Petro seemed pleased for Ti-Charles and the handsome young fisherman.

The tone of the drums was more mellow now, as the two men strolled over to the four soldiers, all of whom were now resting, leaning their backs against the cool plaster wall behind the peristyle. Obry had his arm around Jestin's shoulders, and was dozing, and Dany was asleep with his head in Valentine's lap. Jestin looked up at Ti-Charles, his eyes dark with wonderment.

'The slender young man,' he said, unprompted by any questioning. 'Pierre is his name, I think. He was with us in the grove this afternoon. He was possessed by a spirit and he – he told me things about my grandfather I never knew but always wished I had known. And things I should do to honour him. I felt like my life meant more than I thought it did this morning. I don't know . . .' he ended, his voice tailing off, his eyes glittering with tears. 'It's not an easy thing, life,' he whispered, almost to himself. 'Or to do the right things in it.'

'You can only follow your heart,' Ti-Charles said to him. 'And your spirit. All you need to do is listen, and you will start to hear. *Les Mystères* will speak to you.'

'I felt free,' Valentine said softly. 'When I was dancing and the *lwa* were arriving. Freer than I have ever felt before. Totally part of something, and at the same time totally free of crap. So thank you, *maître*. Thank you for welcoming us when you could have turned us away in anger because of what we originally came to do out of ignorance.'

Ti-Charles nodded, his eyes dark and wise. Then he noticed something had caught Henri's attention off to one side of the peristyle. Ti-Charles followed the line of his gaze to see what it was.

It was still some hours before dawn but there was a faint red glow visible above the *oufo* walls far away to the east.

'What is that, man?' Henri asked Ti-Charles, his handsome features crinkling in puzzlement. 'Some army thing?'

Overhearing this, Jestin shook his head. 'We were over the other way,' he said. 'Towards Sous-L'Eau.'

'It is the mansion of the Sonnelier plantation,' Ti-Charles replied calmly.

'The mansion where the *bokor* lives?'

'Where he lived.'

'So that is what Bertrand had to do, man? Burn it to the ground?'

'Yes,' Ti-Charles said. 'And as the fire shatters the clay pots and glass bottles within, the spirits of the dead the *bokor* captured will be freed, and their bodies will no longer be his slaves to toil in the cane fields.'

Their arms wrapped around each other's waist, Ti-Charles and

Henri Biassou watched the flickering red and orange as it lit up the night sky from below, and the old plantation house, symbol of so much pain and blood and history, was finally consumed by fire.

IDOL NEW BOOKS

Information correct at time of printing. For up-to-date availability,
please check www.idol-books.co.uk

WORDS MADE FLESH
Published in November 2000   Thom Wolf

Best-selling novelist Glenn Holden has an appreciation for the rougher side of sex. But when a handsome stranger breaks into his house claiming to be a character from one of Glenn's own thrillers, the author is suddenly thrust into a surreal sexual adventure that goes further than the concoctions of his own dirty mind – a bizarre world full of mysterious men and even wilder sex.

£8.99/$10.95   ISBN 0 352 33544 0

DIVINE MEAT
Published in January 2001   Edited by David MacMillan

An Idol short-story collection. Gods pleasure themselves with male flesh and vice versa in this astonishing array of tales of human/divine homoeroticism. From Ganymede and Zeus to lustful voodoo deities, sacred genies and the Cerne Abbas giant himself, these stories are hot, horny and (well) hung. *Divine Meat*: where man meets his maker. In more ways than one.

£8.99/$10.95   ISBN 0 352 33587 4

MAN ON!
Published in March 2001   Turner Kane

Greg Williams of Middleton United is young, talented and handsome, a favourite with both fans and players alike. But when he signs his new football contract with Weston City, and when he starts sleeping with his soon-to-be-wed best friend Matt, things start hotting up, both on and off the pitch.

£8.99/$10.95   ISBN 0 352 33613 7

Also published:

DARK RIDER
Jack Gordon

While the rulers of a remote Scottish island play bizarre games of sexual dominance with the Argentinian Angelo, his friend Robert – consumed with jealous longing for his coffee-skinned companion – assuages his desires with the willing locals.

£6.99/$9.95   ISBN 0 352 33243 3

CUSTOMS OF THE COUNTRY
Rupert Thomas

James Cardell has left school and is looking forward to going to Oxford. That summer of 1924, however, he will spend with his cousins in a tiny village in rural Kent. There he finds he can pursue his love of painting – and begin to explore his obsession with the male physique.

£6.99/$9.95

ISBN 0 352 33246 8

DOCTOR REYNARD'S EXPERIMENT
Robert Black

A dark world of secret brothels, dungeons and sexual cabarets exists behind the respectable façade of Victorian London. The degenerate Lord Spearman introduces Dr Richard Reynard, dashing bachelor, to this hidden world.

£6.99/$9.95

ISBN 0 352 33252 2

CODE OF SUBMISSION
Paul C. Alexander

Having uncovered and defeated a slave ring operating in London's leather scene, journalist Nathan Dexter had hoped to enjoy a peaceful life with his boyfriend Scott. But when it becomes clear that the perverted slave trade has started again, Nathan has no choice but to travel across Europe and America in his bid to stop it. Second in the trilogy.

£6.99/$9.95

ISBN 0 352 33272 7

SLAVES OF TARNE
Gordon Neale

Pascal willingly follows the mysterious and alluring Casper to Tarne, a community of men enslaved to men. Tarne is everything that Pascal has ever fantasised about, but he begins to sense a sinister aspect to Casper's magnetism. Pascal has to choose between the pleasures of submission and acting to save the people he loves.

£6.99/$9.95

ISBN 0 352 33273 5

ROUGH WITH THE SMOOTH
Dominic Arrow

Amid the crime, violence and unemployment of North London, the young men who attend Jonathan Carey's drop-in centre have few choices. One of the young men, Stewart, finds himself torn between the increasingly intimate horseplay of his fellows and the perverse allure of the criminal underworld. Can Jonathan save Stewart from the bullies on the streets and behind bars?

£6.99/$9.95

ISBN 0 352 33292 1

SHAME
Raydon Pelham

On holiday in West Hollywood, Briton Martyn Townsend meets and falls in love with the daredevil Scott. When Scott is murdered, Martyn's hunt for the truth and for the mysterious Peter, Scott's ex-lover, leads him to the clubs of London and Ibiza.

£6.99/$9.95

ISBN 0 352 33302 2

THE FINAL RESTRAINT
Paul C. Alexander

The trilogy that began with *Chains of Deceit* and continued in *Code of Submission* concludes in this powerfully erotic novel. From the dungeons and saunas of London to the deepest jungles of South America, Nathan Dexter is forced to play the ultimate chess game with evil Adrian Delancey – with people as sexual pawns.

£6.99/$9.95   ISBN 0 352 33303 0

HARD TIME
Robert Black

HMP Cairncrow prison is a corrupt and cruel institution, but also a sexual minefield. Three new inmates must find their niche in this brutish environment – as sexual victims or lovers, predators or protectors. This is the story of how they find love, sex and redemption behind prison walls.

£6.99/$9.95   ISBN 0 352 33304 9

ROMAN GAMES
Tasker Dean

When Sam visits the island of Skate, he is taught how to submit to other men, acting out an elaborate fantasy in which young men become wrestling slaves – just as in ancient Rome. Indeed, if he is to have his beautiful prize – the wrestler, Robert – he must learn how the Romans played their games.

£6.99/$9.95   ISBN 0 352 33322 7

VENETIAN TRADE
Richard Davis

From the deck of the ship that carries him into Venice, Rob Weaver catches his first glimpse of a beautiful but corrupt city where the dark alleys and misty canals hide debauchery and decadence. Here, he must learn to survive among men who would make him a plaything and a slave.

£6.99/$9.95   ISBN 0 352 33323 5

THE LOVE OF OLD EGYPT
Philip Markham

It's 1925 and the deluxe cruiser carrying the young gigolo Jeremy Hessling has docked at Luxor. Jeremy dreams of being dominated by the Pharaohs of old, but quickly becomes involved with someone more accessible – Khalid, a young man of exceptional beauty.

£6.99/$9.95   ISBN 0 352 33354 5

THE BLACK CHAMBER
Jack Gordon

Educated at the court of George II, Calum Monroe finds his native Scotland a dull, damp place. He relieves his boredom by donning a mask and holding up coaches in the guise of the Fox – a dashing highwayman. Chance throws him and neighbouring farmer Fergie McGregor together with Calum's sinister, perverse guardian, James Black.

£6.99/$9.95   ISBN 0 352 33373 1

BOOTY BOYS
Jay Russell

Hard-bodied black British detective Alton Davies can't believe his eyes or his luck when he finds muscular African-American gangsta rapper Banji-B lounging in his office early one morning. Alton's disbelief – and his excitement – mounts as Banji-B asks him to track down a stolen videotape of a post-gig orgy.

£7.99/$10.95   ISBN 0 352 33446 0

SUREFORCE
Phil Votel

Not knowing what to do with his life once he's been thrown out of the army, Matt takes a job with the security firm Sureforce. Little does he know that the job is the ultimate mix of business and pleasure, and it's not long before Matt's hanging with the beefiest, meanest, hardest lads in town.

£7.99/$10.95   ISBN 0 352 33444 4

HOT ON THE TRAIL
Lukas Scott

The Midwest, 1849. *Hot on the Trail* is the story of the original American dream, where freedom is driven by wild passion. And when farmboy Brett skips town and encounters dangerous outlaw Luke Mitchell, sparks are bound to fly in this raunchy tale of hard cowboys, butch outlaws, dirty adventure and true grit.

£7.99/$10.95   ISBN 0 352 33461 4

STREET LIFE
Rupert Thomas

Ben is eighteen and tired of living in the suburbs. As there's little sexual adventure to be found there, he decides to run away from both A-levels and his comfortable home – to a new life in London. There, he's befriended by Lee, a homeless Scottish lad who offers him a friendly ear and the comfort of his sleeping bag.

£7.99/$10.95   ISBN 0 352 33374 X

MAESTRO
Peter Slater

A young Spanish cello player, Ramon, journeys to the castle of cellist Ernesto Cavallo in the hope of masterclasses from the great musician. Ramon's own music is technically perfect, but his playing lacks a certain essence – and so, Maestro Cavallo arranges for Ramon to undergo a number of sexual trials in this darkly erotic, extremely well-written novel.

£8.99/$10.95   ISBN 0 352 33511 4

FELLOWSHIP OF IRON
Jack Stevens

Mike is a gym owner and a successful competitive bodybuilder. He lives the life of the body beautiful and everything seems to be going swimmingly. So when his mentor and former boyfriend Dave dies after using illegal steroids, Mike is determined to find out who supplied his ex with drugs.

£8.99/$10.95   ISBN 0 352 33512 2

THE PHEROMONE BOMB
Edward Ellis

A crack army unit – the Special Marine Corps, consisting of five British and five American soldiers – are on a top-secret mission to investigate, and if necessary eliminate, an illegal private army on a tropical island in the mid-Atlantic. What the tough, hard soldiers realise when they investigate the island is that the enemy doesn't shoot them with bullets. The enemy has discovered a powerful weapon: the pheromone bomb, which produces a gas – and anyone on whom the gas settles is filled with irresistible homoerotic urges.

£8.99/$10.95   ISBN 0 352 33543 2

------------ ✂ --------------------------

Please send me the books I have ticked above.

Name ....

Address ....

....

....

.... Post Code ....

Send to: **Cash Sales, Idol Books, Thames Wharf Studios, Rainville Road, London W6 9HA.**

US customers: for prices and details of how to order books for delivery by mail, call 1-800-805-1083.

Please enclose a cheque or postal order, made payable to **Virgin Publishing Ltd**, to the value of the books you have ordered plus postage and packing costs as follows:

UK and BFPO – £1.00 for the first book, 50p for each subsequent book.

Overseas (including Republic of Ireland) – £2.00 for the first book, £1.00 for each subsequent book.

We accept all major credit cards, including VISA, ACCESS/MASTER-CARD, DINERS CLUB, AMEX and SWITCH.

Please write your card number and expiry date here:

....

Please allow up to 28 days for delivery.

Signature ....

------------ ✂ --------------------------